Praise for the Peaks Saga...

"I remember fondly reading The Lion, The Witch, and The Wardrobe *when I was in middle school.* The Peaks at the Edge of the World *has a similar mix of fantasy and adventure with a moral tale at its center. This is a book that's appropriate for a younger audience than most sci fi/fantasy novels. Enjoy the read!"*

—*Kathy Dunnehoff*
ZOLA AWARD-WINNING WOMEN'S FICTION WRITER

"...a page turner!" —*Judith Seidel*

"Ms. Erler puts religion in new settings as she uses the characters in both the past and the future to meld the consequences of a religion lost, then found, then challenged. The ride is exciting. The characters real and engaging."

—*Charlene Hecht*
BA MUSIC EDUCATION
LONGTIME WRITER, INCLUDING "GUNSMOKE" FAN FICTION

"M.F. Erler skillfully pioneers a new writing genre, mixing elements of science fiction, dimensional time-travel, and modern Christian spirituality. She uses likeable characters in well-crafted settings in which we can identify with their real-life struggles."

—*Richard Bartlett, MA, PhD*

"...[M.F.] Erler's book, with its futuristic sci-fi focus and true-to-life grittiness, is not your typical Christian novel. At times, it unabashedly describes the realities of the darkness of humanity in order to contrast it with the power of hope and love found in God's grace. This unique book is well worth your time to read and I highly recommend it."

—*Pastor Kevin Bueltmann*
TRINITY LUTHERAN CHURCH - ASSOCIATE PASTOR
TRINITY LUTHERAN CAMP - EXECUTIVE DIRECTOR

"Why can't we have more books like this one? I commend M.F. Erler for her imaginative work."

—Danien Neal Allen

"It is unusual to find science fiction with Christian values. Ms. Erler has wonderful skill with word pictures. Her characters are real people with real life challenges. BRAVO! "

—Rebecca Sturdevant

"Spread over all of Erler's stories are strong religious themes, such as the strength of family, the stories of sin and redemption, the search for truth, and the power of love to change us. These values are woven into adventures that are tapestries of individuals and personal tales, crossing over space and time, linking worlds together."

—Kathleen McCafferty
ORDAINED MINISTER, UNITED METHODIST CHURCH

"M.F. Erler skillfully pioneers a new genre, mixing elements of time travel and modern Christian spirituality. She uses relatable characters in well-crafted settings, so we can better identify with their real-life struggles."

—Richard Bartlett, MA, PhD

Books by M.F. Erler

THE PEAKS SAGA

PEAKS AT THE EDGE OF THE WORLD
Finding the Light

SEARCHING FOR MAIA

MOUNTAINTOPS AND VALLEYS

WHEN THE WORLD GROWS COLD

THE FOUNTAIN AND THE DESERT

BEYOND THE WORLD

WHERE ALL WORLDS END

THE JOURNEYS SAGA

JOURNEYS BEYOND THE PEAKS
Tales of Time-Travel into the Past

BEYOND the WORLD

M.F. ERLER

BEYOND THE WORLD, *Book 6, The Peaks Saga*
by M.F. Erler

Published by

WESTWIND PRESS
an imprint of First Steps Publishing
PO Box 571
Gleneden Beach, Oregon 97388-0571
FirstStepsPublishing.com

ISBN:
978-1-944072-20-9 (hardback)
978-1-937333-84-3 (trade paper)
978-1-944072-21-6 (e-book)

Bible quotes are from New International Version:
"Scripture taken from Holy Bible, New International Version (Registered Trademark) Copyright 1973,1978, 1984 by International Bible Society. Used by permission of Zondervan Publishing House. All rights reserved."

Lyrics to songs by Gregory A. DeMuth,
     Copyright 2005: Sacred Ground Music, used with permission
All other lyrics quoted are Public Domain, or composed by the author.

Cover illustration by Kabita Studios
Cover, interior design by Suzanne Fyhrie Parrott

Please provide feedback

10 9 8 7 6 5 4 3 2

Printed in U.S.A.

This book is dedicated to JT & RB, in gratitude for moral support and good counsel.

CONTENTS

"Oh, that I had the wings of a dove! I would fly
away and be at rest—I would flee far away and stay
in the desert; I would hurry to my place of shelter,
far from the tempest and storm."

— *Psalm 55:6-8*

ACKNOWLEDGMENTS

Thanks to all my readers, and especially –

Richard, who has been a faithful beta reader for me, and who has given me much emotional support.

Emilie, who is more than a daughter, also a friend, who reminds me to think positively.

Nancy & Kathy, old friendships being renewed, reminding me of the value of life and faith.

Pastor Greg, whose music still speaks to me, even after all these years. I appreciate your letting me use the lyrics, PG.

FOREWORD

All my life I've been a misfit, not fitting into any of the niches the world has to offer. And my writing is the same. Some think it too explicit and worldly for the religious genre, and others say it's too religious for the science fiction genre. Well, so be it. I am what I am, and if I lose that, I will have lost everything.

That said, I'd like to present one thought which some of my readers miss. Whenever I depict an intimate encounter between characters in my book, my goal is to show that sex is a gift given by God for married couples to enjoy. When I depict an intimate relationship outside of marriage, my intent is to show it only leads to problems and heart-ache in the end.

If I was to delete all this material from *The Peaks Saga*, I feel the story would only be half-told. Thus, I hope my readers will understand what I'm trying to say, and bear with me. We live in a real world, which isn't always what we'd like it to be. But there is one rock we can hang onto, the Lord Jesus.

Thanks to those of you who have given me moral support.

M.F.E. 2014

The Sullien Family Tree

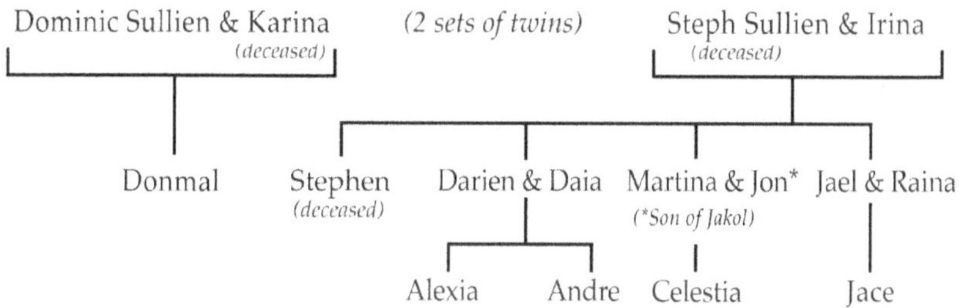

Dominic Sullien & Karina
(deceased)
(2 sets of twins)
Steph Sullien & Irina
(deceased)
Donmal
Stephen
(deceased)
Darien & Daia
Martina & Jon*
(*Son of Jakol)
Jael & Raina
Alexia
Andre
Celestia
Jace

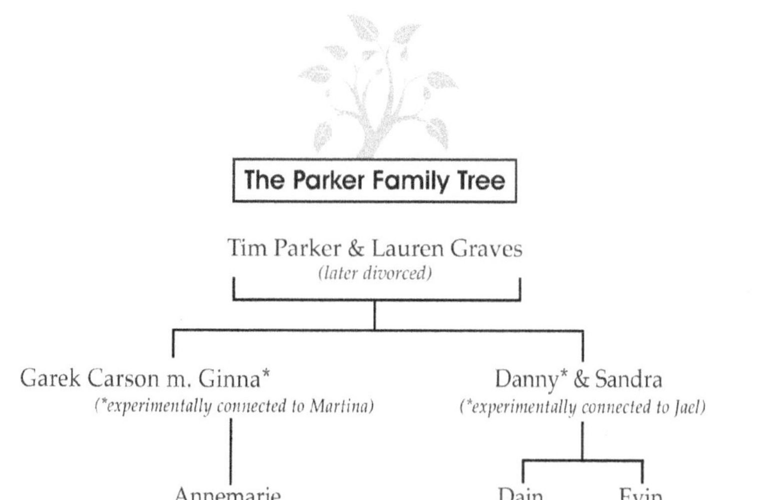

The Parker Family Tree
Tim Parker & Lauren Graves
(later divorced)
Garek Carson m. Ginna*
(*experimentally connected to Martina)
Danny* & Sandra
(*experimentally connected to Jael)
Annemarie
Dain
Evin

PROLOGUE
IMAGES

There was nothing but darkness before his eyes as he moved slowly through the trees. Somehow, he could sense them and avoid walking into their rough-barked trunks. Perhaps it was the way the ground level changed as his hooves neared their roots.

He tossed his head, shaking out his tangled mane and nickered softly. Then he pushed air from his nostrils in a loud *whoosh*.

Lowering his head, he chomped off a few blades of grass. It was still too early in the spring for very many of the new fresh blades, so he had to settle for the dried remains of last year's crop. It wasn't too bad, though—it tasted like the straw his master had fed him—back when he still had a home.

That was now a hazy faded memory, though. He couldn't really measure the time, but there had been numerous periods of light and darkness. The weather had gone through its full sequence—from the chill of the snowy time through the greening up and the hot days of sunlight—and then back to the long darkness and the fading of fresh and green things—into the cold, and back out again.

These cycles had always been a part of his life, but before there was some shelter provided for him from the wet rain and the cold snow. Now he had to find his own shelter—sometimes in a rocky overhang or under some of the taller, thicker trees. The cycles passed over him, and he just took what each day brought. Numbering the passage of seasons was not part of his nature. His only awarenesses were the immediate needs—food, water, and shelter.

This night, there were no lights—he didn't know to call them stars or moon. Neither did he know to call the dark concealing these things clouds. All he knew was his sense of sight had little use at the moment. He was using his keen hearing and sense of smell, along with the touch of his hooves on the ground, and occasionally the brush of his flanks or legs against some low vegetation.

Suddenly his eyes did see something—two yellow lights glowing between the trees ahead of him. Stepping closer, he saw the eyes of some animal. It was lower to the ground than he, and emitted a low growl. At first, he snorted in fear, but when the eyes didn't move any closer, he sniffed more deeply. There was no smell of threat. In fact, there was a smell he hadn't known for a very long time.

Moving closer still, he could scc this was not a wolf but a big black dog with pointed ears. It gave a whining sound and stepped closer to him. Now he knew this scent—it came from humans.

The dog brushed gently against his foreleg and gave a short bark. Then it started off through the trees to his right. Without any hesitation, he followed.

***

Dark and cold and damp. These were the only things the man was aware of. For awhile he'd shivered—his body trying to generate some warmth by movement of his muscles. That hadn't been enough, as the cold settled into his bones. Now there was probably no way to dislodge it.

Sometimes—perhaps in another lifetime—his eyes had seen light. There were faces, too—a young woman who looked vaguely familiar—looming from somewhere deep in his memory. Had she been special to him? Did he know her name?

He shook his head—the effort felt like trying to move a huge and heavy weight. No—there were no memories now. His mind was as cold, dark, and empty as the place where he lay.

***

Stars were falling, streaking across the black of the night sky, pieces of an asteroid that began to break up as it entered the planet's atmosphere.

No human eyes beheld the sight, but in a golden sky a large hawk-like bird circled, riding the thermals.

These were nothing more than particles, following their appointed rounds in space—a cosmos mostly empty, within and without. What was keeping it from collapsing into chaos?

***

It felt so good to stretch his muscles after all the ages of confinement. A laugh rumbled deep inside him, and a sudden puff of smoke came from his nostrils. This made him laugh again with delight, and the smoke became a red-orange flame.

Ah, yes, this was his favorite form. All too often he had to disguise his true identity—posing perhaps as a handsome human male with sleek dark hair—sometimes as a threatening animal, such as a wolf. The form he most detested, though, was when he had to imitate the golden glowing body of an angel, one of the Enemy's trusted servants.

This memory sent waves of rage through him, and bright blue flames shot from his mouth and nostrils. He'd been one of them once—many eons ago—but now was cast out. No matter how he tried to reassume his original form, it never quite fit anymore. In fact, the very thought of it made him itch with an irritation that only got worse the more he scratched it with his long, curving claws.

In anger he spread his huge leathery wings, admiring the dark shadows they cast across the landscape below, as he sat perched on the edge of a craggy cliff. At least now he was free of the chains that had bound him for so long.

'The Enemy thinks he has only released me for a time,' he hissed to himself. 'But he underestimates me. I still have powers he hasn't seen, and when I unleash them…'

The deep chuckling in his throat emerged as a roar. This ominous sound echoed off the mountains all around, as he launched his huge serpentine form into space and took flight.

CHAPTER ONE
CELESTIA EMERGING

The fog before my eyes disappeared suddenly, as though an unseen hand wiped it away. I heard a voice beside me saying:

"Celestia, where are we? Did you see how that fog went away? It's like someone rubbed the mist off a windowpane."

I wanted to ask what a windowpane was, but instead I turned and looked at the slender young man holding tightly to my hand.

"Laken? How did you get here?"

"I don't know. The last thing I remember was the Lord saying it was time for us to go where we each were needed most."

"I think we just crossed a GAP," I said to him.

"But where are we? And when?"

Before I could answer, I began to hear shouts above and behind us. Looking around, I saw a grassy hillside, and running toward us was a woman with long dark hair.

"Celestia!" she was shouting.

"Mom?"

She'd pulled up her tunic past her knees and was moving as fast as she could. "Is it really you?"

Then another female form came into view, and I recognized Daiah, my aunt. Before I could say a word, she'd grabbed me and pulled me into a tight embrace. Mom soon joined her, until I was suffocated in hugs.

As I was trying to disengage myself so I could catch my breath and talk, a gaggle of laughing children surrounded us. "It's our cousin," I heard one of the older girls saying. "Her name is Celestia, and her mother is my Aunt Martina."

"That's right, Lexi," I heard Daiah's voice say.

"Please, let me catch my breath." I took advantage of the moment Daiah turned her attention away from me.

Meanwhile the younger children began to reach out and touch me shyly. As I stepped back, I saw them also staring in wide-eyed wonder at Laken—with his long black hair and striking almond-shaped brown eyes.

"Is he from another planet?" I heard one of the boys ask.

"No," I laughed, "He's my friend from another part of Earth."

After I introduced Laken, Daiah began to introduce her daughter to Laken, but she was interrupted by the youngest child, a girl of about three or four Standard Years, who jumped in front of me and introduced herself. "I'm Morgan. My mommy is Raina, and my daddy is Branden. They got married after his wife died, and they named me for her."

"Wow, that's a lot for one your age to remember," I smiled. As I did this, I saw the cloud that crossed Daiah's face, and remembered one of the last things she'd told me before we left for The Fountain—that her husband Darien had died in a battle.

Just then, Little Morgan pointed to Laken, and asked, "Is he your husband?"

"Morgan! Don't be rude?" Lexi stepped up and grabbed her hand.

"It's all right, Morgan," I smiled at her, and then at Daiah and her daughter. "He's just a good friend." I realized I was still holding Laken's hand, and turned to look at him, seeing his eyes clouded in confusion and embarrassment. "We only met each other recently," I went on. "And we've just been sent here across the GAP so we're feeling sort of tired and confused."

"Confused is right," he sighed.

"Of course," cried Mom. "We shouldn't be making you stand here like some carnival show. Come to our hut, and I'll make some tea. Lexi, take the children back to their games, so our newcomers can get some rest."

Lexi nodded, and as she walked away, I could see how much she'd grown—she was nearly a young woman herself.

"How long have I been gone?" I asked suddenly.

"About four or five years," said Mom.

"That long? Is Dad okay?"

She nodded. "Jon is fine. We're glad to be safe here in Indonia."

"Indonia?" Then I began to remember what Daiah had told me about this place of retreat in the Southern Hemisphere, east of the Indian Ocean. 'When you return,' she'd said, 'I hope to see you there.'

"Let's get you some tea and a rest first," Mom said into my thoughts. "All this detail can wait."

"Thanks," I heard Laken sigh with relief.

CHAPTER TWO
INSIDE CELESTIA'S HEAD

The sun in my eyes finally woke me. I blinked, realizing I was still lying on the sleeping mat Mom spread after we arrived. 'It must be late morning by the angle of the sun,' I thought. No one else was in the hut with me.

My mind was blurry and confused, like I'd already been awake and walking around, talking to people. But it appeared I was lying here asleep all the time. Just as I was sitting up and shaking my head to try and clear it, Mom walked in.

"You're awake," she smiled. "It still seems like a dream that you're really back, Honey. You were gone so long I feel surprised when I see you. And a lot has happened in those five years."

"I was dreaming, Mom. And I'm not sure right now if I'm awake or still asleep. Is Darien really dead? Or was that part of a bad dream?"

I saw the moisture in her eyes as she nodded. "I'm afraid, it's true. Now I have only one brother left, Jael—we think. No one knows for sure if he's still alive or not."

"I'm sorry. I didn't mean to be so abrupt. My mind is still fuzzy. A lot happened to us while we were gone, too. I know I can't tell it all in one sitting, and it sounds like you have a lot more grief than me."

She sat down next to me on the low sleeping platform, giving me a firm hug. "There will be plenty of time here in Indonia. Time seems to flow slowly in this place. Somedays I can't even bear to think of Darien and Jael, or even Stephen, our eldest brother you never met. Perhaps Daiah or Raina would be a better person to ask."

"Where's Laken?" I asked then, just to change the subject.

"He's out taking a walk with your dad."

"All this must be so strange for him."

"Laken?"

"Yes, he's never time-traveled before, and he's from almost one thousand years ago."

"Is he special to you?"

"Uh—I don't know," I sighed. "Laken and I have been through a lot of ups and downs. At first, I think he was just using me for his own ends. But Darroch was leading him to do it."

"Who's Darroch?"

"He was supposedly a police officer in Salt Lake—uh, now it's Salien. That's where we met him. He said he was Laken's friend, and took us all the way to Tacoma to meet him. But in the end, he tried to betray us all."

"Where is he now?"

"He's dead."

She was silent for a few moments, then said, "Is this okay to talk about?"

"I'm fine now. We met the True King."

"You did?" Now her voice was full of wonder. "Was it like when Eli took us to Heaven?"

"No, this was entirely different. We were all in a dungeon in Jerusalem."

"Jerusalem?"

"This is really complicated. Laken worked for MEI, that's the Mind Exploration Institute, back in the Twenty-second Century. He took us to their labs in Toronto, Jerusalem, and on Luna. That's where Darroch betrayed us, and we were taken from Luna back to Jerusalem, as prisoners. But the main thing is the Lord came to rescue us. Darroch was already dead by then—so it was the five of us. Laken and the people I tried to take to the Fountain with me—remember?"

Mom nodded, "Garek, Ginna, and Annemarie."

"The Lord spoke to each of us individually, Mom, and told us we were forgiven. He knew our names-" My voice broke then, as tears filled my eyes.

She put her arm across my shoulders and squeezed gently. "What an amazing moment that must have been."

"For sure. After that, he said he was sending each of us to the time where we were needed most. And here I am—with Laken."

"Where did the others go?"

"I have no idea. But I do have a feeling that wherever they are, Garek and Ginna are together."

I heard her sigh, "I hope so. They really needed each other, and I feel so strongly they were meant to be together all along."

"Me too. I could see their relationship grow through all the journeys we took."

"What about Annemarie?"

"I don't know. She seemed so lost sometimes—like she wanted to trust the Lord but something was holding her back. One time she told me she felt too guilty and 'used-up'—as she called it—to ever be worthy of anyone, especially her first love, David."

"I know how that feels," Mom sighed. "I wish I could've helped her more."

"I guess it wasn't meant to be. I don't know."

"Well, hopefully the Lord has sent her where she can get help."

"You've always told me to trust."

"I've done the best I could, Honey. I know I wasn't always the best example of faith."

"No. When I was out there lost in time, it was thoughts of you that kept me going. Without you and Dad as parents and examples, I never would've survived that journey."

She silently pulled me into a tighter hug, and we just sat side-by-side, deep in our own thoughts.

"The thing I can't figure out is why the Lord sent Laken here with me. I think he sent each of the others to their own time."

"Except Garek, if he's with Ginna."

"Yeah, but they really belonged together."

"So, maybe you and Laken belong together?"

"But I don't have those kinds of feelings for him, Mom. I mean, he's a friend now, and I've forgiven him for the things he tried to do to me-"

"Did he hurt you?" Now her voice sounded angry.

"No, Mom. He tried some kind of mind-reading with me which caused a lot of pain, but he's told me how sorry he is, and I believe him. But despite all that, I don't really know him very well. And because of Darroch's manipulating, we haven't had a real chance to get to know each other."

"Well, perhaps that's why you're both here."

"But why? I mean, this isn't his time or anything."

"It's like you said before—sometimes we just have to trust and wait to see what happens."

Suddenly a wave of sadness swept over me as she said those words. Tears seeped into my eyes and began to trickle down my cheeks.

"What's wrong?" She pulled me into her arms like I was still a child.

All I could do was sob onto her shoulder. We sat for a long time like that, with her stroking my hair. I was ashamed to tell her I was crying for myself and not for the losses she'd suffered.

"I don't know," I said at last. "It just seems that's all my life ever is—waiting and trying to trust."

I could feel her nodding, but she didn't speak.

"Why don't we ever get any answers?"

"Well, the Lord did send you back here—to us," she sighed. "That was an answer to *my* prayers."

I hugged her even more tightly then. "Of course, I'm glad to be here. It's just I don't know what to do about Laken."

"You said he's just a friend," she whispered. "Did you and he ever-?"

"One night we went clubbing in Toronto, with Annemarie and Darroch. We all got too high, and they ended up in one bed, with Laken and I in the other. But I told him I wasn't ready to make love."

She sighed deeply. "You're much stronger than I ever was."

"I felt more like a coward."

"No, don't ever think that. I learned the hard way that sex is meant for two people who truly love each other, who are committed to be together for life. Otherwise, it only causes pain for a lot of people, but especially for yourself."

"Annemarie said something like that."

"She probably knew it all too well, from what you've told me."

"I wonder if the Lord will help her and David work things out. Do you think we'll ever find out if they do?"

She shrugged. "Maybe when we all get to Heaven?"

"Mom?"

"Yes?"

"Is this place you call Heaven really real?"

"I saw it and felt it myself."

"How do you know it wasn't just a dream?"

"Well, it helps that Jon and I shared the experience, so we both know it happened."

I suddenly sat up in surprise. "Maybe that's why Laken is here!"

"What do you mean?"

"Well, if I'd come back alone, I might have thought all my experiences were a dream, too. But with Laken here, I can compare—like you and Dad."

We sat in silence before she spoke again, "I know I'm a pretty bad example to give you advice on relationships, Honey."

"No, you two are good examples for me. I've seen how you work things out together, and how you don't let past mistakes ruin your present."

"Thanks," she sighed. "It hasn't always been easy, though."

"I just wish I could find someone like Dad."

"They say girls tend to marry men like their fathers," she chuckled.

"Did you?"

"Perhaps. I don't remember a lot about my father."

I wasn't sure what to say next, for I knew the loss of her father in the Galactic Wars had been very painful for her and all her family, especially her mother, Irina.

"You'll never find a mate who's perfect for you," she said at last. "In the past, people put too much emphasis on feelings and romance. What you must do is try to keep your sights on the Lord, and someday he'll just give you a tap on the shoulder, saying, 'There's the one I have for you'."

"You're kidding, right?"

"Not really. That's a close description of what happened to me. It wasn't when I first met Jon—because I was too drugged up then, in the Redlarks' Camp on planet Terres. It took a long time, and a lot of good and bad adventures before I heard the Lord's voice, and saw he was pointing me to Jon."

"You really heard the Lord's voice?"

"Well, not exactly *heard* it. It's sort of like I knew in my mind—I didn't actually hear any words."

"When did that happen?"

"The first time I was watching him lying unconscious in an infirmary bed on the planet Platius, where our ship had crashed. I was afraid he and Jael were both going to die, and didn't think I could go on alone."

"Yes, I do remember you telling me that."

"I didn't fall head-over-heals in love with him right away, though," she added. "It took other things, like getting to know the real Jon, and seeing how much he cared about Jael and me."

"And going to the Fountain in the Desert?"

"Oh, that helped seal the deal," she smiled. "But I knew long before the Fountain—even before he asked me to marry him."

"But what about Garek?"

I saw her cheeks flush, and she looked down.

"I'm sorry. I shouldn't have brought that up."

"We all make mistakes," she sighed. "I should've been stronger, and not let that affair take place."

"But perhaps it was meant to be? After all, Annemarie was born, and then Ginna and Garek found each other."

"I suppose. But still I wonder…"

"Wonder what?"

"What things would be like if I'd said 'no'."

"That's a question we'll never know the answer to."

She turned and looked into my eyes then. "You're right of course. We can't change what happened, even if we want to."

"At least that seems to be the case. This Time-GAP crossing, and falling into the Time-Well, has made me wonder if we're making changes in the fabric of time without even knowing it."

"That's kind of a frightening thought," she said.

"But how can we ever know? All we know is the reality we're experiencing at any given moment."

"And the memories we have—of what we believe happened in the past."

"Now that's scary. What if the past we remember isn't what really happened?"

"I wish sometimes the memory of losing my three brothers wasn't real."

"But we don't know for sure Jael is dead, do we?" I was surprised I could actually say these words out loud.

"He and Jon had a strong mental connection, but Jon has felt nothing in all the years since the battle at the Safezone—before you left for the Fountain."

By now, tears were flowing down her cheeks, and I was the one hugging her. We stared at each other in silence for several minutes.

Then she took a ragged breath. "We'd better stop this train of thought, Celestia. All I was really trying to say is—don't rush into things with Laken. Somehow I believe the Lord will let you know if he's the one."

"I know. That's why I didn't sleep with him. And somehow, I have a feeling he understands that, too."

These words were barely out of my mouth when the door of the hut swung inward, and two figures stooped and walked in.

"Dad!" I jumped up as soon as I recognized my father and pulled him into a tight hug.

"It's so good to have you back," he said. "It still seems almost like a dream."

"I missed you both so much. Thinking of you was the only thing keeping me going sometimes."

I saw Laken standing behind my father, who was the taller of the two. I was glad to see Laken smile as he said, "You have a great family here, Celestia. In my time, families are tending to drift apart."

I saw him step forward, and it seemed natural to let him take my hand in his. "Well, we aren't living like typical Thirty-first Century families," I sighed. "We're more like something from your past."

An awkward silence settled until Dad spoke up, "Laken and I had an interesting talk. With his MEI background and my elementary Star Corps training, we've been piecing together what our two respective times know about crossing the GAP."

Laken smiled and nodded. "There are still a lot of holes in our theory, but if we keep pursuing our current line of thought, we may come to a breakthrough in interplanetary travel."

"Really?" cried Mom.

Dad smiled down at her. "Yes, Martina. I know you're the one who keeps wanting to leave Earth."

"Well, it hasn't turned out to be the paradise we expected, has it?"

"No dear. But Johan seemed to have only sketchy knowledge of this place he called 'Maia'."

"Maia?" Laken and I said simultaneously. Then we looked at each other wondering why this word had struck a chord in both of us.

"That's what he called Earth," Mom said.

"Oh," whispered Laken. I was still looking at him as he spoke and wondered what he was thinking. There was a strange glint in those almond eyes of his. Why did this word 'Maia' have such an effect on him?

"Well, I think we need to eat some supper. All these deep conversations have made me hungry." Mom was glancing at me as she said this, and I couldn't tell if she approved of my standing there holding Laken's hand.

To be honest, I can't tell you if I was feeling anything for him right then. It just seemed the right thing to do at the moment—what with his being a total stranger to our time and place. I felt like it was my obligation to take care of him and help him get adjusted. After all, if he hadn't met me, he wouldn't be here   he'd be back at home in his own place, not in this strange tropical forest on the edge of nowhere, with a band of exiles.

As we sat on the floor around the rough, low wooden table Dad had made, all of us joined hands for the mealtime prayer. I have to admit I wasn't listening very attentively to my father's words. My mind was more on Laken, wondering what he was thinking. Suddenly, I was surprised to hear his voice say:

"Amen," when Dad had finished the prayer.

My eyes turned toward Laken of their own free will, and I found him looking back at me. "I'm glad to be here with you," he whispered.

I felt my face getting warm and had to look away from his gaze. Quickly I reached for some of the fruit and bread Mom set out for us and gave portions to Laken and myself.

***

A few days later, Aunt Raina and I were working together hoeing weeds in a vegetable garden. Both of us put our hair up to get it out of our way—mine dark brown, hers still very red. But by mid-morning, the sun was extremely hot, and sweat dripped down our faces. We moved to a shady spot and sat on a stone outcrop. I wanted to talk to her one-on-one about Jael, but I didn't know how to begin.

"Raina," I said softly, "You don't have to tell me if it's too painful. But what happened after the attack on the Safe-Zone?"

"When we all got separated?"

"Yeah. Dad and Mom found Dominic. Daiah told me that—and about losing Darien. I know you and Jael were still missing with the children when I crossed to the Fountain, or rather tried to. We got trapped in a Time Well instead."

"Is that why you were gone so long?"

"No one's told you about it?"

She shook her head. "There's been no chance to talk to Jon recently. He spends a lot of time with your friend Laken."

"Yeah, they seem to have a lot of interests in common."

"Sounds like I need to hear *your* story, too," she tried to smile.

"I'll tell mine after you, okay?"

Silence settled then, and she took a deep breath. "Well, you know Jael is missing. Jon and Martina think he's dead, because Jon isn't getting any feelings of him like he used to. I'll pour out the whole story, if you want to listen. I've never really told anyone *everything*."

"Maybe it will help to get it out."

"You're right. It's time to get this off my chest."

I sat closer to Raina as she began to tell her story:

CHAPTER THREE
RAINA SPEAKS

You don't really know a lot about me, Celestia *[she began]*—except that I was with the Redlarks, back when we were all still on planet Terres. It seems the Lord has seen fit to interweave me with the lives of nearly everyone in this story—especially Jael.

I first met Jael when his parents died on Terres, but I think I'll wait on that part of the story. I'm not ready to tell it.

[She sighed deeply and I began to see that bringing back these memories was painful for her.]

Okay, *[she took a deep breath, as if beginning all over again].* As you know, we all eventually made it to Earth. Daiah and I met because we both knew your Uncle Dominic. I'd met him when Jakob and Myra helped me escape the Redlarks.

As you know, we finally made it to Earth with help from Dominic and the Rebels. And to our surprise Jon, Jael and Martina had also gotten there when they found Darien and the Rebels with him. By the time we all found each other, Jon and Martina were married. And I was overjoyed to be reunited with my dearest childhood friend, Jael.

It seemed that all would be well, but after fifteen or twenty Earth-years passed, the System found us—and attacked Earth.

[I nodded. "I know about that from my youth, and I learned even more when I was in the Time Well. It appears a new evil force was awakening during that time."

"That's right, Celestia. And so, we had to flee the cities and try to find safety in the wilder parts of Earth. I'm sure you remember when Darien's Safe-Zone was attacked by System forces—and we all had to scatter. While you were with the others at Jon and Martina's cave, Jael and I were in another part of Old North America with the children. Let me tell you what happened."

She sighed and began the story:]

I'm going to tell this story just the way it felt to me.

We were creeping on our bellies one early, dewy morning, shortly after our flight from the Safe-Zone. As soundlessly as we could, we crested a hill. Behind us, the trees of the forest were rustling in the wind, hopefully muffling the sounds of the children in our camp.

'Perhaps Jon and Martina's cave would have been a better place for the children,' I thought. 'The waterfall there would drown out almost any sound.'

But Jael said we needed to come to this secluded area of mixed hardwood and conifer forest where there was more likelihood of finding roots, berries, and other edibles. Now though, we couldn't let the children help with any of the gathering because too many Patrols were in this area. Once we'd spotted a Dragonfly-Drone but managed to evade it.

As we reached the dome of the hill and peeked out of the grass stems silently, we saw there was a Patrol camp right below in the next swale. Putting his finger to his lips, Jael motioned for us to creep back down, our hearts pounding so loud that it seemed the soldiers below would hear them.

Neither of us spoke, or even caught a good breath, until we were back under the shade of the forest. "That settles it for us," he whispered. "We have to find a way to get to Jon's cave."

I nodded and tried to swallow, but my throat was so dry I almost choked. We walked another hundred meters under the trees before I said anything. "How can we get there? We don't have anyone firstborn to help us cross the GAP?"

"That means we walk," said Jael.

I knew this was the only option now, but I didn't like it. "That will be hard on the children, and we'll probably be caught. They can't help making some noise."

"Well, it's either that or stay here, waiting to be

discovered," he shrugged. "I guess I'd rather get caught trying to do something, than waiting around and doing nothing."

"Me, too. I wish we had some horses, though."

"That would be too noisy," he shrugged. I realized he was thinking of Splash, his pinto pony we couldn't find when Darien's Safe-Zone was attacked.

"Sorry, Jael, I didn't mean to remind you of Splash."

"Hey, it's all right. Hopefully he's living on his own in the wild."

"With a pretty filly." I tried to smile.

As we continued to work our way back to camp, I found myself thinking of Feier, the telepathic feier-cat I'd given him long ago on Terres. "We sure could use Feier's wisdom these days."

"I miss him, too," Jael whispered. "Too bad there aren't any feier-cats here on Earth."

When we reached camp, five children ran out to greet us—Jace our son; Alexia and Andre, who were Daiah and Darien's children; plus Siene and Toren, children of our friends Branden and Morgan. All were nine Standard Years or older, which was good. Thankfully, we hadn't needed to flee the Patrols when these children were younger.

Many of the Believers in Darien's compound had frowned on anyone having children at all—saying the times were too dangerous for them. Daiah supported me strongly, since she'd just had Alexia when I discovered I was pregnant. Morgan and I became close friends during my pregnancy. Siene was born only a couple of months after Jace.

Right now, Branden and Morgan were on a reconnaissance trip, so there was no way of communicating with them. We hoped that when they found the camp deserted, they'd know what happened. Morgan and her husband had volunteered to help with the children, for obvious reasons, but Darien insisted they also do some recon for him. I often wished they could have stayed. Right now, having Branden's GAP-crossing abilities would really help.

I shook my head to clear these negative thoughts away, and hugged the girls, Alexia and Siene, while the boys clustered around Jael. Before he spoke, he motioned for quiet.

"There's a Patrol camp not far from us," he whispered. "We must pack now and set out at nightfall."

"Where will we go, Father?" Jace asked.

"We need to head for Jon's cave."

"Come on girls," I said softly. "Let's get things organized and see what food will travel well."

"We can't cross the GAP, can we, sir?" The youngest child, Toren, was asking this, as we walked toward our makeshift shelter. I knew Jael's answer, even though he was moving out of earshot.

"Not without Branden," I muttered to myself.

"I'm firstborn," said Alexia. "I could do it."

"No, you can't!" Siene tossed her head.

"Neither can you!" Alexia retorted.

"Stop it, you two. Hopefully someday you can be trained."

Fortunately, neither of them asked when this might be, for it was probably a hollow promise—with the way Believers were being persecuted now.

***

It was full-dark when we each shouldered a pack-sack and followed Jael silently out of the tiny glade. Now there was very little evidence of this camp's presence. Jael wanted to erase all signs, but there wasn't enough time. Hopefully, it looked enough like the place hadn't been occupied recently.

Our walk that first night was long and silent. The stars didn't show themselves through the clouds hanging in the sky, and there was no moon. Actually, this was fortunate because it made us harder to see. The children did a good job of keeping quiet, too. Still, I felt my heart pounding as I pushed through each rustling shrub.

There was no path to follow here, so it should be harder for anyone to track us, but I worried about the noise every time a twig snapped, or dry leaves crunched. Spring had brought out the foliage on the hardwood trees and bushes, so at least there was more concealment than in winter. And hopefully, we were harder to track when there was no snow on the ground.

The creeping light of pre-dawn found us crossing a rocky ridge to the east of where our camp had been. There was one Patrol behind us, but we had no way of knowing if we were heading right toward another one. Again I sighed, wishing Branden and Morgan were here. They might have been able to answer this question. Now, in the dark and chill just before dawn, I shivered, wondering if our friends had been captured—or worse.

Jael soon found a small cave just over the ridge and beckoned us to follow him inside. The place had a dank smell, but the floor was dry enough. After munching in silence on some fruit leather, we each wrapped in a blanket, and tried to rest.

Just before coming to lie next to me, Jael used a couple of fallen tree branches to prop his blanket across the low opening of the cave. "Hope that will keep prying eyes out," he whispered, as he joined me.

"Me too." Then I drew a blanket over both of us.

"This is going to take several days' trekking at this pace," he sighed.

"Well, we have to go at the children's speed. After all, that's who we need to preserve, the next generation."

"Sometimes I wish the True Lord would come now and take care of everything."

"I know. I think that nearly every day. But I guess all we can do is keep trusting and do our best."

"Do you sometimes wonder if there's any point in all this?"

I was surprised to hear him say this—usually Jael had the strongest faith of anyone. My mind went blank, and I pulled him closer, seeking comfort.

Soon he was kissing me and drawing his fingers gently across my back. "Jael, I don't think we should be doing this with the children so close by."

"You're right. I remember how it affected me when I was a boy and heard my sister, Martina with—"

"My brother Jason," I sighed, trying to keep tears from my eyes and voice.

"Are you okay?"

"Just hold me a little longer."

***

Later, as I lay alongside him listening to his even breathing, I was thankful he was getting some much-needed sleep. Too many thoughts were in my mind that night to allow sleep, so I decided to just relax next to him and let the thoughts have their way with me, remembering special times we'd been together. Foremost in my mind was when we each arrived on this mysterious planet some called Maia, or Mother-Earth:

The first time we were reunited here on Earth—when he returned from the Fountain in the Desert—I'd felt the joy of finding a long-lost childhood friend. Both of us were still young enough then, so Darien and Irina—who was my foster mother—felt we needed to go back to school. Irina found a flat for the two of us, but it was across town in Celeton. Jael was used to living at Darien's during the winter, and Irina decided not to disrupt this arrangement. Soon after Celestia was born, Jon and Martina came back to the city, too, staying at Darien's until they found a place of their own.

So, three or four years passed with Jael and I in different schools, only seeing each other when Irina joined her children for a visit or a holiday celebration of some kind. Irina often talked about the True King she believed in, and I finally decided to join their fellowship of Believers.

On that day, when I'd been presented to the assembly, wearing a pure white dress, I felt Jael's eyes on me all through the ceremony. When the ritual was completed and everyone went to the Agape Feast, Jael met me at one of the long tables spread with food.

"Here's some bread for you," he smiled, taking a piece and holding it up to my lips.

I bit gently, and then took the rest of the piece he offered.

"You look so beautiful today."

"Thanks." I felt suddenly shy and wondered why. After all, hadn't we known each other for several years now? Why did I feel like I'd only just met him?

He took my hand and drew me away from the table, toward a bench set along one of the walls of the large room.

Once we were settled on the bench, he put his arm

across my shoulders. "How old are you now?"

"You know as well as I do. We're nearly the same age—eighteen Standard Years," I chuckled.

"I just meant, do you think we're both old enough to think about marriage?"

I was dumbfounded. "What?"

"I was hoping you felt like I did," he sighed, drawing his arm back.

"No, wait." I grabbed his hand before he could stand up again. "Jael, please. You just caught me by surprise, that's all."

I could see his cheeks beginning to redden, the way they did when he was angry or confused. With a start, I realized I probably did know him as well as anyone on Earth—probably better than his siblings did.

"It's just that I've thought of you as a friend and play-mate for so long."

"Do you love me?"

"Of course I do."

"As a friend or a husband?"

"Jael—I—I need time to think about this."

"If you need to think it over, then I know what the answer is," he sighed, standing up suddenly.

"Stop, please. There's something I have to explain."

Slowly he sat down again.

"I've never told you this, and I swore Daiah and Irina to secrecy, too." I swallowed hard, feeling how dry my throat was, and hoping my voice wouldn't disappear entirely. "I may be wearing white right now, but I'm damaged goods."

"What do you mean?"

"When your mother and I were fleeing Terres-City, we joined up with another small group that included Myra and Jakob, who you've met—"

He nodded. "So, what does that have to do with us? That was so many years ago."

"Amian was with them."

"Yeah, I think I heard Jon mention his name once or twice."

"Amian is a beast." I had to stop and take another long breath before I could spit out my next hateful words. "He raped me—when I was only eleven."

He sat in silence then, as I tried to keep from sobbing aloud. Gently he wiped some of the tears from my cheeks.

"I've never been with a man—besides that—and I'm not sure if I can…"

Now, Jael showed his true colors, for he just sat and held my hand. I was afraid he'd try to convince me everything was 'all right', or expect me to act as if none of it mattered now. Instead, he seemed to understand why I couldn't do this yet.

"You said Daiah knew," he whispered.

"She was raped by him, too," I murmured, beginning to feel relief as I told him these things. The pain which had sat in my chest all these years actually was lessening.

"She told me, when we were on Alpha Centauri, before we came here to Earth with Dominic."

"And has she found some peace?"

"I think so, but I'd like to talk to her again. I think it might help me."

"Did you know she's marrying my brother Darien?"

"No, I didn't."

"That would seem to be a good sign, don't you think?" he almost smiled.

"When is the wedding?"

"In a couple of months, Earth time. I'm sure she would want you to come. They haven't sent word out yet."

"So that's why I didn't know."

"She wanted to be here for your ceremony, but there were other things she had to do before the wedding, I guess."

"Will she be in Celeton soon?"

"Next week, I think."

I closed my eyes, hoping I wouldn't start crying again. Suddenly, I felt his breath on my cheek, and his lips brushing mine lightly.

"Remember when we tried kissing at Anha's, our caregiver on Terres?"

I giggled and drew back. "Yes. Neither of us thought much of it, did we?"

He pulled me toward him again. "We were just children then. Now *we're* the grown-ups. Like Jason and Martina."

I jerked back at the sound of my brother's name. "I wonder what happened to Jason."

"I'm sorry," he sighed. "I shouldn't have mentioned him."

"It's just hard sometimes not knowing."

Then we sat in silence, neither of us able to think of anything safe to say. I wondered what I'd do if he tried to kiss me again. "I hope I can talk to Daiah, when she comes," I said at last.

"I'll let her know. She'll be staying with Darien and me."

"Jael—"

"Yes?"

"I do love you. Right now, I'm just not sure what kind of love I'm capable of."

"Dear Raina," he said, pulling me into his embrace. "I'll accept whatever you can give—and I'll wait as long as you need me to."

Those words were exactly what I needed to hear.

CHAPTER FOUR
TEARS IN THE FABRIC

Time passed, and eventually Jael and I were married at a Gathering. Darien and Daiah stood up for us.

It was good to see how the Lord healed both of us—and even helped us each find a soul-mate. But we were still living in perilous times, especially for Believers.

So, now I'll continue with the story of our attempt to reach Jon's cave:

I woke to the sound of screams and explosions. This was the third day of our trek to Jon and Martina's, but we hadn't found a good cave as dawn caught up with us this day, so we'd tried to make do with a swale under some low-branching evergreens. Evidently it hadn't been secure enough, once the sun came up.

Now smoke was billowing toward us as I groped in the direction of the children's frightened voices. I couldn't see anyone clearly. Then came the sound of an amplified voice:

"We know you're in there. Why prolong this, you Rebels? Come out with your hands on top of your heads."

Small hands grasped at me, and voices came in tense whispers:

"Mommy."

"Mom?"

"Dad?"

I realized with a shock that I was the only mother available now, and tried to reach out to any small form I could, drawing them into an embrace. Small hands clutched at me. These probably belonged to Siene or Toren, who were the youngest.

Suddenly I felt the strength of Jael's arm drawing me back, deeper under the sheltering branches of a fir tree. Then I finally saw Jace, seated with his back against the tree's trunk, holding on to Toren and Andre's hands.

"What is it, Uncle Jael?" This had to be Alexia's voice right behind me.

"Patrol!" Jael hissed. "We have no way out." I heard anger at himself in his voice. "They must have tracked us here after dawn-"

"And set up an ambush—just as we were falling to sleep." There was more maturity in Alexia's voice than I'd noticed before.

"There's only one thing we can do now—right, Dad?"

"Are you sure you're ready, Jace?" Jael asked.

"What are you talking about?" I cried.

"Jon and I have been working with Jace and Alexia on this. Sorry, but there's no time to explain."

Just then an explosion came much closer than any previous ones. Before I could say anything else, Jael pushed out away from us, disappearing into the smoke. At the same time, Jace grabbed my right hand firmly. He put Siene on my left, and then reached out to Alexia and Andre, putting Toren between them. I realized with a shock that we were joined in a circle—without Jael.

'He doesn't know how to cross the GAP, does he?' my mind was asking. Suddenly the world seemed to whirl, as I tried to pull away—to go find Jael—but the small hands had a tight grip on mine.

"I need your help, Alexia," Jace called suddenly. "Andre, focus on your mother."

"No! Where is Jael?" But these words never made it out of my mouth, or past the GAP. My mind seemed to close like a door—

***

["I remember now, Raina," I said. "My mother told me people were just getting ready to start the morning meal, there in Jon's cave, when the air crackled with a kind of static."]

Then I began to hear voices *[Raina resumed]:*
"It's Raina!"
"And the children!"

"Mom?"

"Is that you, Andre? How did you get here?" Daiah asked. I saw her gazing in near-disbelief at her son.

"I kept my mind fixed on you, Mom—so we could find you."

Then I heard Jon's surprised voice, "You managed to cross a GAP right to us?"

"Yes, Uncle Jon. Just like you'd taught Alexia and me to do. And we knew from Dad that a younger brother— like Andre—could focus on a person to guide us."

My mind was still numb, looking at everyone around me in confusion, but things were beginning to register. Then I realized, "Jon taught Alexia and Jace to cross the GAP. Of course!"

"Yes, Raina," came a calming voice, and then I felt soft hands reaching to me. I clung to them and asked, "Where's Jael? Is he here? He wasn't in the circle." I was beginning to sob now.

"He had to create a diversion for us, Mom." Could this calm voice really be my young son?

"Jon?" Martina asked.

"Yes, you and Jael have some special connection between you," I cried. "You're the only one who can go back for him."

Suddenly silence fell. Martina drew the children nearer to her, and Daiah stepped over to help her calm them.

Jon moved closer to me, taking my hands in his. "I'm sorry, Raina," he whispered. "I'm not getting anything."

"Nothing at all?" This came from Martina, and I realized suddenly, with the desolate sound of her voice, that Jael was her little brother.

"No."

"Then he must be—"

"Dead!" I wailed, and then fell into silence.

[*"Oh, Raina," I sighed, holding her close. "You must feel desolate."*

"I guess those are the best words for now," she sighed. "But I know I'm not the only one who's lost a spouse or dear friend in this terrible war. I just wish it would stop."

I nodded and stroked her red hair. But I couldn't find any words to say.

Then Raina's voice began to murmur again.]:

During the worst times, I felt like lashing out in anger at everyone around me. See those fluffy white clouds drifting overhead in a pale blue sky? Some of the clouds are making strange shapes. I used to stare at them for hours, but I couldn't focus. I felt as though my mind and my body were separate from each other, my mind drifting and shifting like the cloud forms overhead, and then I could turn and look down at myself, lying prone there in the grass.

'Is this what it feels like to die?' I wondered. 'Or perhaps I'm going insane. Sometimes I wish I could die, so I won't have to keep feeling this pain.'

One day as I looked at the sky, it seemed to unroll like a painting. I could see one of my hands reaching up, as though it could grasp the largest cloud. Desperately I tried to reach it, but the wind blew the vision away, as quickly as it had come. My hand fell back to earth, feeling as though something was ripped out of it. But then I heard a voice whispering:

"You must never despair. You will be reunited some-day. *'I know the plans I have for you—to give you hope, and a future.'*

["Where do those words come from, Celestia?"

"I think they're somewhere in The Book. All we can do now is just keep on living, one day at a time."

I didn't realize I'd spoken this last part aloud, until I heard Raina say:

"Thank you. I know the True King has a plan in this. And somewhere deep inside, I still think Jael lives."

"Here on Earth or in Heaven?"

"I don't know yet. But somehow I know I'll see him again."

"We'll all see our loved ones again, Raina. I'm sure of it."]

CHAPTER FIVE
BACK TO CELESTIA IN INDONIA

The sunlight was scattered by small clouds floating overhead in a turquoise sky, as Raina and I sat on the crest of the green hill several days later. After she'd finished her story, I'd told her of my adventures in the Time Well—in between bouts of working in the garden, of course. How I'd met Laken, and how we'd traveled Twenty-second Century Earth, trying to find a way back to our proper time.

"But in the end," I sighed, as I finally finished my story, "It was the True King who helped us, when we couldn't help ourselves."

"I know what you mean. My life has been like that a lot."

Then we both fell into silence, each lost in our own thoughts. Below us stretched the small valley where our Out-clave had established itself.

Raina sighed as she finally spoke, "So much time has passed since we first came to Indonia. What is it? Four years, at least."

"My mother says it's closer to five," I shrugged. "And I missed them all while we were lost in time."

"Well, it's easy to lose track here. Time doesn't have the same significance it has in the busy world of the cities we've lived in most of our lives. Here it revolves more around the flow of seasons—whether it's the wet of the rainy season, or the drier time for planting crops."

"I guess that's what makes it a good place for Believers. What was it my Uncle Dominic said? This place used to be called New Guinea back in ancient times, hundreds of years ago. Even in the late Twentieth Century, parts of it remained quite remote, totally isolated from civilization."

"So, this has made it an ideal refuge," she agreed. "A place where we've found ways to raise our own food, and hunt animals still living in the wilds—a place to hide from the System."

"I'm still having trouble thinking in terms of the System again," I sighed. "Things were far from perfect back in the Twenty-second Century, but there was no long-distance space-travel yet, no colonies, and no Galactic System."

"So why did you and Laken come here?"

"The Lord sent us here, saying he was sending us to the place we were most needed. We're still wondering what he meant."

"I wonder if it has something to do with those mysterious dark forces we keep hearing rumors about," she whispered, almost to herself.

Below us, we could see several children playing games in the center of the circular compound of huts, laughing and calling happily. Besides Alexia, Andre, and Jace—there were several younger ones now, born here in Indonia.

"Alexia and Andre have really matured since I saw them last in Darien's Safe-Zone," I said.

"Yes, five years is a long time in the life of a child."

"How are the kids handling the losses of their parents?" I was almost afraid to ask this question, but she replied quickly.

"Lexi seems to have compensated by mothering the little ones, especially Morgan. Andre—well, he's a quiet one—so I'm not sure how he's doing."

"What about you, Raina?"

"For me the pain of losing Jael grows a little less each day, but it's sad that those oldest three—Lexi, Andre, and Jace—will never know their real fathers, as I knew them."

"And Daiah?"

"She clings to Andre—sometimes too much I think—as her only connection to Darien."

"He's grown into a striking resemblance of his father, hasn't he?"

She nodded silently.

"At least Siene and Toren have their father, Branden," I whispered.

"Though not their mother, Morgan," she added. "They seem to cling to me more these days—and they don't talk much about their real mother."

"Well, they were quite young when she died, weren't they?"

She nodded. "About nine and ten Earth-years."

I gave her a squeeze around the shoulders. "I can see why they're drawn to you. You're a warm, motherly person."

"Oh, I don't know."

"I see it as your gift from the Lord."

After a short hesitation, she lifted her head and smiled. "Thanks, Celestia."

This set me to thinking about how my own mother, Martina, had lost both her parents while she was still a teenager. But now, at least she had her mother, Irina, back. And Mom and I were together again after a long and harrowing separation, while I'd been lost in the Twenty-second Century.

As these thoughts passed through my mind, I saw my grandmother strolling across the compound toward the hill, up through the tall, waving grasses. She waved a hand to us and smiled, and I found myself thinking of how much she'd been through in her life—losing her husband and later each of her sons. This had been terrible for her, my mother told me.

"Irina will say she's a poor example," said Raina just then, almost echoing my thoughts. "But it was she who helped me the most with my own emotions, especially when we came here to Indonia.

"Branden's wife, Morgan, died in one of the fierce battles of that desperate time, as you've heard. Once Branden went to help me with the children, we began to find solace with each other. By the time we made our way to Indonia, I was six months pregnant with Branden's child. I was embarrassed, and also afraid Daiah would be envious of me. So, we got married at the very next Gathering."

Even though I already knew about this, I turned and looked into her eyes. "Do you really love Branden?"

"In a different way than I loved Jael, but yes, I do love him."

"And you find comfort in each other."

"Yes, Irina said that to me, too. So, I asked her if that was the reason she and Dominic got married—for comfort."

"What did Grandma say to that?"

"She said, 'Of course, I can't deny comfort is a part of our relationship. But for Dominic and me there's more, because we were originally each married to the other one's twin. There's a closeness and understanding that goes deeper than a more typical relationship.' So, I'm glad for Irina," she sighed. "Even though there's a pain I still feel sometimes."

"Some say time will heal us." It was all I could think of to say.

As we'd done many times before, we sat and hugged each other. Then she said, "I still have my children, so I should live for them, right?"

"I didn't mean it that way. Please don't think I meant you to feel guilty for your grief."

"I know you didn't mean to."

"What I really was trying to say is that you and I are missing the same person—my Uncle Jael was a very special man."

"And no amount of talking will bring him back." She leaned her head against my shoulder.

Just then there came happy laughter from the children below us, who were playing some kind of tag game. This made us both smile.

"We do have many blessings, don't we?"

"We certainly do. And as time goes by, I pray these things will help to heal some of your wounds—at least a little."

"And for now, we seem to have found a safe place to live again."

"I sure hope that lasts," I sighed.

***

Later in the day, as a cool evening breeze finally arrived, I climbed the hill once more, listening to the end-of-day sounds in camp—mothers calling children home, fathers gathering wood for their fire-pits and talking back and forth.

I smiled as I thought how much better this was than the isolation we'd sometimes experienced in Celeton. The children here had a much richer life than my family had experienced—even if they didn't have some of the so-called comforts of civilization.

Soon it would be time to begin the preparations for the weekly Gathering, and the Agape Meal. It was so good to have this opportunity to support and help each other. Of course, we were all still human, and nothing was perfect in this temporal world.

Suddenly, I heard someone calling my name. Shading my eyes from the setting sun, I saw it was Laken. He seemed to be very excited about something, but I couldn't make out any of the words he was calling to me. So I rose, waved, and started down the hill toward him.

CHAPTER SIX
UNDER THE CRESCENT MOON

Laken and I met each other about two-thirds of the way up the hill, where he gave me an excited hug.

"What's up with you?" I asked.

"Your dad and I have been working all day on this Space-GAP idea he has."

"You mean space travel? We need ships for that."

"Jon and I don't see why that has to be," he said. "If crossing a GAP is truly instantaneous, why can't a human body survive it? There has to be a way."

I was looking into his eyes with disbelief. "But if that's true, why haven't any scientists ever figured it out?"

"Jon thinks it has something to do with the connection he had with Jael."

"But Jael is dead."

"Jon thinks if he can go back to find Ginna's brother—"

"What?"

"Did he ever tell you how he used the String Theory of Parallel Universes to merge the lives of Jael with Danny—and Martina with Ginna?"

"Of course he did. That's how I ended up meeting you in Tacoma—I was trying to help Ginna and her daughter Annemarie."

"That's right. Ginna told us all about it in Jerusalem."

"You did that mind-reading thing with her, and nearly killed her."

"I know. I'm sorry." He dropped his gaze to the ground, took a deep breath, and then looked up to where the crescent moon was hanging in the deep blue of the evening sky. "Look, let's forget all this GAP and Mind-Exploration stuff for awhile. It's a beautiful evening, and I think we should just sit down here and enjoy a few moments of peace while we can."

The slender sliver of silver was high in the sky. We were basking in one of the rare cool nights that occasionally came to Indonia. Time seemed to flow here like a slow, meandering stream. Several weeks had passed since Laken and I arrived. But each day here was similar to the next—the search for food, caring for the vegetable garden, the cooking, and the cleaning.

I sat down in the grass next to him, and sighed, "You know, the work here isn't exhausting, but the sameness sometimes makes me feel weary. At times, I even find myself longing for the adventures we went through in our Time Well."

Laken laughed aloud. "You must be really bored if you want to go back to all that mess!"

"Well, maybe not the earthquake—or the prison," I grinned back. "Although come to think of it, I wouldn't mind seeing the King again."

His face became thoughtful. "That was quite an experience, wasn't it? To actually see the Lord of Heaven and Earth face to face—to feel his touch."

"I miss it," I sighed.

"He said in The Book that he's always with us."

"I know, but it's just not the same. I can't really feel his presence like I did then."

"Maybe we aren't supposed to go so much on our feelings."

I turned and looked at him, seated there beside me on the grassy hill. Impulsively, I reached out and grabbed his hand. He slid his hand upward along my arm, and then pulled me toward him, so I was leaning on his shoulder.

"I can't help it," I whispered. "I'm a person with strong feelings."

"Are any of those feelings for me?"

I wasn't sure what to say, so I turned my head and looked into his face, which was barely visible in the pale moonlight. Stars were beginning to blaze out in the darkened sky. With no artificial light to wash them out, they were like shining pinpoints of light, outlining Laken's face and almond eyes.

"Don't you miss your home?" I finally asked.

"I'd be lying if I said I didn't. But with the earthquake, there probably wouldn't be anything to go back to."

"Unless there was some way to get back to Tacoma before the quake."

"Well, none of us—your father, you, or me—has that kind of pinpoint accuracy yet. Besides, the quake would still happen—and maybe I wouldn't survive it in another time-line."

"This is getting too weird. It's like trying to understand a maze. But actually, Dad is getting pretty good at Time-GAPs," I whispered. "If you really wanted to go home, he probably could help you."

"No," he shook his head slowly. "The King sent me here, and I need to find out why."

Silence settled between us again, as we gazed up at the shining crescent, the lighted part of the Moon facing us here on Earth.

"I wonder if any of it is still there," his voice came softly.

"Any of what?"

"The Mind Exploration Institute Luna Base."

"Oh, yeah. We were there, almost a millennium ago, weren't we? Until Mauren—"

"Arrested us," he finished. "I wonder if anything is left up there. Nine hundred years is a long time."

"It's hard to believe it was so long ago we were there. Still, with no atmosphere or water, things wouldn't break down or decay. So, it's possible the buildings are still there."

"Wouldn't it be interesting to go and see?"

"That's where I began to trust you," I whispered. "Before that I was afraid you were just using us for your own research."

"Actually, you're right. Up until then, I *was* only thinking of myself, but after I realized Mauren was—well that she had her own secret agenda—it changed me, made me realize I'd been wrong to use you."

"And especially after we knew Darroch had betrayed us."

He nodded silently, and I realized he was still hurt by what his supposed friend had done. Then I heard his voice whispering in my ear, words that I'd least expected, "Do you ever wonder what it's like to really be in love?"

I found myself answering almost immediately. "Well, I thought I was once, but it turned out he didn't really love me. And boy, did that hurt! I guess I learned that love isn't a one-way thing. His name was Patrick. I was still in my teens, and he swept me off my feet. I guess he was my first true love."

"Did you and he ever make love?"

"No. I realize now that was a good thing." Oddly, I wasn't embarrassed by this question. Then I decided to ask him one of my own. "What do you think about making love, Laken?"

"I'd think you figured that out in Toronto," he smiled.

"I was too fuzzy in the head to think that night, you know."

"Yeah, I realized the air-drugs had been too much for you."

"That's why I'm surprised you didn't take advantage of me."

He smiled now and rubbed his hand on his tunic, letting go of me. "I didn't think it was right to force myself on you. I was starting to realize, even then, that there was something special about you."

"About me?"

He nodded silently, putting his hands behind him, and leaned back on his arms gazing up at the sky.

"People sure seem to make a big deal out of sex," I sighed, after a long silence.

"It seems to become the underlying subject of almost any male-female conversation," he smiled.

"Have you ever-" Suddenly, I found I couldn't even say the words.

"Made love?" he finished for me.

I just nodded, with the words lost somewhere in my throat.

"I'm almost ashamed to admit it," he said, "Now that I've seen the King face-to-face."

"What do you mean?"

"Well, I had sex with several women, but now I realize it wasn't really 'making love'."

It was too dark to see his face, but I could hear the embarrassment in his voice.

"Perhaps sex is just over-rated," I sighed, hoping to step back from the subject a little.

"I think humans are just wired that way," he murmured.

"Are you even human, Laken?" I'd never known a man to act like he was—not pressing for more physical contact.

My heart was pounding loudly in my chest, and I wondered if he could hear it, as I quickly pulled away from him and stood up. "I'm still a virgin, you know. I've always been taught to save myself for the one special person."

I was afraid he'd be angry, but instead he shrugged and smiled up at me. "This matters a lot to you, I can see."

"*I* think it does." But frustration was coming into my voice. "It's just how I was raised. My parents told me how they were totally messed up by the Terres Underground, where drugs and everything else were available—so they'd had many lovers before they met. But they say they realize now they were always meant for each other, and it would've been much better if they *had* waited."

"You may not believe it, but I feel that way, too," he sighed. "I can't seem to find the right words to tell you how I feel for you. I've never felt like this before."

"And I don't even *know* what I feel. We've only known each other a short time. There's something here, but I'm confused."

He was still leaning back on his arms, half-reclining and staring up at the Moon. "You asked if I wanted to go back to my home. I might—if you came with me."

"Come with you? But I hardly know you."

"Haven't nine hundred years just passed?" he grinned.

"Yeah, in the blink of an eye—but we didn't live them," I shrugged. "That doesn't count."

He chuckled and then said, "You know me better than you think. Remember what we did at MEI in Toronto?"

"You mean the Mind-sharing?" I didn't like being reminded of this. "Most of what I remember is pain. You probably learned more about me than I did about you. It's not fair." I stomped my foot in frustration and started to walk away. He reached up and stopped me by grabbing one of my arms near the elbow.

"Okay, I admit it. I learned enough to think I love you."

I opened my mouth to answer, but no words would come out, at first. "Sometimes I feel I don't know *anything* about love," I finally managed to murmur.

He rose to his feet then and stood close to me, but this time he made no move to touch me. "There's a lot more to love than just liking someone or believing the same things."

My breath caught in my throat, and I thought again of Patrick. We'd liked each other and had a lot in common, but was it real love after all?

Now Laken was facing me and very gently took each of my hands in his. Holding them up to shoulder height, he gave each a slight squeeze and interlocked our fingers.

"Celestia, the reason I know I love you is that I never want to see you hurt—by me or anyone else. The True King has sent me here with you for reasons only he knows."

"My mom says he only reveals his plans step by step."

"I agree with that. We should go one step at a time, too."

"Okay," I nodded slowly. "But right now, I think I need a hug."

He smiled and drew me towards him, placing his arms gently around me and holding me so close I could hear his heart beating. "May I kiss you now?" he whispered.

"To be honest, I think I'm still a bit afraid of you, Laken. Will you be angry if I say 'no'?"

Stepping back, he looked into my eyes. "I don't want to rush anything either," he smiled.

The stars were still blazing around his head as I looked into his deep brown eyes. "Thanks, Laken," I whispered.

Then he suddenly pulled me toward him, but I was even more surprised when he just kissed me gently on top of my head.

CHAPTER SEVEN
LUNACY

The Indonian days continued to pass in their patterns of misty dawns, warm mornings when we could work, and hot afternoons when it was much better to rest. Then work would resume in the cool of the evenings. I found myself thinking often of Laken and his gentle touch. Sometimes, when no one was around, my heart would start to pound, and my face would feel hot. But I still wasn't sure if what I felt was real love.

Fortunately, I spent most of my time working with Daiah and Raina in the gardens. Vegetables and fruits were beginning to ripen now, and we were enjoying some of the benefits of our hard labors—breaking the soil, planting, weeding, and harvesting. I'm not sure where Laken was most of this time, but occasionally I'd see him with my dad, and assumed they were still trying to work out some new ways to deal with the Space-GAP problem. Laken seemed to have adapted to our life here in the future. In fact, now it was hard to imagine him working behind a desk in a skyscraper like the MEI offices we'd seen in Toronto and Jerusalem.

One night, I found myself gazing up at the full moon as it rose in the east. I'm not sure if this was the first full moon after the evening Laken and I talked on the hill—or a later one. But there was something in the coolness of the air that night reminding me of the earlier crescent-moon night. Not sure what to think, I lay back on the grassy hill, as I often did, to watch the stars appear. Some nights I'd watch for the Southern Cross and think about the northern sky with its Big Dipper—that we couldn't see from here in the southern hemisphere. Tonight, though, I just closed my eyes trying to empty my mind of the many questions darting in and out of it.

'I wonder if Laken and his Mind-sharing have done something to my brain,' I sighed to myself. 'I don't feel like myself sometimes.'

The light sound of footsteps in the grass startled me out of my thoughts, and I sat up, my heart pounding, as I saw a dark shadow moving toward me.

I must have made some inadvertent cry for a male voice spoke, "I'm sorry. I didn't mean to scare you, Celestia."

"Is that you, Laken?"

"Sure is. So, is this where you hide every evening?" he chuckled, seating himself next to me. He'd loosed his black hair from its usual ponytail, and it fell around his shoulders.

"I like to watch the stars come out. Guess I get that from my dad. He says he was always fascinated with space and the stars."

"Yes, he's told me that, along with many interesting tales of his travels."

I could sense him moving closer to me, and my heart started trying to jump out of my chest. I moved away from him.

"What's wrong? I know we haven't been alone for awhile, but I won't hurt you—you know that."

At this I stood and began pacing around the top of the knoll. "You make my heart do crazy things when you're around," I said at last. "Or even just when I think of you."

"So, maybe I'm getting through to you," he smiled slyly.

"I don't know. Sometimes it feels like I'm still afraid of you."

He rose slowly and looked toward the Moon, but didn't meet my eyes. He stared at the glowing globe so long that I finally stepped closer to follow his gaze. There was no sound for what seemed like hours—not even the rainforest animals were making their usual night noises.

"I think we need to get back up there," he whispered, "Where a lot of this started."

"You mean the MEI Luna Base? What does that have to do with me, Laken?"

He shrugged.

"Are you saying this because that's where you think you fell in love with me?"

This time he shook his head and turned to look into my eyes. "I think there's a lot more to it than that. You said it was where you began to trust me—but it seems like you don't trust me anymore."

"I'm just confused. I don't know what I'm feeling. All I know is I've never felt it before."

He slowly took one of my hands. His touch felt very warm in the cooling night air, and my fingers intertwined with his.

"I think the True Lord wants us to see what's up there now," he whispered. "It's not really about you and me, at all."

"But how can we get there? We don't have a spaceship, or even a shuttle—nothing."

He pulled me closer, and again my heart pounded. I was afraid he was going to try to kiss me. But instead he began to lead me down the hill.

"You need to come see what your father and I have been working on," he said in a quiet voice.

***

Most of our little village was made of mud huts, with thatched roofs. In this tropical climate these were adequate shelter. But my father and some of the other men had managed to gather enough rock to build a crude building which sat near the center of the compound. Sometimes, when it was rainy, this was used for our Gatherings, but mostly these were held outdoors under the stars.

On the back of this building, Dad and Laken had built a lean-to with pieces of wood they managed to find in the rain forest. Some were just logs, but a few of the larger trees were hand-sawn into boards for a door. I hadn't paid much attention to what they were doing—with my own responsibilities in the camp. I spent most of my time in the garden, or helping with the children.

The door hinges didn't squeak as I'd expected them to. Then I noticed they were made from strips of leather, rather than from metal.

Laken smiled as I glanced at them. "We had to save our metal for more important purposes than hinges."

Once he'd opened the door, the light of the full moon cast a beam across the floor, which was also made of sawn boards. Now I knew why Laken and Dad had been working so much—sawing boards by hand was long and back-breaking.

Then my eyes began to focus on a strange object sitting in the middle of the lean-to, shining in the moonlight. It almost seemed to give off a light of its own.

"What is it?"

Laken merely smiled, took my hand and led me toward the contraption. In the midst of curved metal bars was a sort of bench, and in front of this were several dials and a small monitor screen. Then he squeezed my hand and said:

"Welcome to the new world of space travel."

My jaw nearly dropped to the floor. "This isn't a space ship. How can a human body survive the vacuum of space in this thing?"

He grinned again. "How long does it take to cross the GAP?"

"Well, it seems instantaneous," I sighed. "But time is being altered, so we can't be sure."

"I know. But your dad and I decided to make a way to test this. Maybe there's no need to protect the body while crossing space. Maybe all that's needed is the proper interface to cross the GAP in an instant."

"Oh, come on," I cried, "You can't be serious." But in the back of my mind I was realizing, 'It's not like Dad to be reckless with crossing GAPs. Maybe I've been careless a few times—like when I rushed to stop Annemarie from jumping from a Denver hotel window. But Dad isn't like that.'

"Jon and I have tested it," he whispered into my thoughts. "It works."

"You what? How?"

"We crossed to the surface of the Moon."

"But how did you breathe? There's no atmosphere on the Moon."

"We had small oxygen canisters, so we couldn't stay

long. But except for the bitter cold, we suffered no ill effects from the crossing itself."

"How do I know you aren't just teasing me?" This seemed too far beyond belief. "For 900 years, scientists at your Mind Exploration Institute have supposedly been working on this. The Star Corps was formed once humans began to migrate to other planetary systems. And you expect me to believe that no one ever discovered this?"

"Most of that may be true," he nodded. "I didn't live through those 900 years, and I don't know anything about other planetary systems, or the Galactic System, for that matter. But your dad does. And somehow—"

"Why don't you just ask me?"

Turning in surprise, I saw Dad standing in the moonlight streaming in the door. "This all seems impossible."

"Laken and I think our minds have some kind of link—that his mind is a forerunner of mine. And now the True Lord has brought the two of us together for a special purpose, something that couldn't have happened otherwise. In the course of ordinary time, Laken and I never would've met, but the Lord sent him here. There have been strange things happening recently—rumors of dark forces that we've never encountered before. Perhaps that's why Laken is here to help me, since I've lost the power of the connection I had with Jael-"

His voice cracked at Jael's name, and I realized how much my father missed this dear friend and brother-in-law.

They'd known each other most of their lives. So I changed the subject.

"There's no denying that Laken's being here in the Thirty-first Century is a miracle. It couldn't have happened without the Lord's intervention. But what does 'forerunner' mean?"

He motioned for us to climb out of the machine, and we found a clear spot to sit on the floor. "Mom and I have told you some of what happened with Danny and Ginna, right?"

Again, I nodded.

"Well, we feel sure that Danny was a forerunner of Jael—they were separated in time by almost a thousand years."

"Like Jon and I," said Laken.

"That's why my Parallel Universe experiment worked—Danny became merged with Jael, and Ginna was 'within' your mother."

"Yeah, we know that has to be true because Ginna got pregnant when Mom slept with-" My voice suddenly stopped, as I wondered if this was still a hurtful subject to my father.

"With Garek," he finished for me. "That's all water under the bridge. I have a feeling Garek and Ginna are married now, somewhere out in time."

"That does seem likely," I nodded. "They got a Civil Marriage License in Toronto—uh, Tornatoh now. But what does this have to do with me—and Laken?"

"Laken has mind-connection ability, so he was able to 'download' all I knew from my time in the Star Corps and our travels in space."

I turned to Laken in surprise. "You mean you can do the mind-blending thing without all that equipment you used on me at the MEI in Toronto?"

He smiled and nodded. "Apparently I can in this time-line. And your father has some unique abilities of his own, too. But we're missing something to make it work over really vast distances. So far we've only been able to go to the Moon."

For a few minutes, all I could do was stare at them in total disbelief. This was sounding like some science fiction book—like the ones Annemarie had talked to me about. "You're just playing games with me, right Dad?"

He took my hand in his. "No, we're very serious. And we need your help."

"Mine? What can I do?"

"For one thing, you've experienced a Time Well."

"That was an accident, and not much fun."

"I'm not asking you to do that again," he smiled. "We've set up safeguards in this new machine to prevent such time accidents."

Laken nodded. "But I need you to go to the Moon with me to see what's left of the MEI base there. I'm hoping that between the two of us, our memories of being there 900 years ago will bring something to light we've missed."

"So, we can learn how to conquer the vast distances between planetary systems," Dad finished for him.

"I'd be happy just to get to Saturn's moons," sighed Laken. "They have some fascinating characteristics, based on information gathered in my time."

By now, I was shaking my head in disbelief. "Are you two crazy?" It was all I could think of to say.

"Think of it as Luna-cy," Laken smiled. "I'm nuts about the Moon, otherwise known as Luna. I just feel drawn to it. Something up there seems to be calling me, and saying, 'Your answer is here'."

Dad was patting me on the shoulder now. "Celestia, you're one of the bravest and most committed people I know. I've seen your unwavering devotion to the missions the Lord has sent you on. This time, Laken and I feel the Lord has called us to this mission, and we need your help, too."

Laken squeezed my right hand tightly. "Please help us, Celestia. Your name means 'stars'. I think there has to be some significance to that."

"Why *did* you name me that, Dad?"

"It was your mother's idea. She said you looked like you had stars in your eyes when you were born."

"Yeah, I guess I do remember her telling me that. But Dad, if Laken is a forerunner of you, does that make him, uh—like my father—or something?"

Dad's eyes clouded for a few seconds, but then he smiled. "I see what you're getting at, Celestia. Laken is not a blood relative to you. It's just a metaphysical thing which connects us as forerunner and postrunner. You're free to make your own decisions regarding personal relationships."

Suddenly, I wanted to move away from Laken, and he surprised me by taking his hand off my back. "I love you enough to make no assumptions," he said softly. "It's up to you, what you do about me."

I could feel both their eyes on me, and then suddenly tears began to slip from my eyes. "What's wrong?" came Dad's voice. "Why are you crying?"

"I don't know." I brushed my tears away angrily. "What do you want me to do first?"

"For now, all we need is for you to come to the Moon with me," whispered Laken. "That's our only request."

"For now?" I echoed his words doubtfully. "That sounds like there may be more to come."

"It depends on what we find," he said. "We really don't know."

"We're going on a hunch right now," Dad added.

Neither of them spoke, as I continued to wipe at tears. "I'm being a baby, I know. I don't even know why I'm crying."

"It could be a carry-over from bad memories you have of the Mind-blend I had with you in Toronto," Laken sighed. "I was much too hasty then. Please forgive me."

"You know I've forgiven you, Laken—in the Citadel in Jerusalem."

I saw him smile and nod.

Then Dad spoke again, "Will you help us by going to the Moon?"

"With Laken?"

He nodded.

"When?" I sighed.

"Well, we have a few more details to work out with suits for you to wear while you're there. Hopefully, we'll be ready in a few more days," said Dad.

Laken was looking at me expectantly now.

"Okay, I'll do it. It's getting a little boring around here, anyway."

Dad patted me on the back and smiled, "That's my brave girl."

Laken was pulling me toward him, but I jumped away. "No kisses for you yet, mister."

Both of them began to laugh.

CHAPTER EIGHT
THE DARK SIDE OF THE MOON

It took another six days for Dad and Laken to get the spacesuits ready for us. We needed a means of getting oxygen to breathe, and protection for our bodies from the cosmic rays, since the Moon had no atmosphere.

I was really surprised they were able to find what they needed, with the limited resources at hand. But Dad always seemed to make a discarded piece of metal or plastic into something useful, and with Laken's background in engineering, they were able to get suits rigged that almost looked like actual spacesuits—at least like the ones we'd worn in the Twenty-second Century.

Of course, it was 900 years later now, and who knew what we'd find on the Moon this time. Their experimental excursion had been too brief to give any clues.

When it was time to try on the suits, Mom and Dad both came to watch. Mine seemed to fit fairly well, and I could manage to lift my feet enough to shuffle a bit.

"You'll be fine on the Moon where there's less gravity," I heard Dad say over my com. "How's yours, Laken?"

"It'll do," came Laken's voice, startling me because it felt like he was whispering in my ear, due to the com.

I think Dad saw me jump, because he stepped closer and tried to pat my shoulder, but I couldn't feel anything through the thick layers of the suit. "Are you okay?"

"Fine." I tried to nod, but this was almost impossible in the helmet. Then I noticed the way Mom was staring at the ground, looking angry. "What's up with Mom?"

"She thinks I'm sending you off on another wild goose chase," Dad sighed. "She doesn't think whatever we may gain in information is worth the risk."

I realized Mom couldn't hear what we were saying on the com, so I added, "She didn't like your letting me go to the Fountain alone, did she?"

He shook his head silently. "It was a tough five years for us. So, try not to stay away so long this time, okay?"

"All I can do is my best," I sighed. "But at least this time I have Laken to help."

"Yes, he does seem to know a lot about the GAP, even if it's mostly intuitive. He's a very gifted young man."

Suddenly we heard Laken laughing in our coms. "Young? I'm over 900 years old now. I was born in 2100."

"It doesn't exactly work that way—" I began.

"I know." He was moving closer to me now. "Time is a flexible background, not a solid entity like the ancients believed. Einstein started that revolution in thought long before my time."

"Boy, I'm starting to get hot in this thing."

"Better get out of them now. Of course, it will be much colder on the dark side of the Moon, so you'll be glad of all the extra insulation then."

Laken and I began the arduous process of taking off our suits, being very careful not to damage anything.

As soon as we were out, Mom stalked over to me, and pulled me into a tight hug. "You know you don't have to do this," she whispered in my ear.

"Mom—" I couldn't think of a quick reply.

"Now, Martina," said Dad, "Don't make it any harder on her than it already is. She's all grown up now, you know."

"Yes, and I missed five years of it—thanks to another of your wild ideas," she snapped.

Dad pulled her into his arms, disentangling her from me. "Hon, I know it's been hard, but you keep saying you wish we could leave this planet Earth. If we're going to find a way, I think our best chance for answers is up on the Moon."

"Why?"

"Because that's where the MEI, which Laken worked for, had their most advanced, top secret base."

Laken was nodding to her. "There's no reason to think it's gone, unless someone purposely destroyed it. With no erosion or weather on the Moon, it's probably sitting just as they left it."

"If they left it!" Mom pushed away from Dad as she said this. "What if the System or something even worse has taken it over? Celestia and Laken could be walking into a trap."

"We'll be careful, Mom. Please try to understand. I think this is why the King sent Laken and me here."

"Oh, another one of those missions you think he gives you."

Tears were beginning to roll down her cheeks, and were also filling my eyes. Now it was my turn to hug her tightly. "Laken and I will take care of each other. We need you to pray for us to be safe. Maybe we'll find something to keep all the Believers safe, too."

She just nodded, brushing back her tears. As the sun hit her hair, I noticed for the first time a few strands of gray appearing there. It was a reminder of how fleeting time really was—and how unstable.

"I've sworn to never let anyone or anything hurt Celestia," Laken said to Mom.

"Well, I hope you can keep that promise," she sighed. Then she squeezed both my hands very tightly. "Just be sure I see you again."

"They're not leaving for a couple more weeks, Hon," came Dad's steady voice. "We have to wait for the next full Moon."

"Why?"

"So, they'll be going to the base when the back side of the Moon is in darkness."

Laken was nodding now. "We'll be less likely to be seen. If anyone happens to be up there."

"But we don't think there will be," added Dad.

I wondered how he could know this. No one on Earth could see the back side of the Moon because it was always facing away from the Earth. Had he managed to cross a GAP to the place, without a suit? Or had he and Laken seen some of the dark side, when they did their first experimental trip?

Seeing how upset Mom was, I knew shouldn't bring this up at the moment, though.

"Let's go get some dinner. I'm really hungry," I said instead.

***

I tried not to stare at the Moon every night for the next two weeks, as it waned down to the New Moon and then finally began to wax to a crescent and the first quarter. Dad had given me a book with charts and maps of the Moon's surface to study, so I spent much of my time with this. One thing I found surprising was how different the topography was on the far side of the Moon, compared to the side facing us here on Earth.

As the first quarter moved into the gibbous stage, approaching the next full Moon, I began to gaze at it a lot, trying to distinguish the 'maria' or 'seas' as the early astronomers had named them. These large darker areas were actually lava flows which had covered some of the Moon's cratered surface, making flat areas among the ridges of craters and peaks. Looking with my naked eye, I could see why the ancients thought they might be actual bodies of water.

The far side of Earth's satellite, however, didn't have any of these lava flows, but was a great expanse of craters upon craters. 'Why are these two sides so different?' I wondered. 'Is it just by chance—a coincidence? Or is there a reason no one has discovered yet?'

When I shared these thoughts with Laken, he smiled. "I've thought about that, too. Of course, the information I had in my time was much less complete. I need to catch up on 900 years of data."

"Here then," I laughed, handing the book to him. "You can start with this book my dad loaned me, but books are all getting out-of-date these days. None have been printed since the System 'rediscovered Earth' about twenty years ago."

He nodded and took the book from my hand. "You sure you're finished with it?"

"Yes. I've tried to put as many of the maps in my head as I can."

"You must be good with maps."

"Well, I had one teacher who thought I had a photographic memory for images."

"Wow, I'm really glad you're coming with me. You'll be just the person I need when it's too dark to read a map."

"I hope I can help," I shrugged. Somehow, I always felt self-conscious when Laken gave me a compliment. "How many days until the Moon is full?" I asked to change the subject.

"Jon says four more nights."

Suddenly I felt a chill run down my spine, a combination of fear and excitement. After all the waiting, the time was almost here. Part of me wanted to hug Laken and ask him to kiss my fear away, but I didn't. Instead I just took his empty hand and looked up at him. "Almost time—"

He squeezed my hand gently and smiled.

***

The light of the full Moon was flowing in through the doorway of Dad's wooden shed, where the new GAP-crossing contraption was stored. Laken and I struggled into the bulky suits and squeezed ourselves onto the bench. Then to my surprise, I saw Dad lighting the amber lamp.

"I thought you said the lamp was for long Time-jumps."

He nodded as he adjusted the dial. "I've adapted it to speed up your Space-GAP crossing this time. You'll be on the Moon almost before you leave here."

"Huh? That sounds impossible."

Laken was chuckling. I could hear him through my com. "Don't think of time as a one-dimensional line.

It has extra dimensions of its own, just like space does. Sometimes they're curled up and virtually out of sight. Jon says this lamp can manipulate some of those hidden dimensions."

"Well, I may be good with maps and ecology, but astrophysics wasn't my best subject."

"That's why you and Laken make such a good team," Dad's voice smiled. I could barely see the expressions on his face through the shielded visor of my helmet. Suddenly though, I wished I could give my father one more hug, but it was too late now. Then, just as I stepped into the GAP, I heard his voice on the com:

"Don't forget, Laken, check for any leads on Jael."

Then I was caught up into the swirling light from the lamp, dancing on the inside walls of the shed. Instead of the usual shades of amber, red, and brown, there was more blue this time. I only saw the colors for an instant, though, and then everything went totally black.

I couldn't see anything, or feel anything—except my heart pounding, and my lungs pulling in air from my suit. Was Laken still with me? Or was I alone in some unknown abyss? Had something gone wrong?

Then I saw a tiny pinpoint of light out of the corner of one eye. Was it an illusion, perhaps something tearing inside my eyes? But now, it began to look more and more like a star as it moved into my frontal view. At the same time, I felt the ground rise up to meet me with a hard push, forcing the air out of my lungs.

I was lying face-down on a rough, rocky surface. Gradually, my limbs regained their ability to move, but it was very awkward to roll over in the bulky suit. 'Now I know how a beetle feels, when it's upside down,' I tried to laugh to myself. But my heart began to pound in fear.

Once I finally managed to get my feet under me and stand, I saw an amazing sight. There were millions of pinpoints of light above me. 'Stars!' I finally realized what they were. I'd never seen so many like this, so bright in an inky black sky, with no atmosphere to blur them.

"Celestia?"

"Laken?" I drew my eyes away from the unbelievable sight above me and scanned around my personal horizon. "I don't see you. Where are you?"

"I can barely see you, so you may be a quarter kilometer from me."

"I'm in a fairly flat spot, but it's really dark."

"Turn on your helmet light."

"Oh, duh! How can I be so stupid?"

"You're just stunned. You landed pretty hard. Stay there. I can see your light now. I'll be there soon."

My head was beginning to spin, so I found a way to half sit, half recline in my suit. Then I concentrated on Daiah's calming breathing exercises, reflecting on how these helped me in many situations through the past several years, in both Laken's time and my own. 'Thank you, Daiah,' I said to myself, and I wished she could be here to hear me.

At last, I began to see Laken's light bobbing up and down as he worked his way toward me. He seemed to be coming down from a ridge, and I wondered how he'd managed to land up there without falling. Apparently, he was better at this GAP-crossing now than I was. 'Dad's been giving him lessons, I bet,' I muttered to myself. Then I felt a twinge of envy. Why hadn't Dad been teaching me some of these finer points, too?

'There wasn't enough time to do everything,' a voice in my head told me. 'Learning the maps had higher priority because that's your gift. You and Laken are a team, not rivals, remember?' Was this the Lord talking to me—like he had at other times before? It was a familiar feeling. 'Thanks, Lord,' I mouthed silently.

By this time, Laken was close enough that I turned and started to move toward him. At my first step, I shot two meters off the ground and reminded myself to work on my lower-gravity walking skills. But I was so anxious to get to Laken that I reached him in about six bounds.

In fact, I almost flew over him, but he grabbed one of my boots as it rose past his arm and pulled me down. "You trying to get away from me?" his voice chuckled into the com.

"No, I'm just so glad to see you." I found myself

wishing I could finally kiss him. But with all our gear, I couldn't even feel the touch of his hand. So I just said, "What now? Do you know where we are?"

"I thought you were the map source."

"Oh yeah. I'm already falling down on my job."

"It's okay. This has to be Mendeleev Crater. It's the largest flat area on this side of the Moon. It's the place where I landed the MEI ship, long ago."

I gave an inward sigh of relief that he recognized this place. "So, the MEI facility should be near here, right?"

"It was located along the eastern rim of Mendeleev, where it blended into the topography better."

"Which way is east?"

Laken pointed to something on his wrist that looked like a watch, but he said it was a compass.

"How can a compass work on the Moon? The poles here aren't magnetic."

"This one works on a totally different principal, but I'd rather start walking than try to explain right now." While he spoke, he was pointing behind me. "East should be that way, where the rim of the crater is a little lower and less sharp. See how steep the cliffs are behind me? I'm pretty sure those are the western wall."

He began walking in the first direction he'd pointed. 'Perhaps my mind is still muddled by that hard landing,' I thought. 'It doesn't seem to be working on all levels yet—just survival mode.'

With a shrug, I bounded quickly to catch up with Laken. I wasn't going to let him out of my sight.

***

For a long time, the cliffs in the distance didn't seem to get any closer, but with only one-sixth Earth gravity, walking was not as much work, and we covered more ground with each bounding step.

Gradually my mind began to register the amazing scene around me. Above me, the sky was inky black, and stars shone as brightly as sparkling diamonds. The ground below us was littered with rocks and gravel, and pocked with craters, both large and small. From what I remembered there had been more fine dust where we'd landed the first time I came here. With a shock I realized that was 900 years ago.

Laken seemed to think, with no atmosphere or weather, there would be few changes to the Moon's surface in that time, but I wondered. What about meteors and other space objects, or perhaps even geologic events right here beneath the surface? Was this hunk of rock really geologically dead, as many assumed?

At last the cliffs were looming closer. Soon I could only see a section of them in my visor. Laken suddenly stopped on a slight rise, and I nearly bumped into him.

"Oh, sorry!"

"Next time I'll try to signal my intentions," came a chuckle through my com.

Then he stood and scanned the cliffs before us for a long time. "I sure hope this is Mendeleev," he sighed. "If it's Korolev, we're in trouble."

"How much trouble?"

"We could be a few hundred kilometers off."

"And we can't walk that far, can we?"

I thought I saw him shake his head, but in the helmet it was hard to tell. "No, wait," he cried. "Let's go south a bit. Korolev has an inner crater in its southern quadrant. If we don't find that, then this is more likely to be Mendeleev."

He set off without another word, and I had no choice but to follow. I was beginning to understand what my mother meant when she called something a 'wild goose chase.' An image jumped into my mind at this phrase, and I pictured myself beside a lake we went to near our home in Celeton:

It hadn't been a huge lake, but there were dozens of geese floating on its surface, feeding and getting ready to migrate south. As soon as we got within their sense of hearing, they began to flap their wings and rise into the air. I must have been quite young, because I laughed and ran toward the flying geese, flapping my arms and pretending to rise into the sky with them.

"I wish I could fly," I remember telling Mom and Dad, as we watched the flock of geese disappear into the distant blue sky, and their honking sounds died away.

As this memory was floating through my mind, Laken stopped again, but this time I was far enough behind him to stop in time.

"Oops, I forgot to signal again," he laughed. "Sorry."

"Do you see something?"

He gazed toward the south for a long time, and then turned back to look east. I tried to see if anything looked like what we'd seen as we came in on the spherical ship from the MEI facility in Jerusalem, so long ago.

There was very little light to help us though, only the starshine.

"Maybe coming here on the Earth's full moon view wasn't such a good idea," I whispered.

"No, wait. Look! There's something over at the base of that rock wall. I see a glint that isn't starshine."

"Are you sure?"

"Not completely sure. But there's only one way to find out."

So once again I loped along trying to keep up with his long bounds. Then I finally saw it, too—looking much as it had the first time—the low building blending into the cliffs. Somehow, after all this time, it *was* still here. My heart began to race as I wondered what we'd find inside.

CHAPTER NINE
EXPLORING THE MIND

With only light from our helmet-lamps and the stars, it was difficult to see much as we worked our way toward the glint of light Laken had seen. Nothing looked familiar to me, until we were almost ten meters from the building.

Now I was sure I *had* seen this place before—from the inside of a tiny spherical ship, centuries ago. But it only seemed like yesterday as we moved toward the access site, the very same one we'd entered that first time. I almost expected to see one of the MEI guards at the door. This sent a shudder down my spine because the last time I'd seen one of those guards, we were being escorted, hands bound behind our backs, to the ship that would take us to the Citadel prison in Jerusalem.

This time, however, the door had a large hole where the security system had been. There were no marks of an explosion, so apparently someone had just removed it. Was this a good sign, or not?

It felt eerie to be stepping gently down the old familiar hallways, holding onto the handrails on the wall, so we wouldn't bounce into the ceiling. Neither of us felt it worth the risk to see if there was any artificial atmosphere in the building, so we kept our helmets on. I was following close behind Laken, and when he suddenly stopped, I bumped into him.

"Sorry. You keep forgetting to signal your intentions," I scolded him.

He chuckled softly. "Oops. Guess I'm just too preoccupied with how spooky this place feels."

"Yeah, I know what you mean. I keep expecting Mauren or some guards to come around the next corner."

"Speaking of Mauren, this is her old office." He pointed to the door just beyond him.

As I looked at the non-descript door, I couldn't see any of the signs which originally indicated whose office it was. There'd been a cryptic sign beside the door then. "How do you know?" I finally asked.

"I've been to it many more times than you, so I just sort of feel her aura here."

"How could that be? Could she have crossed a Time-GAP, too?" The thought of facing the stony-eyes of the woman who'd betrayed us made my stomach drop with a sick feeling.

Laken made no reply, but stepped slowly toward the door, pushing it gently. To our surprise, it swung open.

Holding my breath, I followed him through the opening yawning before us.

There was no artificial light inside, but our headlamps revealed the same imposing desk where the burgundy-haired Mauren was sitting the first time I'd seen her. A chill flowed through my body, and I stepped closer to Laken.

"This place gives me the creeps," I whispered, and tried to reach for his hand. I couldn't feel his touch, or really get a good grip on him, with the bulky spacesuit.

"It's okay," he whispered back. "Her full essence isn't here, just a whiff from the past."

"You can sense that?"

"Somehow it comes to me at times."

"I never knew you had this extra-sensory power. What other secrets are you keeping, Laken?" Suddenly the trust I'd built up in him began to waver.

"Please don't be afraid," he murmured, as though he'd read my thoughts. "I can't always do this. It's a power that comes over me only when I need it. Sometimes it'll be months, or even years, between episodes."

"So, you're not reading my mind all the time?"

"No." I could hear a smile in his voice. "Why would I want to do that? It would take all the fun out of getting to know you as a separate, unique person."

"Well, I'm glad to hear that—I think. Do you sense anything else right now?"

"No. I feel we need to keep going. There are no answers in this room."

So, we left Mauren's old office, and relief seemed to wash over me like a cooling stream of water. Even though I didn't have Laken's extra-sensory power, I'd sensed something sinister in that room.

"I still don't understand why Mauren and Darroch betrayed us," I said at last, as we continued our slow progress through the halls.

"It was the Morotani," Laken replied. "I think they were trying to take over from the True King and set up their own kingdom on Earth."

"Yeah, I remember Darroch saying something about each getting their own planet to rule."

"It's a very ancient religion. But it always comes back to the same basic problem—humans trying to be gods, instead of acknowledging the True King."

"Did the Morotani succeed?"

"They may have for a time. That's part of your history, not mine," he half-chuckled. "It was in the future to me."

"Oh yeah. This Time-GAP does make things confusing."

"It helps if you think of it as a flowing matrix, not a single time-line."

"I have enough trouble thinking in three or four dimensions, Laken."

"But according to String Theory, there have to be at least nine—maybe many more."

"No way." My mind couldn't wrap itself around any of this. "I'm going to leave the astrophysics to you."

Just as I was saying this, he stopped suddenly again, and this time I literally did bump into him, sending him sprawling on the floor.

"You keep doing that to me," I scolded, helping him up.

"Shh!" was his only reply. "I think I saw something—or someone."

"Where?" I barely whispered.

"There was a sense of movement around the next corner."

My eyes followed where he was pointing, but I could only see more darkness. He must be using that extra sense again. "What should we do?"

"Let's move cautiously in that direction. I don't sense any threat."

"Well, this secret ability of yours seems like a good thing to have right now. Did you tell my dad about it?"

"A little." Then he put his gloved hand to his face plate, in the universal gesture that meant not to make a sound.

Eternity seemed to pass, as we slowly and silently worked our way toward the corner, but when we glanced around it, there was still nothing to be seen. Laken motioned for me to follow as he turned the corner and kept going. Meanwhile, my heart was pounding so hard my head was throbbing.

As we rounded the next corner, we saw nothing ahead of us but darkness. I wondered if Laken was sensing anything but knew better than to ask.

After two or three more turns, I was beginning to get disoriented. In fact, I remembered how the guards had deliberately done this when we'd been here back in 2123. This thought did nothing to ease my anxiety. Was there someone out there trying to get us lost in this maze of dark hallways?

Then suddenly, I saw something—a faint bluish glow ahead. I reached out and grabbed at Laken's arm. He turned and nodded to me and motioned toward this strange blue light.

As we turned another corner, I saw something so strange I still have trouble describing it:

The hallway widened here to about twice its former width. In the center of this bulge was what appeared to be a pool of blue liquid, but it shone with a light emanating from it. Swirls of brighter and darker blues curled around each other, and slowly rose above the pool like mist.

I had both my arms around one of Laken's now. It was the only way I could get hold of him. "What is it?"

"I've no idea," he whispered.

As we watched in awe, the shape of the blue pool began to change. The edges seemed to pull in toward the middle, so that it almost became two pools connected by a narrow neck.

"Like an hourglass," came Laken's voice.

"A what?"

"An ancient way of measuring time. People would put a certain amount of sand in a vase this shape so they could measure a given amount of time. Once the sand trickled through the narrow neck to the bulge on the other end, the time had passed. Usually it measured an hour, hence the name hourglass."

"Is that where the saying 'flowing with the sands of time' comes from?"

"You still have that old saying in the Thirty-first Century?"

I nodded, then realized he probably couldn't see this, so I whispered, "Yeah."

"Interesting…"

Before he could say another word the light in the pool suddenly changed to a deep green, and mists rose thickly surrounding us. Some must have condensed on my visor because I couldn't see anything. I just kept clinging to Laken's arm.

Then the blue came back, the mists gradually settled, and there in front of us stood the shape of a man, wearing a beige tunic over a dark-colored jumpsuit.

"You can take those off," his voice came distantly. He was pointing to our helmets.

"How do we know we can trust him?"

"Well, he's breathing something in here."

"But maybe he's an alien and doesn't breathe like we do?"

Laken gently disentangled his arm from my grasp. "I can sense he's human."

And so, with much trepidation, I unsealed my helmet and lifted it off my head, while Laken did the same.

"Who are you?" I heard Laken ask.

But my mouth was already gaping in surprise. "Uncle Dominic? How did you get here?"

What I heard next almost made me faint:

"No, I'm his twin brother, Stephan."

The room began to whirl around me, and I would have dropped to the floor if Laken hadn't pulled me into his firm grasp.

"We were told you died in the Galactic Wars." I was glad Laken spoke up, for I was speechless.

"I did in your universe," came the man's voice again. It sent chills through me to hear him. He sounded just like my mother's Uncle Dominic. "In mine, *I* joined the Rebels, and Dominic stayed behind in the System."

"On the planet Terres?" My voice was finally coming back.

"No, some names are different. Alternate universes don't all follow the same rules or time-lines. Sometimes they run alongside each other, and sometimes they diverge.

And who are you, young lady? You seem to resemble my daughter."

"Uh—my name is Celestia, and my mother is Martina Sullien. She's married to Jon, son of Jakol."

"Hmm." A smile played at his lips. "Same surname."

"Will someone please tell me what's going on?" Laken cried suddenly.

"Oh, sorry, Laken. Stephan, this is Laken Meta. He was sent to my time by the True King—but he's really from the Twenty-second Century."

"And what century are you in now?"

"The Thirty-first. Uh, does this mean you're my grandfather, Steph Sullien?"

"Sort of," he smiled. "My daughter, Miriam, doesn't have a child yet—in my world."

"Oh, this is getting even more confusing. Is Miriam the parallel to my mother, Martina?"

"Well, as I said, sometimes universes run parallel and sometimes they diverge."

"Do they ever converge?" Laken asked suddenly, looking right into Stephan's eyes.

"Absolutely." His voice dropped to a whisper as he stepped closer to us.

Now I could tell he was a real flesh and blood human being. I'd been wondering if I was seeing a ghost.

"This Time Portal in Mendeleev Crater is one of the most powerful in this end of your Galaxy," he continued.

"It's perfectly situated because your solar system is located on one of the spiral arms of the Milky Way, away from the interference of the dense core of stars in the center. Also, there's always been some special force associated with this crater. The man it's named for, Dmitri Mendeleev, was much more than a chemist in the other worlds he visited."

"Didn't he live in the Nineteenth Century?" I mused. "How long has this portal been in existence? How many people have used it—that we thought lived just on Earth?"

"Well—it's Celestia, right?—the Morotani knew about it."

"So that's the big secret Mauren was hiding," Laken cried.

"Why is no one here now?" I added.

"When their attempt to take over Earth failed, the remaining Morotani fled through this portal to another universe," said Stephan.

"I wonder if they're ruling that one," mused Laken.

"I don't know. I'm not even sure which way they went, so to speak."

"Uncle Dominic—I mean Stephan—sorry, but you look so much like Dominic, and he's the only one I ever knew. My grandfather, Steph Sullien, died long before I was born."

The man reached toward me with an open palm and said, "In this world, you may call me whatever is comfortable for you."

"Okay. Now I have to ask—why isn't the System controlling this place? Seems like something they'd want to be in charge of."

He laughed aloud at this. "Oh no! The System doesn't want humans to know of the existence of any other universes. It would undermine their control, you see."

Now I understood. From what I'd learned of the System before we fled the cities, this did make sense. I remembered Dad telling me this was the reason they denied the existence of the True King, too—because they wanted no one but themselves to rule over humans.

"Are you what we were supposed to find here?" asked Laken. "I know I was sent to Celestia's time for a reason, and now here we are with you."

"I'm not sure if this is part of some 'plan' or not, Laken. But I can take you to someone who will know—Johan."

"You mean the old man who lived on the tiny planet?" I gasped. "Long ago, before I was born—and even before they were married—he helped my parents repair their ship and gave them The Book."

"And sent them off to find the planet Maia," Stephan finished for me. "He's much more than just some old hermit, though."

"Must be, if he's still alive now," added Laken.

"I guess he won't mind if I tell you," Stephan continued. "The old man is just his favorite disguise. He's not even fully human."

"What is he then?"

"I think I'd better let him decide how much more to reveal. For now, you two had better put those helmets back on, since you're not as accustomed to Far-space GAPs."

"To *what?*" Laken gasped. "Where are you taking us?"

"To Johan, of course. He's the only one who has the answers you need."

CHAPTER TEN
THROUGH THE HOURGLASS

Just as I was about to step toward Stephan, the blue light in the hourglass shape on the floor turned blood-red. In the same instant, Stephan jumped between us and the roiling liquid light. "Keep back!" he shouted.

"What is it?" came Laken's voice on my com, now that we had our helmets back on.

Stephan was pushing us back toward one of the nearer corners we'd come around before. Suddenly, over his shoulder I saw a terrible creature rising out of the crimson pool. Its eyes were whirling like rotating prisms, sending blinding flashes of red and orange all around the hallways. Its head looked like a huge dragon, something I'd only seen in books.

"What is that?" I heard Laken ask again.

"It's the Serpent, the ruler of the Powers of the Air." Stephan's voice was coming over my com now.

"You mean Satan?" I gasped. "How can we ever escape him?"

We'd just turned a sharp corner in the hallway, and the crimson flashes of light weren't hitting us now. Suddenly, Stephan turned his back to us, and faced the direction we knew the Serpent would come from. He extended his arms to hold us behind him, and just as the first flash of light appeared, his voice boomed:

"In the name of Kristos, True Lord of the Universe, I command you to depart!"

Immediately, everything went black.

"What happened?"

"He's been commanded to leave, and he must obey."

"Really? It's that easy?" came Laken's voice.

"Oh, it wasn't easy." Stephan was panting for breath, and his face was pale. "We must move quickly before he finds another means of attack," he added. "Don't turn on any lights. Just use your hands to follow the wall."

"Is that serpent or dragon—whatever he is—part of the evil we keep hearing about?" I asked, still trembling with fear.

"More than that," said Stephan tensely. "He's the Lord of Evil and the Father of Lies."

As I heard those words, I was more frightened than any time in my life. The blackness around us seemed to throb with threats. Any second, I expected the whirling eyes to reappear, or claws to grab me from the darkness. I couldn't really feel the rocky walls through the gloves of my suit, so I just clung to Laken's arm as I moved along with him. Apparently, he was holding on to Stephan, but I couldn't see anything at all—not even my own hand in front of my face.

At last, the pale blue shimmer of the portal appeared on the floor just ahead of us. I heaved a sigh of relief that the color was no longer red. But my heart was pounding, and I kept expecting it to change at any moment.

Then my eyes made out the hourglass shape on the floor. Now Stephan placed himself between us, took hold of each of our arms, and drew us to the edge of the shimmering blue. It moved a bit like water, or molten rock, but there was no heat rising from it. In fact, there seemed to be an icy chill in the air around us.

"Good," I heard Stephan whisper. "No heat. That means no red, and no Serpent anywhere nearby. We're safe for now."

"What are we going to do?" Laken asked.

"Enter the Time Portal, of course," he replied. "If you want answers, it's the only way."

I saw Laken turn his helmet and glance toward me, but of course I couldn't see his eyes through the reflective surface of my visor. So, I just nodded my head as best I could, and gripped my other-universe-grandfather's arm even more tightly. "Let's do it, Granddad," I said.

"That's my brave girl." I could hear the smile in his voice. Apparently, he liked my new name for him. Then he began to count down, "Five, four, three…"

When he reached zero, all three of us stepped into the blue hole in the floor, which was swirling faster and faster with each number he said.

The icy cold seemed to pierce me like a knife and took my breath away. All I could see was more of the shimmering, whirling blue we'd stepped into. It moved me along like waves pushing out into an ocean.

'No!' I thought, 'Don't take me away from the land.'

But then somehow, I felt an arm gripping me and drawing me near in a comforting embrace. A slight warmth worked its way into my chilled body.

My eyes began to see other colors in the distance—greens, purples, and yellows. They were indistinct shapes flowing and shifting soundlessly. I kept expecting to see the dreaded red of the Serpent, but so far this color was absent.

We continued to drift as if in waves of water, and gradually it became warmer and greener around us. Then something solid appeared in all the liquid. In the beginning it was only a tiny brown spot, and I wondered if it was just a speck of dust in my eyes.

Gradually though, it grew to the size of a small ball. I wondered if it was a planet, but just as we were getting close enough to begin to focus our eyes on it, a sudden flash of crimson zoomed in front of us.

"Oh, no!" I screamed. "The Serpent!"

For a moment we were cut off from the only solid object in sight, but then a blinding white bolt of lightning flashed out of the small planet. With a wail of pain and anger, the Serpent turned and fled.

"What now?" I heard Laken moan.

But Stephan somehow reached up and grabbed the white bolt. I was surprised to see how it illuminated his entire form, but he didn't seem to be in any pain. In fact, I thought I saw a smile through his visor. "Hang on, kids," he called.

"Kids?" I heard Laken say.

Then, just as suddenly as it appeared, the bolt of light zipped back toward the small rocky planet, pulling us along in its wake. I felt like I was riding on a pathway of sparks, but then ground seemed to rise up to meet me, much like it did when I crossed a GAP.

Everything was whirling before my eyes, and I fell to the ground in a heap, unable to keep my balance anymore. My stomach began to heave, but nothing came up, except a bit of bile in my throat. Taking a deep breath, I shuddered, and lay myself out flat on my back. The sky above me was still turning, the stars making pathways and circles, instead of pinpoints of light.

"Are you all right, Celestia?" I heard Laken's concern distantly, even though he was kneeling right beside me.

"Just dizzy," I managed to whisper.

"Lie still, then," he said. "Is it okay to take our helmets off now?"

"Yes," I heard Granddad's voice from what seemed a great distance.

"Was this her first time?" a strange voice asked.

"I think so, though she's crossed the GAP before," said Laken.

'Laken? Has he done this before? How could he?' I wondered. 'What other secrets is he keeping from me?'

I wanted to say these things aloud to him but found I hadn't the strength. Instead I let him gather me into his arms and hold me like a child. Soon I must have fallen asleep, because the next thing I knew I was lying on soft grass beside a small pool.

"This looks like a place my mother described to me once," I sighed. "A place where she and my father—and my Uncle Jael—found rest and help, when they were fleeing from their home planet, Terres."

As I opened my eyes, I expected to see the bent old man they'd described standing near a small waterfall. But instead, I beheld a tall figure dressed in shining gold. Flecks of glitter flashed out from his long robe, and a shimmering red-gold bird with a long tail was perched on his shoulder.

"Johan, this is Celestia," I heard Stephan's voice say. "If we lived in the same universe, she would be my granddaughter."

"Ahh—" was all the glittering figure said. "And you brought her with you? Why?"

"She and Laken are seeking the true Maia, but they're

in danger. The Serpent has been released on Earth, and he knows of their presence. Many Believers are depending on their help. Do you remember Jon and Martina and Jael?"

"Hmm—"

"You helped them get new crystals for their ship," I whispered, finding my voice at last. "They had a feier-cat with them."

"Ah, yes."

"And you gave them a copy of The Book."

"Didn't they find Maia?"

"They thought they did. I was born there. On Earth, I mean. But something isn't right. Believers are still being ostracized. The System has come back. Perhaps this has something to do with this new evil stalking us?"

"I see. Maybe they slipped into the wrong portal. Laken, how did you get involved in this?"

Johan's voice seemed to address Laken with familiarity. How could they know each other?

"Celestia is Jon and Martina's daughter. She was trying to take some others to the Fountain in the Desert."

"So, did Jon and Martina find it?"

"Yes, and my Uncle Jael, too. The Lord wanted me to take Ginna, Annemarie, and Garek there, but we fell into a Time Well. And that's how I met Laken, back in the Twenty-second Century."

Johan glanced in surprise at Laken when I said this, but Laken merely returned his gaze and said nothing.

"Ginna—hmm, that name seems familiar—but who are these others?" Johan asked then.

"It's complicated," I said.

"They've been sent to their proper places and times by the True King," said Laken. "There's no need to worry about them now."

"Very well," Johan nodded. Then the golden figure sat down on a rock near me, and right before my eyes he changed. The tall gleaming figure became a bent old man in rough, hand-sewn clothing. While this happened, the bird took flight and disappeared in a flash of sparks.

"There," he smiled. "This feels much better. I'm uncomfortable in that other get-up."

"Now you look like the Johan my parents described. But what was that bird?"

"You must mean my phoenix. She comes and goes at will. Believe me, you've no need to fear. I want to help you, and your parents, too. Hopefully better than I did last time."

I found myself being raised to a sitting position by gentle hands. At first, I thought it was Johan but then saw it was Laken.

"Who are *you*—really?" I asked him.

"All will be revealed in its time," came Johan's voice. "Just know that Laken has always meant you no harm."

"So, he keeps telling me," I murmured. "But I'm really confused. Here I am with someone on a planet I've never been to, with a grandfather who supposedly died before I was born, and some man I met 900 years ago that seems to know you. I don't get any of this."

"Celestia," Laken took both my hands in his, as he'd often done before. "Just keep trusting the True King's calling for you. We're all part of it."

I took a deep, ragged breath and tried to nod. He squeezed my hands gently, and somehow comfort flowed from him. I looked into his eyes and smiled slightly.

"Now," came Johan's voice again, "We need Jael to complete this task. He is the key."

My heart sank. "Uncle Jael is dead," I moaned. "He sacrificed himself to save his wife and the children."

"Oh," said Stephan. "Now that *is* a big problem."

"Are you sure he died?" asked Johan.

"No one's had any contact with him," I said. "He and my father had a special connection, but Dad's heard nothing for over five years."

"I wonder if he could've been drawn into a Wormhole?" Stephan muttered.

"There'd be no way to locate him, if that were the case," said Laken.

"You sure know a lot about this stuff." I glared at him. "How long have you been lying to me about who you really are?"

"He hasn't been lying, Granddaughter. In fact, his true identity has been hidden even from himself, in order to prevent the wrong ears hearing it."

"Are my ears the wrong ones?" I was feeling hurt now.

"No, Celestia. There were others around you, though. We promise to tell you everything someday," Stephan said. "Laken hasn't lied to you. He's told all the truth that he knew."

"This sure isn't a good way to inspire my trust." I heaved a deep sigh and stared into Laken's eyes, but then I saw a tear shining in the corner of one eye, and another trickling down his cheek.

"I'm sorry," he whispered. "I only did what I could. I feel as confused by these new facts as you do."

Without even thinking, I wiped the tear off his cheek with my finger. "I do care about you. And I'll try to understand."

Meanwhile, Johan and Stephan moved slightly away from us, talking quietly. Laken and I caught only part of what they said:

"…your youngest son, Stephan?"

"No, there are too few parallels between him and Jael."

"Did Jael have any forerunners?"

Suddenly, I remembered things my dad had told me about his Parallel Universe experiment. "My dad took Ginna into my mother," I said quietly. "And her brother Danny 'became' Jael. They lived as one for several years. That's how Ginna's daughter Annemarie—uh—came to be."

"You sound familiar with this, Granddaughter."

I nodded to him. "I was sent by the Lord to help Ginna and her daughter."

"Did you ever meet Danny?" Johan asked.

I shook my head.

"Perhaps we need to find a way to make that happen," said Granddad.

CHAPTER ELEVEN
JOURNEY WITH GRANDDAD

I was looking deep into my 'grandfather's' eyes, noticing they were the same green shade as my mother's. He closed them for an instant, and in that matter of seconds the scene around us changed completely. What power this man had, compared to my puny GAP-crossing skills. There were so many questions I wanted to ask him.

At this moment, however, I was trying to keep my equilibrium, as another wave of dizziness swept over me. This time I held onto him tightly and felt the strength of his arms holding me, and soon the vertigo passed.

"You did much better that time," he smiled.

As unbelievable as all this was for me, he seemed to take for granted that I was somehow related to him. 'How could I explain this to Mom?' my mind wondered—'or to Grandma Irina, who'd mourned her dead husband so deeply that she fell into clinical depression. Will I ever have the chance to tell her I met Stephan? And yet, have I? This Stephan is from another universe. Some things about him are the same, like his name and his eyes, but other things must be different. I know that he also has a twin brother named Dominic, but in his time-line he lived and his brother died—just the opposite of my world.'

Finally, I decided to just start asking:

"Granddad, did your twin brother also marry a twin? Like Steph and Dominic did in my world."

"Yes, I married Irina, and Dominic married Karina. Both of us had four children before Dominic died."

"Where are they—your family?"

"In the world they belong to. And, as you can tell, not all their names are the same, except for our eldest sons."

"Does Irina miss you when you travel like this?"

"Irina has already died." His voice sounded hoarse and sad. "She was attacked by a beast in the wilds. Now Karina is taking care of all our young children."

"In my world, Dominic and Irina are married now, because Karina died in childbirth. Dominic has only one child, an adult son."

"Really?"

By the sound of his voice, I wondered if he was thinking what it would be like to see Irina again.

"Different universes aren't always parallel, are they, Granddad?"

He shook his head suddenly, as though to clear it. "No, and it's better not to cross in and out too often. It muddles the space-time fabric, causing unforeseen problems."

"So why did you come to Luna for Laken and me?"

"It was something which had to be done." His voice cracked suddenly, and he took a ragged breath. I could see he was fighting with some of his thoughts and wondered if he felt the temptation to see the Irina in my world. Just when I thought he'd lapsed into silence, he spoke once again, "Laken is part of Johan's Circle."

"What circle? How can you know Johan or Laken? They're from so far in the past? Granddad, who *is* Laken—really?"

"It's his place to tell you, not mine," he said quickly through pursed lips. "I've said too much already."

I wasn't satisfied with this answer, so I pressed on with my questions: "Is he a time-traveler, like you? How was he able to convince all of us, even Darroch and Mauren, that he was just another scientist in the Twenty-second Century?"

"All I can tell you is he was in a 'deep-cover'—if you've ever heard of that."

"Well, it sounds like something I read in a book about Twentieth Century spies," I said.

He laughed. "It's much more sophisticated than that."

"He did a Mind-sharing with me, and I detected nothing about his being from another time."

"Like I said, it's more complicated than you think."

"You mean even Laken didn't know who he really was?"

"Oh, you're much too perceptive for me to keep secrets from you."

Now it was my turn to smile up at him. "Why did he stay with Johan, and not come with us—if he has such powers?"

"There were some things he and Johan needed to discuss." He took my hand and looked down into my eyes. "Do you care for Laken?"

Confusion filled my mind as I tried to think of an answer. "He cares for me, I know. But I'm still not sure exactly what I feel for him."

"Then it's not time for everything to be told. You must wait until you know for sure—one way or the other. Then Laken can decide what to tell you."

I turned from him then, and realized we were standing on a grassy hill. It reminded me in some ways of the place Laken and I were sent to in Indonia—by the True King. But as I looked more closely, I saw it wasn't the same.

There were open fields of golden-colored grain waving in the winds, stretching in every direction as far as we could see. None of the familiar tropical forests were anywhere in sight. Scattered among the grain fields were small patches of green around little white or yellow houses. Some of these yards had tall trees in them, but the leaves weren't green, as I'd expected. Most were in various shades of yellow and orange.

"Where are we?"

"Eastern Colorado," he smiled. "You've been here before, but it was winter, and all was grey or covered with snow. Now it's autumn."

"You mean we've crossed the GAP back to Ginna's time? Is she here?"

"I believe she is, but several kilometers away. This time, we've come to where Danny and his family live, near a little town called Ault."

"Oh." I was disappointed that we might not get to see Ginna.

"It's better for Ginna and Garek to live their 'new normal' lives in this time, Celestia. They've had enough adventures."

"So, they *are* together?"

He smiled and nodded. "And very happy, too."

"How do you know all these things?"

"It's part of my Circle's job."

"What is a circle?" I asked.

"As I told you on Luna, we guard the Mendeleev Portal and monitor any GAP-crossings in this part of the Milky Way."

"So, is Laken part of your Circle?"

"We both work with Johan, so I've seen him occasionally."

"But he acted like he didn't know you on Luna."

"He didn't know—then."

I shook my head. "This is too confusing for me. How can I trust him if I don't know what *he* truly knows?"

"I hope you'll get used to it, once you know more." He reached out his arm and gave my shoulders a squeeze. "Do you trust me, for now?"

I leaned into his chest and sighed. "Yes, Granddad. Somehow, I know that you're connected to my mother, even if you are in different universes."

"That's my perceptive girl," he smiled. "Now, let's see if Danny is at home, shall we?"

***

We'd been walking for nearly an hour, as the sun sank toward the western horizon, when Granddad finally pointed to a small brown house with a gray roof, sitting atop the next rise and silhouetted against the sunset.

"That's Danny's home," he said softly.

The house looked quite ordinary for the Twenty-first Century, perhaps even the Twentieth, but this was no ordinary sunset. Bands of magenta radiated out from where the sun had just dipped below the horizon. But they were separated at irregular intervals by gaps of bluish-purple sky—some flaring out above the house and the tall trees growing around it.

"I've never seen a sunset like that before," I gasped. "Are clouds causing that effect?"

"It *is* beautiful, isn't it?" murmured Granddad. "I've seen a few like this in my world."

I turned and looked into his green eyes but couldn't find any words to say. The moment was too magical, as though his world and mine—and Danny's—were all touching at once.

"I wonder what Danny will think of GAP-crossers showing up at his door after all this time," I finally whispered.

"If he's even at home."

As we reached the edge of the low-cut grass a large black animal ran toward us, making loud barking sounds. He sounded frightening to me, but Granddad just stopped moving and held out his palm. Once the animal sniffed that hand, its tail began to wag.

"There now, fella," came his calm voice. "We mean you and your humans no harm." Turning to me, he added, "He's a good dog."

"I've never seen a dog before," I sighed, "Just wild wolves and coyotes."

"Hey, Shadow," called a young voice. "Come here, boy!"

From around the corner of the house appeared two boys, one slightly taller than the other. "Who are you?" the taller boy called.

"We're visitors here to see your father," Granddad called back.

As the boys moved closer to us, I saw the older one had blond hair, while the other's hair had a reddish tinge. "He's not home yet," said the blond. He seemed to be more outgoing than his smaller brother. "I can take you to see Mom, though."

"Yes, please," I said, hoping a female voice would inspire more trust. The red-haired boy was hanging back behind his brother, holding tightly to his hand.

"What are your names? Mine is Dain," the blond added.

"Pleased to meet you, Dain. I'm Stephan, and this young woman is Celestia."

"I've heard Dad mention those names once," came a sudden comment from the smaller figure. "He said they were from very far away."

I smiled at the red-headed boy. "Yes, we've come a very long way. What's your name?"

"I'm Evin." His face reddened as he spoke and he looked shyly at the ground.

"Mom's in the kitchen fixing supper," Dain said then. "We'll take you to see her. But first—uh, Stephan—I think I need to show you something in our barn."

I glanced at Granddad in puzzlement, but he just shrugged and went with Dain. So, I turned and followed Evin up some steps to the wooden front porch. He watched me curiously out of the corner of his eye. Even though he was the quieter of the two, I could see he was the one who paid attention to any stories his father may have told him about past adventures.

Inside the front door, we crossed a wood-floored sitting room and passed through an archway into what my mother would have called a 'galley.' This must be what Dain called the 'kitchen'.

Across the tile floor, a slender woman with red hair was stirring something simmering on a stovetop. With a start, I realized I hadn't seen a real stove in a long time, not since we'd been forced to flee Celeton.

"Mom," said Evin, "We have two visitors for Dad."

She turned and surprise filled her face. "You look just like Danny's description of Martina."

I was equally surprised as I looked at her. She looked so much like Raina that I found myself speechless.

"Evidently, there are some strong parallels here," came Granddad's voice, as he and Dain entered not far behind us. I wanted to ask what Dain showed him, but he began talking to the woman before I had a chance. "This young woman with me is Celestia, Martina's daughter. And you are—?"

"Oh, I'm sorry. My name is Sandra Parker. Daniel Parker's wife. I see you've met our sons. Who are you?"

"My name is Stephan Sullien."

"But Danny said Steph died!" she cried.

"I see he's told you much of the story, hasn't he?"

She nodded, and Evin's voice whispered, "Lots of it."

Just then a door slammed, and the sound of boots echoed on the far side of the house. Then a tall brown-haired man walked in and stepped up to Sandra. I gasped at how much he looked like my Uncle Jael:

"Oh my!"

"Martina?" his voice asked.

"I'm her daughter, Celestia. Uh, you never met me, except perhaps as a baby."

"Danny, these visitors told the boys they came to see you." As she spoke, Sandra was holding tightly to his arm, as though she thought he might disappear at any moment.

"Please, don't fear us," Granddad spoke gently. "Your food smells delicious, and I can't remember when I last ate something warm."

"Dain, please set two more places at the table," said Danny, still looking at me curiously. "After we eat, we can talk."

His son quickly obeyed, as Sandra began to ladle soup into bowls. "It's a good thing I made extra," she said. "Something told me."

But her words stopped as we sat down on the chairs. They were like the ones I'd gotten used to in the Twenty-second Century. No floor cushions to recline on here. Danny gathered us into a circle of joined hands and said a prayer for the meal. This was so familiar from my own family, I found myself echoing his 'Amen.'

The soup was delicious, and there was fresh-baked bread, too. No one really spoke much, until all of us had eaten the food set before us. Then for some reason, we all turned and looked at Granddad, as he cleared his throat:

"Since Danny appears to have told his family some of his tales of GAP-crossing, I assume I won't have to explain that's how Celestia and I got here."

The Parkers were shaking their heads. "Celestia I understand," Danny said. "I remember when she was born. I was still 'within' Jael then. But Jael's father, named Steph, died long before that. Unless you came across time from the dead." He was giving Granddad a curious stare.

"Not from the dead, Danny. I'm from another universe—in which my twin brother Dominic was the one who died first."

"But I met Dominic." Then the full impact of the words hit him: "Another universe? Well, Jon did talk about parallel universes."

"There are many alternate time-lines, or universes, whichever you choose to call them," said Granddad. "Time has its own dimensions also, like space does.

"I've been to Jael's time," nodded Danny. "I remember it all like it was yesterday sometimes. So, my family has heard a lot about it. How is Jael, by the way?"

"My parents are in hiding with some other Believers in Indonia," I said.

"Ginna told me a little about their cave, and how she found her new husband."

I nodded and said, "They had to abandon the cave a few years ago to escape the System."

"Was helping my sister mostly *your* doing?" he asked.

"It was a mission the True King sent me on. And now it appears I'm on another one with my Granddad, Stephan."

"How can he be your grandfather if he's from another universe?" asked Evin.

"You *are* the attentive one, aren't you?" said Granddad.

"Well, I call him that, even though he isn't really," I said. "I never knew my real grandfather, you see."

"But why are you here? Jael was always the one who came for me," Danny added.

A nervous silence flitted around the table as Granddad and I glanced at each other. "We're here because we don't know where Jael is," I said at last. "He disappeared five years ago in my time, creating a diversion so Raina and the children could escape."

"Escape from who?"

"A Patrol of soldiers from the System."

I saw his face blanch as this fact finally penetrated, "The System has come back to Earth?"

"In my time-line, yes," I nodded. "I don't know about Stephan's."

"That doesn't matter right now," said Granddad. "We need your help, Danny."

"The Believers trapped on Earth need you," I added. "They're being severely persecuted. And now we've seen the true enemy, the Serpent."

"They need to find an escape," Granddad cut in, apparently not wanting me to scare Dain and Evin with talk of the Serpent.

"But what can *I* do?"

In the silence following Danny's question, I glanced around at his family, and saw the fear in their eyes.

"We're hoping, since you're a parallel forerunner of Jael, that you can help us find him. Jon isn't able to navigate the space-time GAPs alone—those which will make escape possible. We need Jael's special talents."

"I don't have any special talents. I'm just a draftsman for a small architectural company."

"You may have more abilities than you know," said Granddad. "You've just never needed to use them before."

"Does this mean you're taking Danny away from us?" There was fear in Sandra's voice.

I reached over and took her trembling hand. "Please trust Stephan," I whispered. "He has far greater power than anyone else in my family."

"I'll only do what *you* are willing to do, Daniel," Granddad said then. "No one can be forced in these matters. You and your sister were never forced, were you?"

"No."

"And if all goes as I hope your husband will be back by midnight tonight."

"What? Why that's only a few hours from now," came Evin's awed voice.

"Time isn't static, young one," Granddad smiled. "Someday perhaps it will be your turn to learn more."

Meanwhile, Danny had risen from his chair and given his wife a deep kiss. Patting his sons on the head, he stepped over to Granddad. "Jon and Jael did a lot for me. I need to return the favor. What do I need to do first?"

CHAPTER TWELVE
DANNY'S FAREWELL

Danny gently rubbed Sandra's back, right where he knew pain bothered her most—especially when she was stressed. The touch of her smooth skin sent tiny electric sparks into his fingers. She sighed softly.

"I'm going to miss you so much, Sandy."

"Please don't be gone long."

"You'll probably hardly know I've left, and I'll be back already," he chuckled. "But for me it could seem like years."

"I don't understand how this Time-GAP works, Danny."

"Well, I've done it a few times, and I'm still not sure I understand it. Ginna always said the same thing."

"Did she really get pregnant in the future?"

"That's what she says, and I have no reason to doubt her. She insists she was a virgin when we left, *and* when we came back. But she *was* pregnant."

"It seems impossible."

He moved his hands lower down her back, causing her to sigh gently. "That has nothing to do with us," he whispered into her ear. "You smell so good."

"It's just my shampoo," she giggled softly.

He let out a wordless sigh and began to kiss her earlobe. "I love you," he murmured.

Later, as they both lay together across their bed, he saw the tears begin to come into her eyes.

"Why do you have to go with them?" she asked quietly.

"I think I owe it to Jael."

"But what if he *is* really dead?"

"Well, right at the moment—in this time-line—he hasn't even been born yet. When I cross the GAP, maybe there will be a way."

"Do you realize how weird all this sounds?"

He sat up and looked into her eyes, noticed more tears, and began to gently wipe them away with his fingers. "I won't be gone very long. Please believe me. Every time Jon took Ginna and me somewhere—or sometime—he brought us back the same night we'd left."

"But this time it sounds like things are a lot more dangerous. What if something bad happens to you? What if you can't come back?"

She was crying more loudly now, and he put his finger to her lips. "Shh—"

"I know—we don't want to get the boys upset."

"I bet I'll be back before they even know I've gone."

"Oh, you might fool Dain that way, but not Evin."

"Yeah, he seems to have some kind of extra sense for this GAP-crossing stuff."

"And he's not even first-born."

"Well, neither am I—or Jael for that matter. But there was some other power he had. Jon referred to it occasionally, but I'm not sure exactly what it was."

"If this is so important to Jon, why didn't he come himself?"

"I don't think he could risk it without Jael. Or maybe he was needed more at the Believers' hide-out. He did send his daughter, though."

"And this guy Stephan, who says he's from another universe. I can't get my mind around that at all."

"Well, Jon said once his world was actually a parallel universe to this one."

She sighed and pulled him into a tight hug. "Please, just be careful."

"You know I will. And the Lord will take care of me while I'm gone."

"There you go, contradicting yourself again. First you say I'll hardly know you're gone, and then you talk like it will be a long time."

"Well, it all depends on your point-of-view. One observer sees a long time-line, and another sees something completely different. That's been known for over a century—ever since Einstein."

"You know I was never very good at physics," she sighed. "It's all way beyond my comprehension."

"Well, I'm just glad to hear Stephan has much stronger GAP-crossing power than anyone else I've ever met."

"I bet you'll need it, if what they say is true."

Silence settled around them as they lay and just held each other. Soon moonlight began to bathe the room through the gap between the window curtains. Danny knew there wasn't much time left. Then he thought, 'Time—what is it, anyway? Does anyone really know?'

A light knock on their door startled him.

"Danny?" Celestia's voice came softly. "Are you ready? We really need to get started."

Sandra pulled him into one last hug. "I can't watch you just disappear."

"It's up to you. You don't have to come outside with us if you don't want to."

"I'm afraid, but—no, I need to do this." She pulled herself up and got into her jeans and a sweatshirt.

He was dressing, too, in extra layers. "Guess I need to be prepared for anything," he shrugged.

Sandra was shaking her head, and he saw the tears she was still trying to hide.

Then they both stepped to the door, opened it, and followed Celestia onto the front porch. Stephan was standing in the shadows on the stairs, but he turned when they closed the door. "Do you need to say good-bye to your sons?"

"They're sleeping," said Sandra. "It probably isn't a good idea to wake them. They'll be fussy."

"I'll just tiptoe in for a second," Danny whispered, and went back into the house.

The boys were fast asleep in bed, and moonlight was bathing their bedroom in a silvery, white light. 'Each of them looks like a sleeping angel,' he thought. First, he lightly kissed Dain's blond head, and then he stood over Evin's bed a bit longer. 'I wonder what the GAP has in store for you, son.'

Just then the young red-head rolled and groaned in his sleep. Danny stepped back, not wanting to wake him, but the boy settled quickly. Still, Danny was afraid a kiss or touch might rouse him, so he just gazed at him for a few seconds more. Then he kissed his own palm and blew the kiss to his son.

"I'll be back soon, Evin," he murmured.

Then he rejoined the others on the porch, where they all were standing on the front stairs.

"You should wait here, Sandra," said Stephan.

She nodded silently and gave Danny one last kiss. "Don't you go kissing anyone else," she murmured.

He tried to smile.

Celestia took his hand then and guided him out away from the house about twenty meters. She and Stephan joined hands, putting him between them. They were standing just beyond the apple tree he and his wife had planted when Evin was born. 'It's bearing good fruit this year,' he found himself thinking.

He'd just thought about reaching up to grab one of the ripe apples when everything disappeared into a green mist. His head was spinning, and new colors began to flash before his eyes—blue, purple, and hints of red. Then everything went black.

CHAPTER THIRTEEN
POSSIBILITIES

Danny was spinning out of control with nothing to hold onto, no point of reference, nothing to tell him up from down. And no one else was in sight. Where had Stephan and Celestia gone?

Then he saw a slowly turning red ring of light. Inside was a fuzzy scene—a man kneeling as if in prayer, weeping. From somewhere above him came a beam of light and then a voice boomed:

"You are correct, my son. None of these beings are worthy. Come home now, and we will start again."

The kneeling figure began to slowly rise off the ground, but not under any earthly power. His form stayed in its doubled-over position and just moved upward through the beam of light. Behind him there came cries of despair, with terrible sounds of weeping and wailing.

Danny's eyes began to burn with tears, and his voice joined the keening and crying. Suddenly he felt all hope leave him. He'd never felt so desolate and abandoned. It was worse than death.

***

Then he was spinning again, and the scene disappeared into blackness. He brushed at the icy tears on his cheeks but couldn't even see his hand when it was right before his eyes. Soon, another dusty nebulous cloud appeared in shades of violet and green. Bright bursts of white flashed from it, but he wasn't sure if they were stars or not.

In the middle of this nebula was a dark shape, very bird-like. It shimmered slowly, and the wing-shapes faded in and out of sight. Then a deep thundering voice began to boom in time to the wing-beats:

"All is well…no one has disobeyed…we are at peace… all is well…"

Now he felt the greatest contentment he'd ever known. Just as his previous mourning had been the worst feeling of his life, this was by far the best. He hoped he'd be this happy forever.

***

But then something seemed to suction him away, pulling him farther into empty space, more than he'd ever known existed. He saw clusters of stars flash by, and the whirling spirals of many galaxies. 'Where am I?' he cried. 'Have I strayed so far that I've left the Milky Way?' One of the larger galaxies looked very much like pictures he'd seen of the galaxy called Andromeda. There were no planets in sight now, only huge masses of stars and cloudy nebulae.

He closed his eyes, unable to focus anymore on the bright shapes flashing by so quickly. Terror began to grip him, and he trembled violently. All his emotions were magnified to levels he'd never known, beyond his ability to control.

At last, however, he stopped tumbling and spinning. He began floating gently, like a puffy white cloud in an azure sky. Yet when he opened his eyes, the blackness of space was still around him. 'How am I breathing out here?' he wondered. 'Perhaps this is just a vision or a dream, and none of this is real.'

Just as this gelled in his mind, he saw a blue oval floating into his field of vision. Its edges were gleaming yellow, and around it—above and below—were huge reddish rings that flowed outward in concentric circles. Then it seemed to form a shape he recognized—an hourglass. The shimmering blue oval was sitting in the middle where the narrow neck should be, but it was much wider than any hourglass he'd ever seen.

Some force was slowly pulling him toward the red rings. There was nothing he could do but let it draw him ever closer. The rings seemed to flare and pulse. Were they like fire? Would he be burned up by them?

But as the red colors began to close around him, he

felt no heat—or cold, either. Gradually, he was drawn toward the shining blue oval, and then another scene began to unfold before his eyes.

Once again, a man was kneeling in prayer, with bloody tears dripping from his face onto the ground. But this time there was no great voice, only a hoarse whisper: "Thy will be done, Father." A shining white being appeared beside the man, and this presence seemed to give him the strength to rise.

Above the white being were many more, hovering and apparently waiting to descend when ordered to. 'They look very powerful,' thought Danny, 'Like an army of angels.'

The man who'd been praying was walking slowly toward a grove of trees. Everything was hazy and in a fog. Then came shouts, and a crowd of noisy humans coming up a hill toward the man.

'Surely these mighty warrior-angels will help him,' Danny said to himself.

But the man raised an arm in greeting to the crowd, and behind him a huge flaming shape—like another hand—came between him and the heavenly army, holding them back. "The prophecy must be fulfilled," boomed a deep voice.

To Danny, the angelic army looked angry and confused. Especially when some ugly-looking men began to grab at the tall figure. "I am who you want," he said in a steady voice. "Let these others go." They seized him roughly and quickly bound his arms behind his back. Soon they were dragging him away.

Then he could see nothing but shimmering blue—as though he was falling under a huge wave in the ocean. His breath left him, and he thought he would drown. But just as suddenly he was pushed through the neck of the hourglass and into the red rings on the other side.

The scene of the lone man, the angry crowd, and the confused angel-warriors was gone—as though a light had been snapped off. Instead, he was in a glowing pool of green and gold, but this pool felt warm and safe—no danger of drowning here. It pulsed with positive energy, something that began to fill him with a peaceful joy. And then he heard voices beginning to sing:

Praise to the Father, who has done all things well.
Praise to the Son, in whom all his fullness dwells.
Praise to the Spirit, who calls us by name –
Holy, unchanging, forever the same.
Praise for the Kingdom which forever will remain.

You are holy: you dwell in the light.
You are worthy: our hearts to unite.
You are beauty: all the stars in the night
They bow down and they sing of your glory. Amen

Surrounding your throne there are rainbows
and angels of light.
The Elders bow low and fall down in their song of delight.

The heaven's infused with the incense of prayer;
The Lion has triumphed—his Word is declared.
Bright Morning Star, you are far beyond compare.

You are holy: forever you'll reign.
You are worthy: The Lamb that was slain.
You are beauty: that can't be contained.
We bow down and we sing of your glory. Amen.

As the music washed over him, Danny felt like a small child being held safely in his mother's arms. He closed his eyes and soon fell into a deep sleep.

***

When he opened his eyes, he was lying on a hard rock floor. Blue light was shimmering across the rock. He sat up slowly, and though his head was still spinning, he made out a shining blue hourglass opening in the floor nearby.

"Danny?" called a voice.

"Here."

A hand groped toward him and clutched his arm. "You made it!"

"Yes, but where are we? Is that you, Celestia?"

"Yes, it's me. Stephan is here, too. This is the Time-portal in Mendeleev Crater."

"Where's that?"

"On what many people call the dark side of the Moon."

"You mean the back side of Earth's Moon?"

"Of course. Why do you ask?"

"Apparently you didn't see all the places I did on the way. I thought I'd left the Milky Way Galaxy altogether."

Stephan stepped closer. "Perhaps you crossed a Nexus."

"A what?" he and Celestia asked together.

"You may have been at a junction of several possible time-lines. Some might call them alternative universes. Can you remember any of what you saw?"

"Right now, it's sort of a blur. But maybe I can get it sorted out when I don't feel so weak."

"What's wrong?" Celestia's voice was suddenly full of concern. "Do you feel sick or something?"

"No. Just kind of confused. I'll be okay with a bit of rest." He was still sitting on the floor, while they were standing over him.

"Here," Stephan reached down and helped him up. "Can you stand on your own?"

"I feel sort of wobbly."

"Lean on me then. We need to head for the lab wing and see if Laken is back."

He could walk if he took it slowly and hung onto Stephan's waist with his arm. Celestia stood on his other side and helped support him by holding his elbow.

"Who is Laken?" he asked, when he had enough breath to speak again.

"He's a friend I met when I was stuck in a Time Well," Celestia replied.

"How did that happen?"

"I was trying to take your sister and her daughter to the Fountain in the Desert. You remember that place?"

"Oh yes, I remember it well. You know I heard a song a little while ago that reminded me of it."

"You'll have to tell us about it," said Stephan softly. "It might be something important."

"As soon as he gets his strength back," added Celestia.

To Danny, it seemed they wound through a maze of hallways for a long time. His eyes felt heavy and bleary. At last, however, Stephan and Celestia turned into a doorway. Inside was a room with several black tables, like ones he'd seen in a science lab at his old school. A young man with long, black hair was sitting on one of the lab stools, looking intently at a screen hovering in front of him.

"Oh, Laken," cried Celestia, and Danny could hear the joy in her voice. "You're here!"

The man looked up and smiled at her warmly, "Safe and sound."

Celestia moved quickly to Laken's side and planted a quick kiss on his cheek, which seemed to surprise him greatly. "I'm fine," she said. "And so is Granddad."

But Danny had reached the end of his strength and was leaning heavily on Stephan by now.

"Here," Stephan said, quickly helping him into a low, comfortable-looking chair. "He's worn out. We're not sure where he went on his way here, but it sure doesn't sound like the route Celestia and I took."

Laken had moved to his side by now. "I'm glad you're here, Danny," he said softly. "How are you feeling?"

"Really tired," he managed to murmur. "May I please sleep?"

Laken made no reply, but he smiled, picked Danny up, and took him to a couch located along the back wall of the room. As he looked into the dark brown eyes above him, Danny felt warm comfort flow into him. He'd closed his eyes and fallen asleep before Laken even left his side.

CHAPTER FOURTEEN
CELESTIA'S QUESTIONS

"Are you sure he's all right, Laken?" I asked. "He seems so pale."

"None of his vital signs are alarming. I think he just needs to rest—like he said."

I was looking closely at this tall, thin young man I thought I knew. There was something different about him now—some aura that hadn't been there when we first met. But he smiled the same smile I'd come to know, and now usually trusted. His eyes were the same deep brown that seemed to see into my soul.

In fact, I couldn't quite explain what was different about him now. Was it only because Granddad hinted Laken was more than he seemed? Finally, I couldn't stop myself from asking:

"Laken, who are you really?"

"Who are you?" he smiled back at me.

"Why are you asking that? You know me. I'm from the Thirty-first Century, born on Earth. I met you when my friends and I fell into a Time Well, and we ended up in the Twenty-second Century. Which was supposedly your time. At least that's what you told us then."

"Yes, it was my time, but now I'm here in your time, I think." He turned and looked at Stephan as he said this. "With Mister Alternative Universe here, I'm not sure of anything, anymore."

"Hey, you two are the ones who came to the Mendeleev Portal. And that's what brought me here. So, I think I need some answers, too," said Granddad.

"Oh, come on, you two. You're being so male about this," I cried in frustration. "Will someone just tell me where and when we are, and why?"

Laken quietly took my hand when he heard the tone of my voice. "Please try to be patient. This will all make sense in time."

"What time?" Tears were threatening to burn my eyes. "When can I go home?"

"There now," he pulled me into a warm hug. "You know I've promised to take care of you. Your father wouldn't have let you come with me otherwise."

"So, I bet he knows more about who you really are than I do, doesn't he?"

He nodded but didn't speak.

"That's not fair," I cried.

Now he was stroking my long hair. Then he kissed me lightly on the lips, something he hadn't done since we'd left Toronto. It sent a thrill up my spine. "Your granddad is here to take care of you, too." he whispered.

"Really?"

"That's why I was the one sent here, when you two showed up," Stephan replied.

"You guys are sounding like there's some plot here that no one is letting me in on."

"Well, that's true. But if we tell you too much now, it could endanger everything."

"Why?"

Laken stroked my cheek softly and smiled into my eyes. "We can't tell you that either."

"Oh, this is so frustrating." I tried to push him away from me, but he kept hold of my waist, and pulled me back into another hug.

Then I felt Stephan's hand on my shoulder. "Soon we can tell you more, Celestia. Just try to be patient."

"Okay," I sighed heavily.

Just then, a voice came from the couch, "Hey, where am I?"

"Danny?" I moved quickly to his side.

"Is that you, Martina?"

"No, I'm her daughter, Celestia. Don't you remember?"

He shook his head in confusion for a moment, but then nodded. "Oh yeah, I remember now. You and Dominic came to get me, and we crossed the GAP."

"Not Dominic," I whispered. "Stephan—from another universe."

Again, he looked confused, but then finally nodded.

By this time, Laken and Stephan had joined us. "Are you feeling better now, Danny?" Laken asked.

"I'm beginning to feel more like myself again."

"Do you think you're strong enough to share with us what you saw on your way here?"

Something about the way he said this made me turn and eye him suspiciously. "Are you going to try one of those mind-reading sessions? I know what they're like, and I don't think Danny is strong enough for one."

"Don't worry, I can do a much less painful job than Laken," Granddad said.

I was surprised to actually hear Laken chuckle at this. "He's right. They are much better at it in his universe."

"How do you know about Stephan's universe?" I demanded.

"He's been there," Granddad replied.

"Oh, great, another of your surprises." I turned and pushed at Laken's chest.

"What's this all about?" Danny asked, sounding a bit frightened.

"Steady now," came Granddad's deep voice. "No need to fear. I'm a good mind-reader, and it won't hurt anyone."

"Why do you have to read *my* mind?" demanded Danny. "Can't I just tell you what I saw?"

"You could," he smiled. "But this will be more ac-curate. No details will be missed. And all four of us can see the same memories. That way we have more observers to catch everything. Besides, you can tell us if anything I project is inaccurate."

"Celestia?" Danny looked into my eyes, and I knew what his unasked question was.

"It'll be okay. They can be trusted."

I felt Laken squeeze my hand and saw Granddad smile.

"All right then," said Danny. "What do you need me to do?"

"Just let me sit down there beside you, and then lay your head in my lap. You may close your eyes or keep them open. It makes no difference, because what you'll see is already recorded in your mind. I'll project your memories into holograms so the rest can see them, too."

"Wow, is this for real?" I wasn't surprised that Danny sounded incredulous.

He sat up so Granddad could join him on the couch, then calmly laid his head in his lap.

"Can *you* do this?" I whispered to Laken.

"Not as well as he does," he whispered back. "Shh, now. Let him concentrate."

Laken pulled up a couple of lab stools for us to sit on, and silence descended on the room. Was it my imagination, or did the lights somehow begin to dim themselves?

CHAPTER FIFTEEN
DANNY'S VISIONS REVEALED

Before my eyes, the air shimmered, and then cloudy shapes began to flow and fold, shifting colors and sometimes sending out flashes of bright, white light.

"These are nebulae," I heard Stephan say. "Danny was definitely moving out of our galaxy."

Then we saw the figure of a man, weeping intensely, and bowed to the ground. "He's deeply troubled," I heard myself say.

"Yes, indeed," nodded my grandfather. "This is the True Lord himself, praying on the Mount of Olives."

"Why did I see that?" Danny's voice asked weakly.

"It's a key Nexus," Stephan replied.

"What's a Nexus?" I asked.

"It's a place where many possibilities meet, Celestia. Time can change its path at a Nexus and go another way."

"But we know what happened at this place," I said. "He did the Father's will, and let himself be arrested and killed by the—"

"Shh! That's in the time-line you know," said Laken. "Let *us* see which one Danny saw."

Just then, the figure on the ground began to rise up, as if traveling on a beam of light energy.

"What's happening?" I hissed into Laken's ear.

"Come!" boomed a huge voice above us. "We will begin again."

"In this time-line, they drop the Plan," Laken whispered.

"What Plan?"

"The only Plan, which has existed since before time began, Celestia. The Plan for the Son to pay the price for the sins of all humankind."

"But what does it mean—when the voice said, 'We'll begin again.'?"

"It means, Granddaughter, that no one is saved. All of humanity—and the entire Earth—belongs to the Serpent."

Just as he said this, I saw the awful vision we'd seen before of the flaming red dragon. He seemed to rise right out of the ground where the man had been kneeling. Larger and larger he grew, until the vision showed him encircling the whole of planet Earth. The blues, whites and greens of the globe began to shoot out crimson flames, and these dropped off the edges like dripping blood. The Earth began to whirl faster and faster, and the splotches of red flew all around it into space. When the whirling finally slowed and stopped, nothing was left but a blackened chunk of rock.

"It's dead, isn't it?" I hid my face against Laken's chest. This vision filled me with an aching despair.

Now the nebulae returned and swirled in their changing colors, but this time there was more red, except for a shining blue disc in the center of two red sets of concentric rings. As we drew closer to the blue disc, I realized we were seeing the same man, and again he was weeping and praying.

"No," I whispered hoarsely. "I can't bear to see this all again."

"This is another Nexus," said Laken softly. "Watch and see."

Sure enough, this time, the Son was whispering, "Thy will be done, Father."

We could see him moving back in among the trees of the garden, and behind him were many shining beings who looked extremely powerful.

"Are those angels, Laken?"

He nodded to me silently and put his finger to my lips.

So, I watched in silence as the Son walked into the crowd of enemies, who grabbed him roughly, bound his hands behind him, and hauled him away. I knew that feeling. My hands had been bound this way when Mauren took us all prisoner, right in this very building. But that was hundreds of years from here.

"Why did he let them take him?" I heard Danny whisper. "Why didn't he call the angels to help him?"

"Look deeper into the Nexus," said Stephan. "See what the possibilities were."

Danny closed his eyes again, and the blue disc seemed to pulsate and grow in size. Inside we could see a shining hand holding the angel-army back, so the forces of darkness could have their way with the Son of light.

Then the disc heaved itself upside-down, and we saw the great hand lift and motion the angelic hosts into battle formation. They moved with such force and speed everything had to flee before them. All the humans melted and sank into the ground. The angels lifted the Son up on their shoulders like a hero and bore him high into the sky, where he shone like a bright star.

But down below, the ground was oozing red. As the colors rose and swirled, I began to see the shapes of snakes appearing. And there he was again, the terrifying Serpent. Slowly he rose from the ground and hissed, raising his head into the sky:

"S-S-So, you've left them to me, after all. I knew you didn't care enough to die for this human filth. Now they're mine, and I'll show you what *I* can do."

Once again, the awful scene appeared of the Earth whirling and dancing with the red Serpent, splotches of blood-red liquid flying off into space all around it. And at the end, the dead black rock.

"I don't understand," murmured Danny. "Why does the Earth lose when the angelic armies win? It was the same outcome as when the Son abandoned the Earth to the Serpent."

"Because the only solution to the problem of Evil—the Serpent—is the Plan."

"You mean the darkness has to rule for a short time, before the Serpent can be overthrown?" I asked.

"Evil must think it has won, before it can be beaten."

"But then, how did it win in the other time-line? Why can't the True Lord just step in and defeat the Serpent once and for all?"

"Oh, he can. But didn't you see what happened when he did?"

"The Earth died—a bloody terrible death that left nothing behind."

"Yes, the only way to save the Earth *and* defeat the Serpent is the Plan."

"Oh, I see," cried Danny. "The Serpent thought the Earth didn't matter enough to the Father. He thought he would save his Son instead."

"You see it now," nodded Laken. "The great surprise of the Plan is that the Father loved the Earth enough to sacrifice his Son to save it."

As we were talking softly, the blue disc returned to its original position. Deep inside a shape began to appear—a shimmering golden plus-sign. "There it is," whispered Danny, "Just like we saw it in the clouds when we went to the Fountain in the Desert."

"Yes, I see it, too," I sighed. "The sign that means we are saved."

"But what about my second vision?" Danny asked then. "You skipped that one. Where the eagle shaped nebula was moving or flying, and saying, 'All is well…'-"

"That was a totally different world," said Stephan, "A universe with no Serpent and no need for a Plan."

"Are there really such places?"

He smiled and nodded at all of us. "Not all worlds fell prey to the Serpent, I'm happy to say. But far too many have."

"Maybe the Believers can escape to one of those worlds," I cried suddenly.

"I don't know if it's permitted," he sighed. "But that's not our question at this point."

"What is our question?"

"My question is which Nexus we've gotten ourselves into," he said. "What was that song you heard, Danny?"

"Let me think. It started something like this: *Praise to the Father, who has done all things well*.'"

"That sounds promising," said Laken. "What else did it say?"

"There was a chorus which kept coming back, something like: *You are holy: forever you'll reign. You are worthy: the Lamb that was slain*'—"

"Yes," cried Stephan excitedly. "That's the Plan. And this song—was it the last thing you heard?"

Danny nodded, as he lay with his head still in Granddad's lap. "Yes sir. I'm sure."

"Ahh—" My grandfather seemed full of relief. "Then we've passed through the correct Nexus. The Hourglass Nebula is the one which holds the key."

"The what?" I said.

"The key to the Plan—and our plan, as well," he smiled. "But I can't tell you any more yet."

"Figures," I sighed, looking over at Laken. He was smiling into my eyes with those deep brown ones of his, as I added, "I'm not sure how much longer I can wait."

CHAPTER SIXTEEN
LAKEN'S SECRETS

I glanced up at the two men on the couch and saw both of them were fast asleep. "Looks like they'll be out for awhile."

Laken smiled. "You and I know how mentally exhausting the Mind-blending process can be, don't we?" He took my hand and led me toward the door of the lab. "Let's find someplace else to talk."

'Talk?' I thought to myself. 'This sounds promising. Perhaps I'm finally going to learn something about this stranger I thought I knew.'

The hallways were dimly lit, and I wondered where the power to provide any light was coming from. "There was a long-term backup generator I was able to turn on," Laken said, as if answering my thoughts.

"How do you do that?"

"What?"

"You seem to be able to read my thoughts now, without any of that paraphernalia you used at the MEI in Toronto."

"I'll tell you soon," he smiled. "First I need to show you something."

We came to a lift which was evidently powered by the long-term generator, because it slowly rose up four levels. When the doors slid open, I saw a bank of windows across from us, like an observation deck. Through the thick plastiglas windows we could see the black lunar sky, and bright pinpoints of stars that seemed close enough to reach up and grab.

"Watch the horizon," he whispered. "It's coming soon."

"What's coming? Is it Earthrise?"

"No, we can't see Earth from the back side of the Moon, remember?"

"Oh, yeah." I sighed inwardly, wishing I'd seen more than just pictures of Earthrise—a blue marbled planet gradually rising into view, looking so lonely and far away out there in space. It was hard to believe my home was really somewhere on that tiny chunk of rock.

"There," he said suddenly, taking my hand. He pointed to the horizon before us, and sure enough a brightly shining globe of silver began to emerge above the grey edge of the Moon.

"What is it?"

"Venus." As he said this, he pulled me closer to him, wrapping his arms around me. Strangely, I felt no tension or fear from his embrace now. In fact, I felt safer and calmer than I had in a long time. "The ancients named this beautiful shining planet after their goddess of love," he added.

"I can see why. It looks so pure and white, like true love should be. And it's beautiful, like lovers see each other."

"That's just the first rush of love, though," he murmured. "It takes work, cooperation and sacrifice to keep it alive."

"I've seen that with my parents."

I wondered what he'd say next, afraid of what reply he might expect, so I was thankful he remained silent. We stood there until Venus had fully risen into the dark sky and shrunk in diameter from the huge shimmering ball we'd first seen.

"Why does it seem to get smaller as it rises?"

"It has to do with the angle we're observing from. Have you ever played with a head-lamp?"

I nodded.

"When you shine it on the ground at a low angle you see a larger but dimmer circle of light, right?"

"Oh yeah, but when you shine it directly down, say at a 90-degree angle, the circle of light is smaller and brighter."

"That's right," he smiled. "When Venus is low on the horizon, we see it at a low angle. But as the Moon rotates, Venus appears to rise in the sky, our angle increases, and the circle appears smaller."

"And brighter, too. Oh, that's why on Earth we can watch the sun rise, but once it's higher in the sky, it's too bright to even look at."

He squeezed my hand. "Smart girl. That's one thing I love about you."

An awkward silence came over us then, but I was thankful he seemed to be waiting for me to speak, and not forcing me.

"Laken," I whispered at last, "I think I love the *you* I know. I definitely feel some attraction. But how can I truly love the real you, if I don't know who that person is?"

He smiled. "That's another thing I admire about you, Celestia. You're not afraid to confront the truth. Come here and sit with me on a bench. This could take awhile."

And so, we sat where we could still admire the vista through the observation windows. Venus was gradually climbing higher, and I wondered if he'd planned this all along—to talk to me here, as we gazed at the planet of love.

As he'd often done before, he took my hands in each of his. I found this familiar gesture comforting. It didn't seem too forward. The way he caressed my palm and locked his fingers through mine reminded me of that evening on the hill in Indonia, when he promised he'd never hurt me. His dark eyes were gazing into mine. Was he expecting me to say something first?

"All right," I sighed. "The big question—who, or what, are you, Laken?"

"Well first, Laken Meta was the identity I was given for the Twenty-second Century. And I was totally enmeshed in it. At the time you met me, I knew nothing about any of the rest of my life. All I knew was the reality I was in then. Now I remember other names I've had, like Logan, Michkail, Raphael—"

"Well, to me you'll always be Laken, so can we stick with that?"

"Sure. I'm beginning to like it best. It always felt natural whenever I heard you say it. Perhaps it's the root of my real self."

"And what is that self? You're still dancing around the truth."

"I'm sorry. Okay, what I'm called is a Time-GAP Guardian. I'm sent to various key places—Nexes, if you will—to perform specific tasks that are part of the Plan."

"The Plan? You mean the one we saw in Danny's visions?"

"What we saw from Danny's mind is just a part of it."

"So how old are you really? Hundreds of years?"

"It depends on how you count it. Right now, if you stay with my Laken identity, 'born' in the Twenty-second Century, I'm over 900 years old."

"But I mean before that. How many other lives have you lived?"

"To be honest, I've lost count. When one assigned life is over, it's forgotten. That way we can avoid most disruptions of the space-time continuum."

He had one arm across my shoulder now, caressing my cheek gently with his hand. "You have such beautiful skin." Then his hand moved up into my hair, and he ran his fingers through it slowly. "I love dark, long hair—and your deep brown eyes make me want to be drawn right into your soul. I've never felt this for anyone else."

"Ever? In all those lives? Maybe you just don't remember?"

"Oh, no. I'd remember deep feelings like this," he whispered. "Not everything from each life is forgotten. I retain all the details which will help with the next assignment."

"Are you even human?" I asked, a bit of fear gripping at my insides.

"As human as you are, my sweet thing."

"Please don't call me that. It reminds me of Darroch."

"Oh, sorry. Okay, back to your question. Yes, I'm human now, but I haven't always been in this body. My spirit is the part which moves into whatever body is necessary for an assignment."

"So Laken, the slender scientist, is the body they sent you in for the Twenty-second Century. But that's the form I'm used to—the one I love. There, I've said it. I do love you."

He didn't say a word but began to softly kiss my lips, his hands moving across my back. I felt myself begin to glow with a rush of emotion I'd never felt before. Was this love, or just my hormones kicking in?

Suddenly I was overwhelmed and began to kiss him back, pulling him as close to me as I could. "This must be what desire feels like," I murmured in his ear.

"Perhaps it is."

But at this, a darkness crept into my mind, and I pulled myself away from him.

"Back in Toronto, you seemed like you'd done this before." My voice broke off in what was close to a sob.

I saw his eyes grow concerned, but not angry. "Those were other lives, other assignments."

"But why haven't you forgotten them?"

His silence gave me the answer I didn't want to hear.

"So, when they—whoever your managers are—tell you it's time to move on, will you forget me? Or remember me as just one other woman you had?"

"Right now, I'm not sure."

"Why not?"

"Because I've never felt so strongly about anyone before—not like this."

"I suppose that's your favorite line, isn't it?" Now I was feeling snappish and angry, and pushed him away from me.

"No, I'm telling you the truth. What I remember of any other lives is like pieces of shiny glass. But you're a diamond to me, and the beautiful shine of diamond is so far beyond glass. There's really no comparison."

I looked searchingly into his face and sighed. "I want to believe you."

"You're like that beautiful planet up there," he nodded toward the windows. "Any others were just tiny, distant stars."

We sat in silence for a long while. Time was becoming a strange sensation for me. Sometimes it flowed like a river, and other times it seemed to be isolated bubbles that hung indefinitely in an imaginary sky.

"But I don't want them to take you away from me when your next assignment comes. What sort of things do they make you do anyway?"

He sighed and took a deep breath before he spoke. "A Guardian must protect the Time Portals, try to prevent their abuse. And now it appears we have the Serpent to deal with."

"So, were you supposed to protect this portal here at Mendeleev Crater, and that's why you brought us to Luna that first time?

He nodded. "Unfortunately, the Morotani outsmarted me, and that mission wasn't a success. I was also assigned to begin teaching a few people to cross the GAP, but that backfired, because Darroch betrayed me."

"So, the Lord sent you with me—to this time—instead?"

"Yes, and for some reason I've stayed the same person, even in this next millennium."

"That hasn't happened before?"

"No." He began to run his fingers through my hair again. "And I think that means something important."

I felt tingly sensations in my chest and couldn't draw back from him this time. "What do you think it means?"

"I think it means you're to be my partner."

"Me? A Time-GAP Guardian? I don't know enough about any of that. I'm the one who fell into a Time Well, remember?"

"But maybe that was part of the King's plan—so we we'd meet."

"Hmm, I hadn't thought of that."

"His plans often surprise us," he smiled. "What seems to be one thing turns out to be another, often completely opposite of what we expected. Besides, I've seen what you already know."

"Oh, yeah. You've read all my memories."

"And I see how quickly you learn. You won't be an apprentice for long. But I was also thinking of something more, when I said 'partner'."

My heart stopped beating for an instant and breath suddenly left me. "You mean—"

"I've lived a lot of lonely lives. I believe the King has sent you to be my permanent partner, my wife."

My mouth dropped open, but no sound came from it. "Your what?"

"Believers still get married, don't they? We must do what's right. I'm really glad you're a virgin, by the way."

"Uh—what can I say? I don't know."

He made no reply but kissed me lightly on the lips. "How about, 'yes'?"

"You've dropped a lot of unbelievable stuff on me here. I need time to think, Laken."

As I was saying this, he'd drawn his lips back and was gently stroking my cheek with one hand. "I can accept that. I guess I'm too used to jumping around in time and doing things quickly."

"You could say that."

"Before, you were frustrated because I couldn't tell you all this. Now how do you feel?"

"Still confused, I'm afraid."

"Afraid of me?"

"No, I trust you. I just need some time to get my mind wrapped around all this. I'm still a simple human woman, not a Time-GAP Guardian."

"Not yet anyway," he smiled.

"By the way, if I do say 'yes' how can we get married? There aren't any justice-judges around here."

"We can go to a higher authority."

"Who's that?"

"Johan."

"The hermit on the planetoid? Is he a prophet, or a minister, or something?"

"Sort of. He's my supervisor."

"Another Guardian?"

"But he's much more than I am. He's a Guardian of Guardians, and beyond humanity. He's the one who makes it possible for my soul—my psyche—to continue on, when I move to a new body."

"So, you're saying Johan can marry us?"

He nodded and pulled me closer to him, so our cheeks touched.

"I haven't said 'yes', you know." My face was turned to the side, so I couldn't see his eyes, but I could hear his heart beating rapidly.

"I know," he whispered. "For now, let's just sit here and rest together."

"Yeah, my mind really needs time to think. And, Laken—"

"Yes."

"Can Johan keep you in this body? This is the one I love. It would feel too strange if you turned into someone else."

He put one hand on my shoulders and began to rub in slow, gentle circles. "I'll ask him. I see your point. If you weren't in the body I associate with you, it would feel strange."

CHAPTER SEVENTEEN
RETURN TO INDONIA

The next thing I knew, Granddad was shaking us awake. We must have fallen asleep from exhaustion, still sitting on that bench. "We have to get going." His voice sounded urgent.

"What's wrong?" Laken mumbled sleepily.

"I've had a signal from Johan. There's going to be an attack on the Indonia Out-clave. We have to get them out of there as quickly as possible."

"Where's Danny?" I murmured, trying to wipe the sleep out of my eyes.

"I'm right here," came the voice that sounded so much like Jael's.

"Grab any gear you have with you right now," Granddad continued, his voice even more urgent. "There's no time to talk."

All I had was the clothes on my back and the same was true for Danny as far as I could see. Laken pulled a small tablet out of his pocket and powered it down. He was never without some kind of technology. From what I could see of Granddad, everything he needed was stored in his mind. This thought made me wonder if he was entirely human, or perhaps part-machine.

There was no time to talk about it, though. By this time, he had the four of us in a tight circle, but instead of holding hands, he told us to link arms at the elbows and push our own hands into the waistbands of our pants. "This could be a difficult crossing, so we need to stay linked at all costs," he said tensely.

Just as I tried to take a deep breath, it seemed the floor suddenly dropped out from under my feet, sending me whirling in some kind of black and violent maelstrom. The arms linked through mine—Laken on my left and Danny on my right—were shaking. My hands were trying to pull out of my waistband, but I shoved them in deeper, actually digging my fingernails into the flesh of my thighs.

Then just as suddenly the world turned green, and I began to recognize some of the rainforest plants, whirling around my head. At last, the green settled into patterns at my feet, and blue appeared above my head—the sky finally in the correct position. We were standing upright in a small grove of trees.

"Whew! That was the roughest crossing I've ever had," Laken sighed. "And I've made quite a few."

'Quite a few?' I asked myself. 'I thought Dad and I taught him only recently.'

"Who goes there?" a voice suddenly cried from a tree above us. There was no more time for me to think about anything, as I heard the click of a gun safety being turned off.

"Blessed be the True King," cried Granddad before I could warn him this might be System Soldiers. Usually they were the ones who had guns in my world.

"Believers?" came the voice again. Then a lithe form slid down the trunk of the tree.

I was prepared for the worst, so I was surprised to see my own father staring at me. "Celestia? How did you get back so quickly? Is Laken here, too?"

"Yes, I'm here, Jon. We cut back as close to our departure time as possible."

"What did you find on Luna?"

"Let's find a safer place to talk," I said quickly. "We've heard an attack is coming your way."

Dad's face grew troubled, and he briskly led us through the trees on a path toward camp. "How did you find me so quickly?" he asked over his shoulder.

"Laken must have concentrated on you."

As I spoke, my father's eyes widened in surprise when he saw Danny. He whispered in awe, "Jael? Is that really you?"

"Uh, Dad, this is Danny—remember?"

"My, you've grown to look so much like Jael."

"Perhaps it's because I spent so much time 'within' him, Jon."

"Well, I suppose it could be that, but Ginna doesn't look as much like Martina."

Just then, Granddad stepped closer to Jon and shook his hand. "So this is Jon, son of Jakol."

"Uh, yeah—so what? You've known me for a long time, Dominic."

"Ah, but I'm not Dominic. I'm his twin brother."

"But Steph has been dead for ages. He died when my wife was still a teenager on Terres."

"In your universe, yes," Granddad smiled. "But I'm from another universe, one that's not totally parallel to yours."

"Dad," I took his hand, "I know this sounds really crazy, and I don't understand all of it either, but we need to keep moving. An attack is coming."

"Who's coming?" Dad finally realized the time for curious questions was past, and action was needed.

"The System is going to attack. Johan warned me," Granddad nodded.

"The 'One Who Shows the Way?' The same Johan who repaired our ship?" Dad's voice sounded incredulous.

"Never mind that. We've been sent to help your outclave escape before the attack," said Laken then. "But we need to get started. We can't explain right now. Time is slipping away."

"Okay, that's why I'm taking you all on the shortest route to camp. But there are going to be a lot of really surprised faces when they see all of you. It will be quite a stir."

"I just hope we don't waste more time on questions," mumbled Granddad, as we fell in behind Jon, continuing our run through the dense forest.

***

As soon as we reached the circle of huts, I began thinking how this place certainly wasn't prepared to withstand an attack. 'How did we become so complacent?' I wondered to myself. But then I remembered that five years ago when we'd come here, it was a remote and unknown wilderness. 'I wonder if someone betrayed us. Or has the Serpent followed us? Now that's a scary thought.'

Just as we entered the open area in the center of the compound, Dad gave a piercing whistle. People came running from all directions, so I surmised this was a signal to gather. I saw the children I remembered from when Laken and I first arrived here. They seemed older and taller now. Perhaps we'd been away longer than I thought.

While I was thinking, there came a sudden surprised cry from my left. "Jael!"

Turning, I saw Raina staring at Danny and holding her hands toward him. Her freckled face had suddenly gone pale.

Likewise, Danny was staring at her and slowly mouthing his own words, "Sandy, how did you get here?"

I stepped quickly to Danny's side and whispered in his ear, "That's not Sandra. It's Raina, Jael's wife—uh, I mean widow. She's remarried now."

He shook his head as if to clear it. "Of course. But isn't it strange how similar she is to my wife?"

"Apparently, you look like Jael to her," I added, as Raina came running up to us.

"Jael, is it really you? How can you still be alive? Where have you been all this time?"

Before Raina could grab Danny, I stepped between. "This is Danny," I said to her quickly. "He was 'within' Jael when you first got back together in Celeton. My dad says they're parallel—that Danny is a forerunner of Jael."

"But he looks and sounds just like—" Then suddenly, her eyes rolled back in her head and she crumpled to the ground in a faint.

Seeing her fall, her husband Branden came running. "What's wrong? She looks like she's seen a ghost."

"Well, in a way she has. This is Danny, Ginna's younger brother." I gestured for Danny to step up beside me. "He's a forerunner of Jael."

Branden eyed the lanky young man before him and nodded. "The resemblance is striking, though his hair's a bit darker."

"She was just taken by surprise," I sighed. "Hopefully when she comes out of her faint, she'll realize the truth."

"Yeah," nodded Branden. I could tell by the tone of his voice that he didn't want to share Raina's affections with anyone else, even if Jael were to come back from the dead. This set me to worrying, 'What if Jael *is* still alive somewhere? That could really complicate things for Raina and Branden.'

My thoughts were interrupted by another sharp cry. "Steph!"

'Here we go again,' I thought, as I saw my grandmother Irina and her husband Dominic running toward us.

Dominic, being the more fit of the two, reached Stephan first and grabbed him in a tight bear hug. "You old son-of-a-spaceship! What have you been up to, hiding from us all these years?"

Stephan smiled graciously. "Pleased to meet my twin brother's counterpart. I'm from another universe, Dominic. In my time-line, you were the one who died first."

Just as he was saying this, Irina reached them and threw herself into Stephan's arms. "Wherever you're from—you still look and sound like my dear first husband."

He smiled down at her and planted a kiss on the top of her head. "And you look much like my dear departed Irina."

"Irina died in your time-line?" said Dominic's surprised voice.

By this time, Stephan extricated himself from the hugs. "Our universes aren't exactly parallel. In mine, Karina is taking care of the youngest of my children."

Dominic stepped closer to Irina and slipped his arm around her waist, in a protective-looking gesture.

"But why are you here?" Dominic demanded.

"Never mind," Dad cut in. "We don't have time to talk about all this. Stephan says they've been sent to evacuate us before we're attacked."

"Attacked? But the System doesn't even know we're here," cried Dominic.

"Somehow the enemy has found us," said Laken. "All I know is Johan warned us to get you all away from here as quickly as possible."

"Johan?" came my mother's voice. "The one we met on the tiny planetoid?"

Dad took her hand. "Yes, but there's no time to talk."

"All right," said Stephan, suddenly assuming a voice of command. "Do you have an evacuation plan?"

"Yes sir," Dominic nodded.

"Then let's get it into motion."

I was thankful Dominic didn't seem to mind letting this 'stranger' Stephan take over. It was obvious to all that he had more authority behind him than we knew, that hc was accustomed to leading. A large bell began to ring, and everyone started moving back into their huts, packing what they needed, and leaving behind what they must.

I was standing in confusion for a few moments. Then Laken took my hand. "Where is your hut, Celestia?"

"I'm not sure. It depends on what time we're in. How long has it been since we left?"

Laken shook his head and led me toward the small lean-to he and my dad had built. "The only thing I know about is our little laboratory. Why don't you help me with that?"

"Sounds fine to me. I can't think of any possessions that are important, anyway. Seems like all I've been doing is time-traveling for ages."

He squeezed my hand as I said this—it was a comforting gesture. "I'm glad I've been able to keep traveling with you," he smiled.

"Me too." I wanted to hug him now, but there wasn't time. We'd just reached the door of the hut.

Stepping inside, he grabbed a couple of pack-sacks and started putting electronic gear, a tablet-screen, and some piles of papers in his.

"What should I pack?"

"See if there's any food over in that cabinet. There used to be non-perishable items in there for quick meals, when your dad or I didn't have time to go eat."

Sure enough, there were a few boxes of light-weight food items. Stuffing these into my pack-sack, I noticed some bottles of water and juice behind them, so I put these in also.

I'd just finished filling my pack when the outer door opened, and Granddad stepped in. "You two ready?"

"Sure are." Laken replied. "But where are we going?"

"I'm taking them all to where we just were."

"The old MEI base? Why?"

"It's the closest place, and one where the System is

unlikely to look," he said. "Remember? They don't want anyone to know about the Time Portal."

"Oh, yeah." But as I said this, I was hoping that dragon-like Serpent wouldn't show up again.

***

In less than an hour, everyone from the Indonia compound was standing in the center gathering area, each with at least one pack-sack. Even the children were carrying what they could. I noticed that Lexi, Daiah's daughter, had naturally assumed the role of leader for the children. 'She comes by leadership from her father, I bet,' I said to myself. Catching her eye, I smiled at her and she nodded, returning a shy grin.

This was to be no ordinary GAP-crossing, however—not with this many people. There were at least 50 of us, counting the children. I found myself frequently glancing at Stephan, wondering how he was going to accomplish this escape.

The first thing he did was get each family together. "It's important that you stay with your family," his voice boomed, filled with authority. "We don't want anyone getting lost, trying to find someone else *they think* is lost. So, do *not* break your handholds—for any reason."

"Does this mean he's going to take each family separately?" I whispered to Laken.

But he shook his head. "That would be too slow.

Speaking of family groups, shouldn't you be with your parents?"

"I guess," I shrugged. "But what about you?"

"What about me?" he grinned.

"You don't have any family."

"Not here, anyway."

"Great. Another secret you're not telling me," I hissed. "I suppose you have a wife or girlfriend in every place you've been sent."

He frowned and shook his head. "No, I don't. Please believe me, this is the first time I've found someone I care so much about."

Silence settled between us, and I felt ashamed of the way I'd been teasing him—or had I truly been doubting him? He seemed to be honest now, so I took his hand in mine, and wordlessly led him to where my parents were standing. Soon the four of us joined hands in a tight circle, our pack-sacks on our backs.

Dad smiled at Laken, and I remembered then how they thought Laken was his forerunner. 'He's much more than that, Dad,' I thought to myself. 'You have no idea. Will I ever get the chance to tell you what I know about Laken now?'

Just as I was thinking this, we heard a low rumbling sound. As it grew louder, I knew where I'd heard it before—when System forces had attacked my Uncle Darien's compound.

"Dad? What do we do?" I cried, looking into his deep violet-brown eyes.

"Just follow Stephan's directions," said Laken, squeezing my hand tightly.

It seemed Granddad had found some kind of megaphone, for his voice was suddenly amplified: "Everyone hold on tight like I've told you, and close your eyes. No matter what happens, or what you think you see, just keep concentrating on Luna—Earth's Moon."

I noticed, just as he spoke, that the full moon was rising in the east, appearing when we most needed it.

"Dad, look," I nudged him with my elbow. "Luna."

He smiled and nodded, then closed his eyes.

Suddenly my feet lifted from the ground—just the opposite of the sensation I usually felt when crossing the GAP. My head began to whirl, and it felt like my whole body was turning in circles. Was I caught in some kind of cyclone?

But now I began to see rainbows of color swirling around. Were my eyes open, or were these sights all in my mind? Then the shape of the Moon began to rise through the rainbows, pulling me with it, as though I was riding on a tall blue wave.

The wave heaved me up and down and then began to crest. I saw the foaming white as it broke above my head and pulled me into the curl. I was going under! My lungs waited to be engulfed with water, but nothing happened. Soon I bobbed back to the surface, like a piece of floating wood.

Was I still with my family? I couldn't feel their hands, either Laken's on my left or Dad's on my right. I almost pulled my hands toward me, trying to see if anyone was there. But then I felt Laken rubbing his thumb across my knuckles. There are no words to express the vast relief I felt at his touch.

I tried to say something to him, but the winds were whirling so hard around my head that any words were torn away and flung into the distance. What was happening? Were we lost? Then I remembered all the strange sights Danny had seen on his crossing to Luna. Either this was a vision with meaning, or it was just an illusion. Hopefully this meant it would end soon.

And as soon as I thought this, the whirling began to slow. The colors faded to black and white. I was gliding slowly above a silvery surface, rocky and pocked with craters. Between tall ranges of mountains were large flat areas I knew were marias or seas. But this landscape had no water or atmosphere, for now I recognized the surface of Luna.

Just after this we passed the terminus, the edge of the sun's reflected light, and moved into darkness—to the back side of the Moon. This night it was truly all dark, for the Earth was having a full moon.

Then my feet touched ground, but they weren't on the rocky surface I'd seen in the light. We were inside a building, on smooth man-made floors.

"Where are we?"

"Is this place safe?"

"Can we let go yet?"

Many voices, young and old were asking questions all at once in a confusing babble.

"It's all right, everyone," said Granddad's comforting voice. "We've reached our first stop on the journey. You may let go of hands and open your eyes. Sit down and rest for a bit, if you like."

"Where are we?" Several voices asked this question again.

"You're at an old institute building on Luna." he began.

"Institute? Is that connected with the System?" someone asked.

"No," said Laken. "The System had nothing to do with the Mind Exploration Institute. This facility is over 900 years old. It was here long before the System ever 're-discovered' Earth, before the Galactic System itself even existed."

Finally, people began to calm down. Most found places to sit leaning against the walls of the hallway or curling up and lying on the floor. Lexi, I noticed, had two of the smaller children on her lap. One I knew was Morgan, daughter of Raina and Branden.

Thinking of Raina made me suddenly wonder where Danny was. Whose family had he joined? I didn't think he'd join Branden and Raina. That would be too awkward.

Then I saw him seated a few meters down the hallway, talking to a youth with blond hair. I motioned Laken to move closer with me. Soon we'd seated ourselves next to them.

"So, have you two met?" I asked.

Danny nodded and smiled. "This is Jael's son, Jace."

"When I saw Danny, I knew he wasn't my dad," said Jace. "But I could see the resemblance."

"And I noticed the same thing with Jace. He looks like my older son, Dain."

"We've been comparing memories, Celestia," Jace smiled. "I think it's sort of interesting that my name and my dad's both start with the same letters—'j' and 'a'—and Danny and his son do, too."

"Yeah, Dain and I share the same first letters: 'd' and 'a'."

"Well, it could be coincidence," Laken spoke up. "After all, fathers tend to choose names for their sons based on their own. Not that I've had any first-hand experience." He glanced at me quickly as he added this, and I knew he was thinking of my comments about his 'girlfriend' in every time-line.

To keep things from getting more awkward, I said, "Mothers have a say in naming their sons, too, you know."

Danny looked wistful for a few seconds after I'd said this. "Come to think of it, Sandra was the one who thought of 'Dain'."

Laken patted him on the back. "Don't worry, we'll get you back before she's even had time to miss you."

"What happens next, anyway?" Danny asked.

"I'm not sure—" began Laken, but just then Granddad stepped up and interrupted him:

"Danny, it's time to reveal what I need you for, to help me find Jael."

"You mean my dad's alive out there somewhere?" Jace cried excitedly.

"We hope so," said my granddad softly. "But please don't let your mother hear any of this, Jace. I'm not sure how she'll handle it."

'Or how Branden will handle it, either,' I thought.

CHAPTER EIGHTEEN
WAITING AND WONDERING

It was impossible to tell how much time was passing in Earth-hours. None of us had a chronometer, and of course 'nights' on the moon were measured in terms of weeks instead of hours. Besides, we were inside the atmospherically sealed buildings of the old Mind Exploration Institute most of the time.

Dad said we shouldn't go outside or use any suits. "We don't have much extra oxygen. So, we must save it for emergencies."

And so, time seemed to crawl. We ate lightly from our food supply, too.

Meanwhile, Dad and Danny seemed to always be off somewhere talking. Sometimes they took Laken with them, but he didn't talk to me about it.

One time, as Laken and I were lounging on the floor, just to get our backs into a different position from sitting, I finally asked:

"I know I probably shouldn't pry, Laken, but what are Dad and Danny up to?"

"Jon is trying to bring out everything Danny remembers of his time 'within' Jael."

"I'd guessed that. But why?"

"Jon is sure Jael isn't dead after all. He says he's been hearing voices in his head, and he thinks it may be Jael trying to reach him."

"What kind of voices?"

"He hasn't told me specifics."

"Sometimes I hear something like a voice in my head when the Lord has a mission for me."

"Really? You think God talks to you?"

"It's not actually a voice or words—more like just a feeling."

"Like an image or picture in your head?"

"No, not that either. I can't explain it. I just sense something I'm supposed to do."

He sat silently looking into my eyes and then kissed me gently on the forehead. "I knew you had some special power from the time I first met you," he smiled.

"I'm nowhere near your powers, Laken."

"Oh, I don't know about that. You may be surprised someday."

I sighed and pulled him closer to me. Was I beginning to feel more strongly for him? "You're still avoiding answering my question you know."

"Which question?"

"The one about what Dad is up to with Danny."

"Oh, yeah. Your eyes distracted me," he grinned.

"Well?"

"If Jon can get enough of Jael into the forefront of Danny's mind, he thinks he can re-forge the link they had. Then maybe he can sense enough to find out where Jael is."

"But where could he be?"

"There are lots of possibilities."

"Are they using you to help them connect?"

"That's part of my job. Also, Stephan and I are trying to locate a Time Portal closer to the 'signals' Jon is getting."

"Do you think it will work?"

He shrugged and stared at the floor for a moment before he answered. "Jon knows it's a long-shot. Even his 'voices' may be just his own mind's wishful thinking."

"So, you haven't made any great progress?"

"Not yet. But Stephan thinks we should keep working on it. He's more optimistic than I am."

"Do you think that maybe Stephan has some connection to Jael, since the Steph in this universe was Jael's father?"

"I hadn't thought of that. Maybe it's possible. But Stephan keeps saying our universe isn't a true parallel to his."

Just then we heard a soft sigh above us. Looking up we saw Jace was standing nearby.

"Jace, when did you get here?" I asked, trying to sound casual.

"I was taking a walk and heard you mention my dad's name."

"Have you been eaves-dropping?"

The boy looked at the floor and muttered, "I'm sorry. I shouldn't have."

"No, it's okay," I stood and took his hand as I saw him beginning to blush. "You and your dad were very close, weren't you?"

He nodded but couldn't speak.

"Come sit with us," said Laken. "What's on your mind?"

I knew then Laken was sensing something more in Jace's presence. This sixth sense of his wasn't always with him, but it sure seemed to crop up when needed.

Jace sat and leaned his back against the wall beside Laken. But then I saw Laken signal to me with his head to sit on the other side of Jace, putting him between us.

"There Jace," he whispered. "Now you can talk to us without fear of anyone else eaves-dropping."

"Thanks," he whispered. "I'm worried about my mom."

"What's wrong?"

"Well, of course she was really sad when we lost my dad."

"Yes, she told me some of it," I nodded. "But she seems happy now with Branden."

"Oh, she *was*, back at the cave, and when my half-sister Morgan was born. But something's changed."

"Like how?" Laken asked.

"Well, I see her staring blankly off into space a lot. Sometimes, there are even tears in her eyes. But whenever I get close, she pretends to smile or talks about something unimportant. I know she's avoiding me."

"Hmm," I heard Laken murmur.

"She won't tell you anything?"

"No. But one time, I thought I heard her saying my dad's name in her sleep."

"Your dad—you mean Jael?"

Jace nodded stiffly. "Branden's not my father. He never will be."

I was surprised to hear the anger is his voice. "Has he hurt you, Jace?"

"No. It's just—well, I think he wants to replace my dad. And I don't want that."

"Totally understandable," said Laken.

"What?" I asked. "That Branden would want to replace Jael?"

"No. That Jace knows no one else can ever replace his true father. So Jace, you feel like Branden is trying to push himself on you?"

"Yeah, I guess that's it. But there's something else."

"What?" This time it was Laken who asked.

"He keeps talking to me about stuff."

"Stuff?"

"Yeah. Stuff I don't think he should be saying about The Book and the System."

"You mean he seems to be challenging your beliefs?"

"Sort of. He never comes right out and says anything bad. But he drops these hints—like how can the Lord really care when he's so far away. How can we believe in something we never see or hear?"

"Jace," I sighed. "I feel deep in my heart that the Lord does care. Sometimes I can almost hear his voice."

"What does he sound like?"

"Well, it's not actually an audible voice. I was just trying to explain it to Laken. It's more of an impression or a feeling, but I know it's real."

"Don't worry, I still believe," Jace said, with a half-smile. "But it makes me uncomfortable to hear Branden talk that way."

"Well, losing his first wife in battle couldn't have been easy," I said.

"Yeah, he's probably still getting over his grief," Laken nodded.

"But he has my mom now. Shouldn't that be making him feel better?"

"You'd think so," muttered Laken. "Maybe I should try to talk to him."

"Would you?" Jace's voice sounded hopeful. "And maybe my mom, too? They both seem sad, and they don't talk to each other like they used to."

"I can try, son. I'm no expert, but sometimes I get this sixth sense, where I can read people's feelings."

Jace stood up then, and we joined him as he gave us each a hug. "Thanks." Then we all walked down the hallway toward one of the offices we'd been using as a sitting room.

***

Jace left us soon, however, for Toren and Andre came and asked him to join them in a game.

"It's fun to play tag in all the empty, twisting hallways," he smiled.

Laken and I stood and talked softly about what Jace had told us. At last he sighed, "I need to walk and clear my mind."

All the things we'd discussed were rumbling through my mind as I left the room with Laken. He was silent, apparently full of his own thoughts. Part of me wanted to reach out and take his hand, but something held me back. Knowing what I now did about his powers, I was in awe of him—almost afraid to speak.

When we reached a junction in the hall, he turned toward me. "I think I need to go see Jon and Danny about this. Something feels wrong with how Branden is acting."

"Should I come with you?"

"Please don't right now," he sighed. "And don't be angry. It's just that you wouldn't understand what we need to discuss."

I hung my head for a moment, not able to deny it

made me envious to be left out of these plans they were making. But then I looked up into his dark eyes and tried to smile. "Okay, you men do your thing. I think I'll look for my mom."

"That's a great idea," he smiled. "She's probably feeling a bit left out, too. I think I saw her in the blue conference room." He pointed down a hallway leading in the correct direction. Just as I was about to turn and walk away from him, he pulled me into a quick hug. "I really appreciate your understanding, Celestia."

Shaking my head, I murmured, "Sometimes you're a tough person to figure out, Laken Meta." Before I could add anything else, he gave me a quick kiss, then turned down the other hallway, leaving me standing there—confused and feeling the memory of his lips on mine. But there was nothing else I could do but walk down toward the conference room.

Mom was talking to her cousin Donmal when I entered the room. He'd been late in joining our Indonia Out-clave. If fact, he'd only been with us a year or so when we'd been forced to flee to this back side of the Moon.

As a firstborn, his skills in crossing the GAP had been in high demand as the few remaining out-claves scattered around the world had to be evacuated quickly. It all happened so suddenly, I could see why most of our leaders suspected there was a traitor in our midst. Someone had to be feeding information of out-clave locations to The System.

In spite of the demands on Donmal's time, my mother seemed to spend as much time with him as he could spare. I was usually busy with my own duties, but I often wondered what they found to talk about so much.

One thing I knew for sure, Mom saw a lot in Don which reminded her of her eldest brother, Stephen, who died in a tragic shuttle crash many years ago on Terres. She'd only been a teenager then, and was already mourning the loss of her father. Besides that, no one knew what The System had done with Irina when they took her away after a mental breakdown.

Could I have handled all these trials my mother experienced? She never talked much about them. Perhaps some of the trauma still ran too deep.

After their parents were gone, she and Stephen were the ones who tried to hold their family of four together, for their little brother Jael's sake. Apparently, Darien, her second brother, had been traumatized as well, for he'd become very moody and withdrawn. After Stephen's death he left altogether to join the Inland Raiders, a unique corps of System troops.

Mom tried to tell me once of the despair she'd sunk into at that time:

"I felt totally alone. My boyfriend, Jason, was no help. All he wanted was my body. I tried to hang on for Jael, but one night Jason and I fought, and I just snapped. My only choices seemed to be suicide—or fleeing to the Wilds of

Terres. I knew there were refugees from the City out there called Redlarks. I felt too lonely to go on living, but afraid to die. So, I ran away, leaving poor Jael all alone."

Tears had filled her eyes then, but her voice was gone. I knew she was aching to talk to Jael again—to apologize. Would my father and Laken find him somehow with Danny's help? I hoped so for Mom's sake.

That day—we were still in Indonia then—I pulled her into a tight hug. "Mom, please try to let this go. Jael forgave you long ago. And the Lord brought some good things out of your wrong choices. He's powerful enough to take even our mistakes and turn them around for good."

She'd nodded and tried to smile. "Yes, you're right, of course. It was with the Redlarks that I met your father."

"And he'd even brought Jael with him."

"That was indeed a miracle, how he used the disaster of the Double-star to bring Jon and Jael together."

"And that's when Raina and Irina found each other, too—remember?"

So now, as I looked from the doorway at Mom and her cousin, all this flooded my mind in a flash. It's amazing how the brain thinks. In an instant, it can see memories which take hours to tell.

'Could this ability have something to do with the powers we've been learning to harness in crossing GAPs?' I thought. 'Our minds can move through multiple dimensions all at once, instead of step by step in a single line. I remember learning something about this in a Quantum Physics class,' I chuckled to myself.

Mom and Donmal were standing near the opposite wall of the conference room, and an untrained eye might have mistaken Don for his father, Dominic, and my mother for her mother, Irina (who was now Dominic's wife). There was a strong resemblance in many members of my family. In fact, people often mistook me for my mother.

And apparently Don also looked very much like his cousin, my dead Uncle Stephen—with his curly blond hair, lanky frame, and piercing green eyes. I stood in the doorway, just gazing at him, wondering if I was seeing a vision of this uncle I'd never known—this older brother who seemed to have meant so much to my mother.

"—but The Book seems to say the True King *will* return to Earth to reign—" I heard Mom say, as I stepped closer to them.

"It's confusing, though, Martina," said Don. "There are so many passages when the Lord says, 'The Kingdom of God is within you.' He doesn't seem to be talking about a political kingdom."

"But then it talks about the saints reigning with him a thousand years, a Millennium."

"But is that a literal number? Or does it represent eternity?"

I stepped closer to them, interested in what they were

saying but not wanting to interrupt. So I kept behind Mom, where she wouldn't see me.

"Don, if that's the case, why does it say that 'at the *end* of the thousand years' Satan is released for a short time? Eternity implies no end."

He smiled at her, and then caught my eye over her shoulder. "You've got me there. What do you think, Celestia?"

I was just about to open my mouth to mention the Serpent that Laken and I had seen at the Portal, when a sudden loud wailing filled the air. Even the walls of the room seemed to vibrate.

"What's that?" cried Mom.

"It must be an alarm of some kind." Don grabbed both of our hands and pulled us with him into the hallway.

People were pouring into the passageways from rooms all around us, everyone looking frightened and confused. Then, a loud voice boomed from some coms above us in the ceiling:

"We're being attacked! System ships are now landing in the crater!" I recognized Dominic's commanding voice, and this gave me a slight bit of comfort. At least we had a capable leader.

"What?" voices around us were asking.

"How did they find us?"

"Somehow they tracked—"

"How could they?"

"Someone is tagged."

"Do you think we have a traitor?"

All these things were going through my mind, too.

Then Dominic's voice came over the com with authority. "Everyone, head for the Hourglass Portal. Stephan will meet you there."

I realized with a start he meant his parallel-universe brother, the other Stephan, who hadn't died. But what was Dominic going to do?

CHAPTER NINETEEN
BATTLE FOR THE PORTAL

As we rounded the corner where the shining blue light from the portal appeared, I thought I was seeing double. Both Dominic and Stephan were standing there, and their identity as twins was obvious. Irina was between them, as though wondering which one was her true husband.

Then a shimmering light began to appear around one of their graying heads, and I knew this was Stephan, the Guardian of the Hourglass Portal. Thankfully, the people behind us were moving in a fairly orderly fashion. Panic could have easily turned this flight into a stampede, and I knew this wouldn't help any of us escape safely.

"Just step right into the blue," came Stephan's voice, with a calm command. "There's nothing to fear. The Portal will take you to my world which, for now, is unknown to the System."

People seemed to hesitate then, many of them having never seen this twin of their leader Dominic.

"Please, don't be afraid," I heard Laken's voice call.

"Yes!" came my father's deeper voice. "Stephan can be trusted. He's one of us, and Guardian of this Time Portal. Please, we must move faster."

I saw them moving toward the front of the crowd. Dad was the first to turn and face the group. "My daughter has traveled with Stephan before, so I know he's trustworthy. Now follow me, before it's too late." Then he turned and stepped into the shimmering blue spot on the floor—and disappeared.

Laken grabbed my hand and was about to follow, when a sudden sizzling sound filled the air. "What's that?"

"Sounds like lazer-fire. The soldiers must have found us."

At this, Laken pulled me aside, and began shepherding others in the group into the Portal. No one hesitated now—not with the threatening sounds of the lazers getting closer. Soon, everyone had gone into the blue light, except Don and his father, Irina and Stephan, Laken, and me. Danny had just stepped in with Jace, when we saw the shapes of soldiers coming around the nearest corner. Worst of all, there was the same reddish glow behind them that I associated with the Serpent.

Dominic glanced quickly at Stephan and nodded, as though they already had a plan. Without a word, Stephan grabbed my hand and Laken's, and pulled us with him into the Portal. Dominic tried to push Irina and his son toward us, but they refused to move from his side.

"You're not dying alone, Father!" I heard Don shout.

"And I'm not becoming a widow again," cried Irina.

My heart leaped into my throat. "Can't you help them?" I shouted to Granddad.

But there was no time. He had to use all his power to get the three of us across the GAP. And then I realized that to prevent the soldiers from following, he must close the Portal. Lazers were firing rapidly now, and I saw my grandmother fall, lying eerily still.

Then the shimmering blue engulfed me, and unbearable cold cut right through my bones. It was all I could do to hang onto my granddad's hand. My eyes saw nothing now but black, and then I was falling into emptiness.

***

Gradually, a yellow light began to appear before my sight. It was blinding after the blackness, and I reached my hand up to shield my eyes. As I did this, I felt a firm hand take mine.

"Granddad?" I murmured.

"No, it's me, Laken. Are you okay?"

All I could do was nod feebly. "So that was a space crossing to another universe?"

"Yes, and you did fine."

"I don't think I've ever felt so tired."

"It does consume a lot of energy." By this time, he'd pulled me onto his lap, and was cradling me in his arms. "But you're a strong one."

"I don't feel very strong right now."

"Well, some of the others are going to be asleep for several more hours, but you're already awake. That says something," he smiled into my eyes.

"Thanks, I think." But then my eyes began to close. "Where's Stephan?"

Laken nodded his head toward the right, "Just coming back from reporting to his superiors."

Turning my head slightly I could see him walking slowly toward us, and I noticed we were sitting under a leafy tree in a gray field. The colors were strange. Instead of green, everything was a deep golden color, against a gray background.

"He looks really tired," I whispered to Laken.

"I'm sure he expended a lot of energy keeping the Portal open long enough, and then closing it."

"I think I saw the red glow from the Serpent behind the soldiers, Laken."

"Me, too. I'm sure Stephan was trying to hold him off so we could all escape."

"Did Dominic and Don—"

"No," he whispered. "I saw them go down."

"I think I saw Irina die, too. Why do we have to keep losing people dear to us, Laken?" My voice dissolved into a sob, and I buried my face in his tunic.

"We'll see them again in the world beyond, where death has no power," he murmured into my hair.

I nodded against his chest but could find no words to express my grief.

"Just think of Stephan, though," he went on. "He's had to watch Irina and Dominic both die twice—in our world and in his."

"Oh my. Once was bad enough."

'Shh now. He's almost here."

I clung to Laken and tried to draw some comfort from his embrace. "I could never bear to lose you."

"We'll always be together somewhere—sometime," he whispered.

By this time, Stephan had reached us and slowly sat lowered himself to the ground. We were silent for a long time, and I must have drifted back into sleep. The next thing I remember was their voices whispering:

"There has to be a traitor among us, Laken. Otherwise they couldn't have found us so quickly—even with the Serpent's help. I made sure there were no traceable pathways when we went to Luna. Someone in our group must have a tracer on them."

As I listened, I realized Laken was stroking my back gently. It felt so comforting I decided to keep my eyes closed, so he wouldn't stop.

"I've been getting the same feeling."

"Do you have any idea who it might be?"

"I think I may, but I'd rather not say just yet. I need to follow-up on some information I got just before we left Luna."

Now I opened my eyes and found myself looking up at Laken's face from beside his jaw. I could see the tightness in it and wondered if he was thinking the same thing I was.

"Oh, Celestia, you're awake," he smiled. There was a slight cloud that crossed his eyes, though. "Have you been eaves-dropping?"

I shook my head, not wanting him to be angry with me.

"Well, just let Stephan and I handle this," he smiled. "We're the ones who know how. And this enemy we're facing is much more powerful than the System."

"Sure, whatever you mean," I nodded, still pretending I didn't know what he was talking about. "Is this your world, Granddad?" I decided to change the subject.

He turned as though I'd interrupted his thoughts. "Uh—yes, this is Materna."

"Hmm—Materna. Doesn't that mean 'Mother', too—like Maia?"

"Yes, I've been told that. Guess it goes back to the old Mother-Earth story."

"Yeah, my dad told me all about their search for Maia," I nodded. "But what they found on Earth wasn't what they were expecting."

"Perhaps they missed a Nexus," added Laken.

"So how many Mother-Earths are there?" This was beginning to sound confusing.

"As many as there are alternative universes," said Granddad.

"And I suppose that's an infinite number," I sighed.

"Some think so," Laken said. "But I'm not sure they're right."

"At least, we hope they're wrong," Granddad added, as he finally cracked a small smile.

I reached over and took his hand, disentangling myself from Laken's lap. Granddad seemed to understand my wordless gesture, and his green eyes gazed deeply into mine for a few moments.

"I should go look for my parents," I said at last, breaking the spell.

"They're in that domed building over there." He pointed to his left. Not far from us was a large building, topped with a crimson dome that shimmered in the light of Materna's sun. Then I noticed the sky wasn't quite the same shade of blue as on Earth.

"Everything is a different color here," I said. "Earth was so green, but there isn't anything green here."

Granddad nodded. "Our sun's spectrum is slightly different, and our chlorophyll absorbs green light, instead of reflecting it. As I said, we're an alternative world, not a parallel one."

"It's really beautiful." I slowly stood, still feeling a bit of dizziness.

"Are you sure you're okay?" Laken asked.

"Yes, I'm fine. I really want to see my parents."

"Should I walk with you?"

"No thanks, Laken. I just need to catch my breath and be alone for a few minutes, okay?"

"All right, Ms. Stubborn," he chuckled.

I walked very slowly at first, as I moved away from them, just to make sure I wouldn't get any dizzier. That's why I heard Granddad ask, "Do you think she heard us?"

"It's possible. She's a smart one—"

CHAPTER TWENTY
SEARCHING OUT A TRAITOR

By the time I reached the crimson-domed building, my heart stopped pounding, and my breathing slowed to almost normal. I really was anxious to see my parents, for I hadn't seen them since the beginning of the battle. I wanted to confirm for myself that they were safe.

As I entered one of the automatic doors, I found myself in a large rotunda. The red dome above bathed everything in an eerie pinkish light. I was surprised it wasn't a darker red, but something in the lighting must have been diluting the color. Once my eyes adjusted to this strange light, I saw my parents seated on a long bench near the curved wall to my left.

Mom jumped up as soon as she saw me, grabbing me in a tight hug. I gripped her just as tightly.

"I'm so glad you're safe." It was then it hit me—she'd just lost her mother—for the second time.

I held her for as long as she let me, and wet her face with some of my own tears. "It's okay, Mom. I'm here."

By the time we parted Dad joined us and gave us both an embrace. Then we sat down again on the bench, and I noticed that even though it looked pink in the light from above, it was actually a neutral cream color once I saw it up close.

For a long time, we just sat in silence with Dad between us, holding each of our hands. "We've been fortunate," he murmured, at last. "We're one of the few families that's still intact."

"Really?"

"If you call just the three of us intact," mumbled Mom.

"Now, Hon. We have each other, and our daughter."

"I know. Raina has lost Jael, Daiah has lost Darien, and there are motherless and fatherless children—like Toren and Siene."

"And Jace." As I added this name, I began to remember the conversation Laken and I had with him, not so long ago on Luna. "Have you seen Jace since we got here?" I tried to make my voice sound casual.

"Yeah. He and Raina were here. Then they went to look for Branden."

"Is Morgan—" I heard fear in Mom's voice.

"She's fine, Hon. You know Lexi takes care of her like her own."

"It's a good thing, since her own parents don't seem to take much notice of her."

"Have you noticed that, too? How Raina and Branden are drifting apart?"

"They do seem preoccupied lately," added Dad.

"It's a good thing Lexi and Daiah have more or less adopted Siene and Toren," Mom sighed. "I just don't understand Raina. She seemed to have gotten over Jael."

As her voice broke, I murmured, "Mom, you know it's not that easy. You haven't gotten over it either."

She glanced at me angrily, but then her anger dissolved into tears. "I don't know if I ever will. I think I hear him calling out for me in the night sometimes—like he used to when he was small and had nightmares."

Jon put his arm around her shoulder. "I keep wondering if I hear him, too. And I don't think it's my imagination."

"Say, where's Danny?" I asked suddenly.

"Oh, he's around," Dad nodded. "He and I have plans to meet after the next meal."

"Do you really think Jael is still out there somewhere, Dad?"

"I have this feeling in my gut, and it just won't go away. It's gotten stronger now that Danny is here."

"So maybe these dreams I have and voices I hear aren't my imagination?"

"Martina? You didn't tell me about any of this. Why not?"

"I thought I was going crazy. Like when Stephen died back on Terres. I was afraid."

He pulled her closer, his arm across her shoulders. "Don't give up on yourself, Martina. You're stronger than you think. And what you know may help Danny and me, so I think you should come meet with us tonight, okay?"

"Dad, can I please come, too?"

He glanced over at me and shook his head. "Not yet. Let us get your mother's information first. Then you can come."

I resisted the temptation to fold my arms and pout like a child being denied a treat. Instead I just nodded silently. Then I shifted slightly out of his hand's grasp on mine.

"You know, I think I'll look for Raina. She sounds like she could use someone to talk to."

"That's a good idea, dear," said Mom. "I think she and Jace were going to walk in the gardens."

So, I left them to each other, trying to walk away as casually as I could.

***

Sure enough, after I walked about halfway across the colorful flower garden surrounding the crimson-domed building, I saw Raina's flaming red hair several meters away. At first, I didn't see Jace, because he was on the side of the path talking to someone. As I got closer to them, I saw him facing Lexi, who stood next to a purple-flowered shrub. Beside her was little Morgan, holding tightly to her hand.

"No!" I heard Morgan shout, as I came within earshot of them. "I stay with Lexi! I want my daddy—not Mommy!"

I didn't want to get into the middle of this argument so I stepped closer to Raina, where she stood at the junction of two trails. Just as I was about to speak to her, I saw tears shining in her eyes so I took her hand. As soon as she felt my touch, she grabbed my arm and pulled me with her down a path leading to our left.

"What's wrong?" I whispered.

"I just need to get away from her."

"Morgan? Why?"

"It's like she sees something evil in me." Now she was beginning to sob and had to stop walking.

"Raina, don't be upset. Children Morgan's age often get these tantrums. They're learning to assert themselves. Don't take it personally."

"Oh, there's much more to this than you know, Celestia," she sighed. "I've heard him—the things he's telling her about me."

"Heard who?"

"Her father, of course."

"Branden?"

"Yes, he's using her to drive a wedge between us."

"But why?"

"I have no idea. All I know is he's not the man I married a few years ago. Something's happened to him. He's so moody—not himself. I—I'm afraid of him."

By now, she was clinging to me and sobbing into my shoulder. All I could do was stroke her hair gently. Then the sound of footsteps approaching startled me so much I jumped. Raina looked over my shoulder, fear registering in her eyes, and then buried her face in my hair.

I glanced behind me, expecting to see Branden, but instead saw Jace.

"What's all this about?" I hissed to him. "Has he been hurting her?"

Jace shook his head and gently pulled his mother toward him. "Come here, Mom," he murmured. "Let's sit on this bench over here. Maybe Celestia can help us."

Raina was still silently sobbing as we seated her between us on a stone bench, sheltered from the trail by some low trees full of fragrant yellow blossoms.

"I just don't know what to do," she said, after a long deep breath. "Branden is acting very strange."

"For how long?" I asked.

"It started just after you and Laken came to Indonia," Jace cut in. "He began to get angry at Mom over little things that weren't even important—like what she fixed for dinner. Then he started taking Morgan for long walks, and each time they came back, Morgan would seem angry with Mom."

"What about Siene and Toren?"

"He's pretty much ignored them," Raina sighed. "It's like he can't stand to be around anyone who reminds him of his dead wife."

"They must be pretty hurt, don't you think?"

"I don't know," he sighed. "They won't talk to me."

"Why not?"

"They just don't. But a couple of times I've heard Siene muttering to her brother, things like, 'Well, Dad's not his *real* father, anyway.' Stuff like that."

"How does that make you feel?" I asked.

"Oh, I don't care. I never wanted Branden to be *my* father." I could hear the undercurrent of anger in his voice.

"Siene and Toren have gone to stay with Daiah and her children now," sighed Raina. "All I have left is Jace."

He reached over, patting his mother's hand. "You'll always have me, Mom."

I found a small catch in my throat as he said this. He sounded so grown up—almost like his father.

"I know, sweetheart," Raina murmured. "You're all I have left of him—of your fath—" Her voice ended the last word in an abrupt cry.

This time she collapsed completely into my lap, her head across my thighs, and her shoulders trembling with sobs.

"I can't go on like this anymore," she cried between the tears. "My life is worthless—except for you, Jace. If anything ever happens to me—"

My heart took a frightened jump as I heard these words. My mother had told me once how her brother, Stephen, said this to her: 'If anything happens to me—' and then he'd been killed in a shuttle crash.

"Please, Mom," Jace cried. "Don't talk like that. It scares me."

"I'm sorry…" her words were barely audible now.

A deathly silence settled over the three of us. At last, I heard Jace take a shuddering breath. "What should we do? I can't just let her go on like this."

"Let's go find my dad," I sighed. Even as I said these words, I knew they were the thoughts of a child who felt a big, strong parent could fix anything.

Jace nodded and helped me get his mother up and supported between us. She seemed as weak and limp as a wet blanket. "I wish *my* dad was here," he murmured.

"I know. But at least we have my parents with us still."

"Jon and Martina were the two people in the world Dad was closest to."

"And there's Danny, too," I thought out loud.

"Yeah. I wonder if he can help."

We didn't see any of the others as we crossed the center path through the gardens. But perhaps it was because we were heading away from the crimson-domed building, despite the fact that it was probably the wrong direction for finding my parents. At the far end of the path was a circular stone gateway leading into a stone-paved area. I'd seen it from a distance earlier in the day. I'm not sure why we chose to walk this way. It was almost as though some other force was drawing us in that direction.

As we walked, I heard a far-off cry like an eagle. Looking up, I saw a red-colored bird circling overhead. In the strange golden colors of Materna, its fanned-out tail seemed to be aflame.

"What's that bird?" asked Jace.

"I'm not sure," I shrugged. "Some kind of hawk, I guess. Everything is different here."

By this time, we'd reached the stone gate.

"I've seen pictures of round stone openings like this," I told Jace. "They're called 'Moon Gates'."

As soon as we passed through the Moon Gate, we were surrounded by a circle of tall standing-stones. They were a deep purplish color, with glowing red streaks running through them. A hush fell over everything around us. The birds and insects we'd heard in the garden were silent here. Even the breeze stopped. There were no plants within the stone circle, and the paving stones beneath our feet felt cold, right through the soles of our shoes.

"What is this place?" whispered Jace.

"I have no idea."

Then suddenly a deep voice interrupted me. "Who has entered my sanctum?"

For an instant, everything went black before my eyes, and then just as suddenly a shining golden figure was revealed, standing right in front of us.

"W-we're sorry!" I cried.

"Y-yes, sir—we didn't mean to intrude," Jace added.

Then the shimmering before us faded, and instead we were staring at a stooped old man dressed in ragged brown clothing. His face was nearly hidden by his long white hair and beard. "My children," came the voice again, but this time its deep tones echoed with more gentleness. "Come to me, Celestia."

"You know my name?" I was still a little frightened. Raina seemed to be unconscious and was leaning heavily on my shoulders. Jace's eyes, I saw, were wide with fear.

"Don't you remember me? You came to see me with Laken and Stephan. Besides, haven't your parents told you about me?" he rumbled.

"My parents?"

"Long ago, they were led to my Maiar—Jon, Martina, and Jael—along with some hidden companions, and a feier-cat—"

"My father is Jael!" Jace suddenly blurted out. "They were told to come to the Centauri Sector to look for Maia."

"Oh, you're Johan!" I cried. "But you look so different. And how did you get to this alternative universe?"

Now a bright smile appeared in the twinkling eyes above the beard. "I can go to many places—if I choose."

"But was Earth really Maia?" Now I found I had many questions, some almost angry. "It was no paradise. We had to flee the System again—maybe something even worse—and here we are, in Stephan's alternate universe. Or so he says."

"Now, now," he chuckled again. "Come and sit with me. Life is never a straight and easy path. There are always twists and turns, holes to fall into, logs to trip over."

"But why?" Jace demanded, echoing my feelings exactly.

Johan made no reply but moved all three of us, with uncanny strength, toward a circle of rocks within the huge standing stones. They were small enough to sit on comfortably.

Once we were seated, Raina suddenly woke from her stupor and sat blinking at each of us. "Where are we?"

"I'm not sure," I whispered in her ear. "The old man says he's Johan."

"The one Jael met on their space travels from Terres?"

"Yes, my dear," Johan said to her, and I noticed there was more gentleness in his voice now. He reached out and took her hand for a moment, and some of the normal color returned to her cheeks. I wished he'd touch me.

And then he did, placing his wrinkled hand on my cheek. "There now, my brave servant of the Lord," he murmured. "Don't forget where your strength comes from." At this, a warm glow built deep within my belly, and a strange calm radiated throughout my body.

Lastly, he turned to Jace and patted him on the shoulder. "You have a special mission only you can perform, my son. Each of God's children does. Keep the faith." Jace's eyes glowed suddenly with a hope I hadn't seen there before.

"Sir," Jace said softly, "Why is Branden hurting my mother? He used to love her. Even I know that."

"Though you never loved him, did you, son?"

"How could I? He's not my real father."

"Yes, I know. Your father was—is—a very special person."

"Is?" Raina's voice cracked when she spoke.

"Existence doesn't end at death," said Johan.

"But he *is* dead, then?" I didn't want to say these words, but they came out anyway.

"I can't say for sure from this universe, dear ones. We must wait for other answers to that question. But as for Branden—"

"What about him?" snapped Jace, with near-hatred in his voice.

"He's been sucked down into a pit," Johan muttered softly. "Not entirely of his of choice. Darkness of heart can do terrible things."

"But what should we do?" I asked.

"Pray for him *now*," he replied. "It may be too late before long."

And in that instant, Johan began to utter words I didn't understand. I could tell they were a prayer, but in some language I'd never heard. Still, even though I couldn't understand what he was saying, I sensed they were words of power. I was swept along with them as though I was riding a surging wave.

When Johan's voice stopped, I heard some of the words echoing and realized they were coming from my own mouth. I didn't even know what I was saying, but some kind of power was moving me deep within.

"There," the old man said, at last. "We've done what we could, putting him in the Lord's hands. Now, each of you must be on your guard. Watch what everyone around you is doing. Someone has become a traitor and given the Serpent a foothold."

"Branden?" said Jace sharply.

"We don't know for sure, son. It could be him, but it could be another. Don't jump to conclusions. That can lead to terrible consequences."

"Yes sir," Jace nodded, humbled.

"And Raina," Johan added, "I know it won't be easy but try to respond to Branden with as much love as you can—no matter how he tries to hurt you. It's himself he hates right now, not you."

Raina nodded silently, as the gnarled hand rested on her red hair for a moment. When she looked up, I could see more strength in her eyes.

***

The days and nights here weren't like Earth, but somehow our bodies adjusted their circadian rhythms to this place. At least the change wasn't as drastic as the Moon. We slept when the strangely colored sun set, and woke when it rose.

Apparently, Stephan had brought us to an isolated part of his world, for we didn't see any of the other inhabitants. Finally, one day, I asked him, "Granddad, where exactly are we? Why aren't any of your people here?"

"This is the remains of an ancient civilization from thousands of years ago, Celestia. I can't risk your people meeting the people of this alternative universe. It could change the time-scheme."

"Time-scheme? Is that like a time-line?"

He chuckled, "You still see time as one dimension, don't you?"

"Uh—I guess. It's just the term my dad always uses."

"Well, he hasn't been introduced to the Full Quantum Theory then. Time has as many dimensions as space does. A Guardian, like me—or Laken—can explore many dimensional directions at once, not just one time-line at a time."

"I think this is all beyond me, Granddad."

"Laken sees a lot of potential in you."

"Maybe his eyes are blinded by love."

He laughed aloud this time. "Oh, knowing Laken like I do, I seriously doubt that. He's extremely perceptive."

For some reason I felt embarrassed at this remark. Granddad and Laken were so far beyond me that they could see right into my soul.

"Don't fret, my other-universe granddaughter," he smiled. "Laken will never harm you."

"Yeah, he's told me that," I shrugged. "But you guys are so powerful and different. It's kind of scary."

He reached out and gave me what I knew was a grandfatherly hug—though I'd never had one before. "Don't fear. The True King guards you."

"Thanks." I hugged him back as tightly as I could.

As we dropped hands and began to walk across some of the golden hills beyond the garden, I suddenly noticed something was missing.

"Granddad, where's the stone circle?"

"Stone circle?"

"There was a round stone entrance, just beyond the gardens—over there." But now there was only bare hillside where I was pointing. Could I have my directions mixed up?

"Mmm. Did you perhaps see Johan there?"

"Yeah, Jace and I did."

"That's fascinating," he murmured, almost to himself.

"What do you mean?"

"Apparently Johan chose to reveal something important to you."

"You mean he isn't really here?"

"He was when you and Jace saw him. Did anyone else see him?"

"Not that I've heard of."

"What did he tell you?"

"That there—"

Suddenly he looked around, and silently put his finger to his lips. "Not here," he whispered. "Let's walk a little farther."

I couldn't see anyone else around us, but I let him take my hand, and we walked over two or three more hills before he stopped beside a tall golden tree. Then he pointed to his ear, indicating I should whisper to him.

"He said there was a traitor in our midst, and for us to be very careful."

"Did he tell you anything else?"

I thought for a moment, not sure if I remembered any more. "Umm. He told Jace not to jump to conclusions."

"Well, that's interesting," he muttered to himself. "Have you noticed anything unusual?"

"Oh, wait. Raina was with us, too. And he told her to be as loving toward Branden as she could—that he was angry with himself, not her."

"Anything else?"

"Hmm, I think there was something else about Branden—about being sucked into a pit."

"Did Johan say Branden was a traitor?" Stephan was barely keeping his voice in a whisper now, and I put my finger to my lips to remind him.

"No. He said it could be someone else."

He heaved a deep sigh. "Well, just be sure to follow the directions Johan gave you very carefully."

"But some of what he said was in a language I couldn't even understand."

"Really?"

"But when he stopped talking in it, I was echoing him, even though I didn't know what I was saying. And I felt all warm inside."

He was looking into my eyes intently now. "That's a very powerful thing he did, Celestia. When the time comes, you'll know what to do."

"I sure hope so."

"Don't worry—you will," he smiled. Then he took my hand and we walked the long way back over the hills to the garden, and finally arrived at the domed building.

"This place looks so well-kept—not like an ancient civilization."

"Well, my people have restored and preserved it, as a memorial—"

"To those who built it?"

"In a way. And to what they stood for."

I wanted to ask him more about this, but we'd reached the dome and a door slid open.

Inside, my parents were seated at a table, just ready to start a meal. "Stephan, Celestia. You're just in time to join us," smiled my dad. "Are you hungry?"

"Famished," I laughed. "Granddad has been trekking me all over the place."

And so, we joined them for dinner, first giving thanks to the Lord for his provision, as we always did.

***

A little later that day, I was lying on one of the benches in the rotunda, with my eyes closed, enjoying the feel of the warm pinkish light filtering down from the dome overhead. Just as I was drifting off into a nap, I heard voices, and recognized them as Jace and Branden. Since the two of them actually talking to each other was rare, I quickly decided to keep my eyes closed and pretend to be asleep.

Branden's voice was calm and friendly: "You know, Jace, I owe you a big apology. I haven't been the kind of person I should be to you."

"Well, you're not my father," said Jace, with the angry tone I'd heard from him before.

"Of course, I'm not," came Branden's voice, still calm and friendly. "No one could ever replace your real father. I just want to be a friend—someone you can come to if you feel upset or lonely."

"Uh—well—okay."

"Come on. Let's have a seat over here where the sun's not so hot."

They sat on a pair of chairs about twenty meters from me. There was a half wall behind the couch I was lying on, so they couldn't see me. I had to listen carefully now. Sometimes I couldn't catch everything they said.

"…your mother says you've been upset lately," I heard Branden say.

"—she worries about me too much—"

"Is there something I can help with, Jace?"

"Some people are saying there's a traitor—"

"—wonder who—"

"—no idea."

"You know, all our troubles started when your cousin brought that stranger back with her." Branden's voice was louder now, as though he wanted everyone to hear this part of the conversation.

"Laken?"

"Yeah. I mean—who is he really? How can he be from 900 years ago, like she says? That's impossible."

"Well, uh—"

"And then they went and got the other stranger—that Danny," added Branden.

"But Danny says he was a close friend—"

"Of your father—yeah, so they claim."

"—but Mom says—"

Their voices were getting softer now, and I was missing words again:

"—your mother has been under so much stress—shouldn't always believe—"

Jace's voice suddenly rose in anger, "Are you saying Mom's a liar?"

"No! No, son. It's just that she gets confused sometimes." I could hear Branden's voice getting that overly-calming smoothness he had at the start. "Hey, Jace, I know you love her very much—so do I. Let's both just do our best to take care of her, okay?"

"Yeah—sure."

Then I heard their footfalls as they walked away from the chairs, and their voices faded into the distance.

***

I was troubled about what I'd heard, so when sunset came, I joined my parents in our sleeping-room and asked them about it. I was surprised to see that Granddad was there, too. Apparently, he and Dad were talking over their plans about searching for Uncle Jael.

"Well, I'm glad to see Jace and Branden are finally beginning to develop a relationship," said Mom, after I told them what Branden said.

Dad nodded. "Jace needs some kind of male role model."

"But Dad, you and I know Laken and Danny can't be traitors. They've never had any contact with the System. Why was Branden planting such ideas in Jace's mind?"

"Maybe he's trying to help him feel less fearful," Stephan mused.

"I don't know. It didn't have that effect on me—just hearing them."

"Hey," Dad smiled. "Don't try to take all the world's problems on your shoulders. That's what I'm here for."

"Oh, all right," I sighed. Inside, I was wondering if I should tell my parents about the encounter we had with Johan, but something in my mind held me back. After all,

Granddad knew about it, and he wasn't saying anything. Instead I asked, "So have you guys made any progress on your attempts to locate Jael?"

Stephan looked over at Dad for an instant as if asking his permission to answer my question, and I saw him give a slight nod.

"Okay, it's finally your turn to hear the story."

"What story?"

"You remember when we went back to Colorado for Danny?"

I nodded. "By the way, where is Danny? I haven't seen him much since we got here."

"I've been keeping him out of harm's way in a secret place."

"Harm's way?"

"I'll explain that later. Anyway, just before we got to their house, something strange happened to them."

"What?"

"Are you going to let me tell—or keep interrupting?" He was beginning to sound perturbed.

"Sorry. I'll stop."

He gave a sigh before he began again. "Your curiosity is a great strength, but sometimes it gets in the way of my thought process. All right. Just before we arrived at their house, do you remember the dog who met us?"

I nodded, not wanting to speak after just being admonished.

"He's a big black dog named Shadow," he nodded to Dad. "And just the day before we showed up, he'd brought home a strange visitor—a pinto pony, colored black and white."

I turned to Mom in surprise as she added, "From the description Stephan has shared, he looked a lot like Splash."

"Uncle Jael's horse?" Then I bit my lip—I was interrupting again.

But this time Granddad smiled at me. "Yes, their son Dain showed him to me. Remember when he asked me to follow him to their barn?"

I nodded. "But how—?" Why could I not keep my mouth shut?

"Laken and I have no idea how a horse was able to cross the GAP. Perhaps the dog picked up some power from Danny's younger son Evin. You remember how he seemed to have a special connection to the GAP?"

"But he isn't the firstborn—oops! Sorry."

"Well, Jael wasn't firstborn either, but he had some kind of special power I've never encountered before," said Dad. "I sensed it the first time we met on Terres."

Mom took my hand and squeezed it. "Laken has probed my mind, along with Jace's, Raina's and Danny's. Since all of us have experienced visions, dreams, or messages. This gives hope that Jael may be out there somewhere."

"Maybe he's just in Heaven," Dad sighed. "But the

horse showing up—and at Danny's of all places. Seems like an omen to me. Perhaps the System took him prisoner instead of killing him when he left Raina and the children at the fir tree."

"Laken said perhaps he crossed a Nexus into an alternative universe," I blurted out.

"Okay." Now Dad laughed aloud at me. "I can see that you can't keep your thoughts out of this. But perhaps that's because you're part of the picture."

"So, what are you going to do?" Mom asked.

"Well, it seems Danny and I should try to find a Nexus close to Jael's last known location."

"How can you do that?"

"Laken and I have been working on crunching the numbers and dimensions."

"Are you taking Laken with you?" My stomach was beginning to ache at this thought. Suddenly, I didn't want Laken in danger, but then I felt guilty that I wasn't having these same feelings for my own father or Stephan.

"Yes, Laken is needed very much—to help me," said Dad softly, "And don't ask me how, because I can't tell you about it yet."

This time I did just nod. There was a big lump in my throat keeping me from speaking anyway.

"Stephan will come with us, too," Dad was saying, "Won't you?"

"Of course."

"But he's our only contact with the people of this universe." Mom sounded upset. "What if something goes wrong, and he's not here to help?"

Granddad reached over and patted her hand. "I've taken care of it, Martina. Karina will come over to stay with you."

"Karina?"

"My Irina's twin sister," Stephan said softly.

"Yes, but she's dead," murmured Mom.

"Not in this universe. Remember?"

"So, I'll get to meet my aunt, in a way," she smiled.

"In a manner of speaking. You'll be meeting her counterpart in this alternative universe."

"Like I've gotten to meet my 'Granddad'."

"Anyway, the plan is for our group of men to gather tomorrow and see if all the pieces are finally in place. And Celestia, Laken wants you to keep an eye on Raina while we're gone."

"Why me?"

"I don't know, but he was insistent."

"So, who's actually going, Jon?"

"Well, I am for sure. I'm the one with the strongest link to Jael. And we need Stephan and Laken to help us navigate the Nexes. That's all for this first attempt, besides Danny, of course."

Granddad was moving toward the door and nodding, "See you as we've planned, Jon." Then he was gone.

I could see fear beginning to show in Mom's eyes and knew exactly what she was thinking. Dad took her gently in his arms and kissed her. "Celestia, be sure to help your mother, too."

"I know, Dad."

For an instant I wondered again if I should tell him about our encounter with Johan, but he was murmuring softly to Mom now, and I didn't want to interrupt them. So, I crawled into my blanket, trying not to let my fear for Laken overwhelm me. As I lay there on my sleeping mat, trying to fall asleep, I wondered when—or if—I'd ever know the meaning of those foreign words Johan had put into my heart.

CHAPTER TWENTY-ONE
THE TRAITOR REVEALED

The next morning, I slipped out the door of our sleeping room and headed to where I knew Raina and her family were staying. Their door was closed, but I could hear voices, and the tinkle of dishes. I made out Branden's deep voice first, and Raina's soft one. Morgan's child-voice was easy to distinguish, but I was surprised when I also heard Jace. To have him and Branden both there seemed out of the ordinary, but then I remembered their conversation I'd overhead yesterday.

"Good breakfast, Mom," Jace was saying.

"Yeah—it's okay—for leftovers," grumbled Branden.

"Yeah, Mommy." It seemed Morgan liked to echo her father.

"Thanks, dear," I heard Raina say in her sweetest voice. Apparently, she was doing her best to follow Johan's directions. "What are your plans for today?"

"I thought Jace and I might take a hike."

"Me too!" cried Morgan.

"Sorry, little one," Branden chuckled. "This hike will be too long for you."

I could hear Morgan beginning to whine. "I want Daddy, not Mommy!"

"Morgan, don't say unkind things," Jace scolded.

"Yes, my little one," came Branden's voice, deep and calm. "Sometimes Daddy needs to be with the men. I'll take you for a walk when I get back."

Morgan didn't say anything else, but I could hear her still whining softly.

Then came the sounds of dishes begin cleared, and heavy footsteps coming toward the door. Quickly, I ducked around the corner, just in time to see Branden stride out, his arm across Jace's shoulders. Jace seemed to have a slightly puzzled look on his face.

"Where are we going?"

They were moving rapidly away from me, so I couldn't hear the answer.

"I have an idea," came Raina's voice from inside the quarters. "I think we have enough sugar here to make your favorite treat for tonight. Would you like to help me?"

"Okay, Mommy." The brighter sound of her voice made me feel better. Perhaps following Johan's advice was helping mend things between Morgan and her mother.

Branden and Jace were disappearing into some yellow and orange trees at the base of a nearby hill, and I decided it was more important to see what they were up to.

It was difficult to follow them and keep out of sight. A couple of times I lost them in the thickly-growing tree stems, but then a voice, or the crack of a twig would tell me which direction they went. This continued for what seemed like half the morning, until finally I saw what looked like a small clearing ahead in the forest. Sure enough, when I crept up to the brightness between the trees, I saw an opening with a thick carpet of red-gold leaves.

I expected there to be crunching sounds ahead of me as I tried to see where Jace and Branden were. But everything was silent, like in the stone circle where we'd met Johan. Was this another magical place like that?

Just as I was about to step into the clearing, I heard Branden's voice off to my right. Ducking back into the tree trunks, I turned carefully toward the sound. He and Jace were also standing at the edge of the clearing, as though deciding what to do next.

"Okay, Jace," his voice hissed. "See that dark spot on the cliff across the clearing? That's their hide-out—the traitors. They've been plotting in there ever since we got here."

"Who has?" came Jace's slightly quavering voice.

"Danny—of course!" snapped Branden. "And that fake time-traveler, Laken, his crony Stephan, and Jon…"

A tight ball of fear was forming in the pit of my stomach. 'Could Branden be right? Is Laken or Stephan not what they seem? Sure, they have unique powers, but have they fooled me into thinking they're good rather than evil? When *did* we first met Stephan—before or after we saw the evil red Serpent coming out of the Hourglass Portal? And isn't Laken the one who tried to deceive me back in the Time Well? Has he somehow blinded me to his true mission?'

"Look," said Jace suddenly. "They're coming out of the cave."

"Just as I expected."

I crept a bit closer to them while they were talking, and now was near enough to see them. Branden was reaching into his pocket and handing something to Jace.

"What's this?"

"A lazer-pistol. All we need to do is stop them from disappearing into the GAP."

"But how?"

"Just press the green button and pass across the whole group. They'll all go down at once."

Jace stared down at the weapon in his hand for a moment and then looked out at the small group, which moved to the center of the clearing. All four joined hands in a circle, as I'd often seen GAP-crossers do in preparation for the crossing. Laken's back was to me, close beside Stephan, who began glowing with a familiar bright golden light.

Just as Jace was aiming, it came to me—this light was what we'd seen coming from Johan. Words that had been foreign before began to race through my mind: "The Guardians must be protected—falling stars will guide the way—the traitor is among you."

I leap to my feet just as I heard the lazer's sound. A flashing beam of green light hit Laken in the back and I screamed:

"No, Jace! Remember what Johan said—don't jump to conclusions."

The young man turned to me in total surprise. "Are you the traitor, Celestia?"

"No, of course not—and neither is my father. Can't you see who has deceived you?"

The hand he held the weapon in was beginning to tremble, but when I tried to grab it from him, he turned and ran toward the other three men, who were beginning to shimmer out of sight.

All I could think of was Laken, and I staggered to where he was lying prone on the carpet of red leaves. Just before I reached him, I saw Jace plunge into the space left in the circle, but he wasn't firing the weapon. Instead I heard him crying, "Take me with you! You have to let me come! Johan told me!"

There was a sudden flash like lightning, and then all four of them were gone. A mist of gray smoke hovered for an instant where they'd been, and then I heard a sinister voice behind me.

"So, you thought you'd search out a traitor, did you? Well, you failed. Jace will take care of the rest of them. I know he will obey me. All I have to do is finish you off now—like he did your skinny boyfriend."

Tears were beginning to blind me as I looked down at Laken's prone form. Was he really dead? There seemed to be nothing I could do, but I rose from my knees and turned toward that voice behind me. And what I saw made my blood run cold.

Branden was looming over me, seeming almost a meter taller than normal. His face was shining in a sickening greenish light, and in the center of his forehead glowed the emblem of a Serpent. Total disbelief washed through my body, from my head all the way down to my feet. I wanted to run and hide amongst the trees, but something was keeping my feet firmly planted in the ground between him and Laken's body.

"How could you do this, Branden? How could you betray your loved ones—your children—your wife?"

His eyes blazed out at me with a dark fire. "Don't talk to me about love. I haven't felt any such thing for years."

"But what about little Morgan?"

"Oh, she and her mother brought some comfort for a little while. But this black hole inside me eventually swallowed up everything."

"Black hole? What do you mean?" I was hoping I could keep him talking long enough that someone would come along to help me. If nothing else, it kept him from killing me that instant.

In fact, he turned away from me briefly, clenched his fists fiercely, and then looked back into my face before I could even think of fleeing. Besides I couldn't bring myself to leave Laken, even if he was dead.

"It was God who betrayed *me*!" Branden suddenly bellowed, in a voice with so much power it nearly knocked me over. "You have no right to call me a traitor."

"But God is love," I murmured.

The darkness in his eyes flared like fire as I said this, and his whole body seemed to shake, as he continued:

"Don't try to tell me about your King of Love," he cried, anguish in his voice. "Where was he when the System captured Morgan and me at the Battle for South Europa? Where was he when they forced me to watch as an entire squad of soldiers raped her? And when they tied me next to her and made me watch her bleed to death?"

"I didn't know!"

His face was drenched with tears now, and his voice fell to a hoarse whisper. "I never told anyone. After I managed to escape and get to the North Out-clave, I just told people she'd been killed in the battle."

I reached out and tried to take his hand, but he jerked away, turning his back on me.

"You shouldn't have bottled all this inside, Branden. We could have helped you. God could have helped."

"I want nothing to do with your God." His harsh voice didn't sound human at all. "It's too late for me now."

By this sudden change, I knew this wasn't the real Branden talking—maybe it never had been. Perhaps he was right, and it was too late. The despair in his heart had opened the door to darkness, just as Johan warned us. One of the Serpent's evil servants must have taken over Branden's heart.

As my mind realized this, all of Johan's prayer suddenly flooded my mind in words I understood. A bright light seemed to come down onto my head from the sky above. Power that wasn't my own filled my body, and when I opened my mouth it wasn't my own voice coming out:

"Servant of Evil, leave him! I command you in the name of the King of Heaven and Earth."

A light as bright as the sun seemed to be shining from my eyes. As I looked, Branden turned his eyes toward mine and I saw the flashing blackness leave them. A dark shadow fell on the ground behind him. Then with a loud hissing sound, it sank into the ground and disappeared.

Branden crumpled into a heap at my feet, gasping for breath. This time when I reached for his hand, he didn't pull away. In fact, he clutched at me and pulled my whole body toward him.

"Thank you." I could barely hear him whisper. "You've freed me. Now I can be with Morgan."

His voice died away in a long sigh. The grip of his hands on mine suddenly loosened, and then he was no longer breathing. I tried to shift myself to where I could try resuscitating him, but a voice spoke behind me:

"Don't waste your effort. The demon ate his heart out from within. When the demon was cast out, Branden had no way to go on living."

A great weakness engulfed me as I turned in disbelief toward that voice. "Laken?" Now *I* could barely breathe. "You're alive?"

"The weapon must have been on stun."

I literally fell into his arms and melted into sobs. "You mean I killed Branden?"

"No, you didn't," he whispered into my hair, as he held me close. "The Lord helped you do the only thing that could be done. You saved him."

Then a wave of utter exhaustion washed over me, and I collapsed against Laken's chest, all my energy drained. Vaguely, I felt him lifting me and carrying me in his arms. We seemed to be moving slowly downhill, but then everything became hazy, and turned to the cool healing comfort of sleep.

CHAPTER TWENTY-TWO
THROUGH THE NEXUS

Jace had never felt this kind of deep, bone-chilling cold in his life. But then he'd never crossed a GAP quite like this before. Instead of being focused and united with trained GAP-crossers in a circle, he'd just thrown himself into the middle of one.

Stephan was giving off a strange golden glow. Where had he seen it before? 'Oh, yes, I remember—Johan in the Stone Circle, before he changed into the kindly old man. Now Stephan is emanating the same power that awed and frightened me there.'

Then it was as though dark scales fell from his eyes—this power was the essence of good, not evil. Suddenly, he knew—'Branden was the one who deceived me—for this glowing light reveals the words that Johan said:

"Don't jump to conclusions."

'And then there were other words—ones that were in an unintelligible language before:

"Stephan is my servant—trust him—his judgments are true—the people he trusts can also be trusted by you.'"

Suddenly, the vision of his green lazer-beam cutting into Laken's back filled his mind. 'I shot an unarmed man—when his back was turned. I'm worse than evil.'

The gray and white mists swirling around him began to slow then, and his arms went limp. He watched with no emotion as the lazer-pistol drifted out of his grasp, disappearing into the misty cloud. Then it stopped moving, as a hand grabbed it.

"Shoot me!" his voice cried. "I deserve to die!"

Just at that moment, a painful thud lurched through his body, and he found himself lying flat on the ground. Above him loomed a dark shape.

"Please shoot me," he pleaded.

"No!" said a deep and powerful voice. "You were deceived by the Evil One."

"But I killed Laken," he moaned.

"He lives," the voice came again. "You're repentant—and forgiven."

"Are you sure Laken is alive, Stephan?" came Jon's familiar voice.

"I'm positive. And we need Jace. Johan has sent him for a reason."

"Johan? How could he? He's far away."

"No time to explain. I know what I know."

"But what reason could it be?" asked another voice, which must be Danny.

"That's yet to be revealed," said Stephan. "But I know from Celestia that Johan has touched Jace."

"How?"

"Never mind. We just need to get to shelter—we're on a System planet now, remember?"

The mist around them cleared, and Jace saw they were in a mixed conifer and deciduous forest which looked vaguely familiar. As Stephan helped him to his feet, he murmured:

"This looks like the place where—"

Before he could finish, Stephan pulled him off his feet, carrying him in his strong arms, and strode toward a patch of evergreens. Danny and Jon were close behind them. Soon, they were crawling back among the low-hanging branches of some spruce and fir trees.

"Ouch!" cried Danny. "The spruces are sharp."

"Move closer to that big fir tree," Jace heard himself say. "Its needles are softer and more flexible."

"Is this the place?" Stephan whispered in his ear.

Jace looked around in wonder. Things did look like they had several years ago, when he and Lexi formed their circle and crossed their first GAP—the way Uncle Jon taught them. Looking up, he saw a slight smile on Jon's lips:

"You did well, Jace."

"This is the place," he nodded to Jon and the others, "But not the time."

"That's what we intended," Stephan smiled. "Our goal is to avoid the System."

"Are they near?" came Danny's nervous voice.

"Not at the moment," replied Stephan. "Hmm, now I see what Johan is up to."

"What do you mean?" Jon asked.

"Jace, show me exactly where you were sitting," was Stephan's only answer.

Jace settled into the depression in the soil at the base of the huge fir tree. Sure enough, his back fit right into a slight swale in the tree's trunk. Branches came out over his head. They seemed closer now—but of course he was older and taller.

Looking up at the others, he nodded. "This is right where I was—I know it."

Stephan smiled and with a shift of his head to the right, indicated for Jace to make room for him. As he settled into Jace's spot, his eyes began to glow with sparkling golden-brown flecks. When he took Jace's hand, the young man felt a hot tingling sensation, almost like electricity.

"What's that?" he couldn't help asking.

"A gravitonic force," Stephan replied tersely. "Come on, you two—help me. Jon, you must be the GAP-crosser. Danny, focus all your being on everything you remember about Jael."

"What about me, Sir?"

"Jace—listen to any words you remember Johan telling you, and obey them without question."

"What will you be doing?" Jon asked. "And don't we need Laken, too?"

"I must navigate the Nexes without him—there may be several. It would be better to have Laken's help, but I think I can manage. You're accustomed to following one path—like someone climbing a mountain. You can't see the whole area, only your path."

"I get it," Jace cried. "You'll be seeing the whole mountain from above—like someone looking at a map."

"Ah, you *are* a smart one," chuckled Stephan. "Actually, I'll do better than that. A flat map has distortions of distance because of its lack of a third dimension. Steep trails appear shorter than they really are, for example. What I do will be more like seeing the whole mountain from a moving perspective—I won't be limited to a single observation point."

"But according to Quantum Physics, that's impossible," Jon cut in.

"Not in my universe," Stephan laughed. "Enough talk now. You each know what to do—so get to work."

***

Jace tried to close his eyes, as he knew he should for a GAP-crossing, but something felt strange. Usually, the ground would drop away and in the next instant, he'd feel the new ground rise to meet his feet. But this time, he found himself whirling in ever-tightening circles—like when he jumped into the broken circle before.

The next thing he knew, flashes of red lightning were filling his field of vision. Some of them seemed like bolts hurled directly at him. He began twisting and turning to avoid them, and suddenly he couldn't feel anyone holding onto his hands.

Panic seized him. 'Where are the others? Why am I alone?' For a few seconds he tried closing his eyes, hoping to block out the blinding flashes, but to no avail. The red bolts seemed to come through his lids and right inside his eyes. But when he opened his eyes, the scene he saw was even more frightening.

The lightning bolts were merging and writhing together, turning and slithering like snakes, and the shape they formed before his eyes was worse than a snake—more like a dragon. Its eyes were reptilian slits, and they seemed to stare right into his soul. A forked tongue darted in and out of a gaping mouth lined with pointed fangs. Then two huge leathery wings spread from the creature's back, and it began to fly toward him.

'You fear me, don't you?' the creature hissed, in his mind. 'And well you should. I can devour entire worlds. I can consume your very soul.'

Jace had nowhere to hide. Everything around him was the black emptiness of open space. His crossing-companions had disappeared. He wished he had a shell like a turtle to crawl into, but knew it would do no good. This creature could devour him shell and all.

He was about to close his eyes and accept his fate, when he saw a pinpoint of light above the creature's head. It looked like a small star at first, but then it began to grow. Beams shot out above and below it, and he saw the familiar shape—a golden plus sign.

Then words began pouring into his head, and he recognized the voice of Johan speaking a message somehow planted in his mind that day in the stone circle:

"You have already been defeated, O Prince of Darkness. You deceive us into thinking you're all-powerful with your evil might, but one has overcome you with humility and love."

As Jace felt these words pour from his mouth, the creature shrank in size, then it hesitated and stopped moving toward him. New words oozed like the steam of a dragon's breath into his mind, 'You are protected—for now. But I'll be back.'

Suddenly the fiery dragon was gone, leaving behind nothing but a puff of smoke. From somewhere overhead came a lonely cry like an eagle's, but Jace wasn't sure if it came from the dragon or not.

'Great,' he thought to himself, drifting in black emptiness. 'I'm alive, I think—but where am I, and where are the others? Has the Lord saved me, only to leave me here alone?'

Then he felt something nudge at his hand. In sheer panic, he turned, thinking the Dragon had already returned and sneaked up behind him. But instead, he saw a big black dog.

'A dog? Out here? How can he breathe? For that matter, what am I breathing? Or is this like the visions they said Danny saw when Celestia brought him to Luna?'

He reached out, expecting to feel nothing but emptiness, and was shocked when his hand touched real fur and felt the ripple of muscles beneath it. This dog was real flesh and blood. It quickly licked his face and barked. 'How can I hear a sound in the vacuum of space?' he thought. 'I have to be dreaming.'

He was even more surprised as a shock of red hair appeared above the dog's head, and a smiling young boy revealed himself.

"Who are you?" he asked. "How can I even be talking to you?"

"We're using telepathy, of course," the boy smiled. "My name is Evin. What's yours?"

"Uh—I'm Jace, son of Jael."

"My father is Danny—I think you've met him."

Jace nodded hesitantly. "How are we breathing out here? We have no ship. Are we in the middle of a GAP?

"We're in a Time Nexus," said Evin. "No time is passing here. When we leave it, our crossing will have been instantaneous."

"But where are the others?"

"You mean my dad, Jon and Stephan?" said the boy.

Jace stepped back in surprise, "How do you know their names?"

"They went through another Nexus—the one Stephan selected," the boy went on, ignoring his question. "But it's the wrong one for us. You must come with Shadow and me."

"Shadow?"

"He's my dog. Isn't he amazing? He's telepathic, too."

Suddenly Jace remembered things his father had told him of his early life on Terres. "Like my dad's feier-cat!"

"Guess so," nodded Evin.

'I can communicate with you, son of Jael,' came a rumbling dog voice in his mind. 'But we must move on. Splash told me where they've taken Jael.'

"Splash?"

'His horse.' Now the voice was more like an excited bark.

"I remember Splash," said Jace, angry now. "But he never talked—or communicated. Why isn't anyone answering my questions?"

Shadow growled. 'The pinto communicates only with me. Enough of these questions. Now climb on my back.'

"Are you sure you can carry both of us?" Jace sighed, resigning himself to receiving no answers right then.

'I have no doubt,' came the gruff voice again. 'We've spent no time here in this Nexus, but I'm growing impatient.'

Jace said no more, and quickly climbed onto the huge dog's black back, settling himself behind Evin, who seemed quite small. In fact, now that he was on Shadow's back, he felt smaller than usual, too. Perhaps this creature had some power to make his passengers lighter and easier to carry. Another unanswered question.

As soon as he settled onto the strong back of soft fur and placed his hands around Evin's waist, everything shifted and whirled. The next thing he knew, the three of them were standing on a barren rocky surface.

"Is he always this quick?" he asked, climbing off the dog's back and turning to Evin.

The red-haired boy smiled up at him. "He crosses GAPs better than any human."

"Where did you get this dog?" Jace was still wondering if he was dreaming.

"He just appeared at our house in Colorado one night." As Evin was talking, Shadow stepped up and nuzzled his hand, and Jace realized this was what he'd felt from behind after the Red Dragon disappeared. "He's no ordinary dog," Evin added.

"I can see that."

"Some people think he's part Labrador, but see how his ears stand up? Labs' ears droop down. And he has longer fur, too—more like a wolf."

"Do you think he's part wolf?"

"It doesn't matter. I'm the only one who knows what

Shadow can do, and he's never taken anyone else with him besides me—until now."

"Why did you come for me, Shadow?" he asked.

'You're the son of Jael, the one who must find him. Those others don't have what you do.'

"What can I possibly have that they don't? Stephan is a Guardian and knows more of Time-scapes and GAPs than anyone—Danny was 'within' my dad for many years—Jon and Dad had some kind of special connection ever since they first met long ago on Terres."

'But you have your father's blood in your veins. None of those others have any of his DNA like you do.'

Jace was speechless for a few minutes. Then his mind began to overflow with questions again. "How can Dad still be alive after all these years? Did they have him in prison? He must be very sick—and old."

'In your time, about eight years have passed—it's not as long as your grief has made it feel,' Shadow continued, his thoughts rumbling in Jace's mind. But now the voice was more comforting and less threatening. 'Besides, the System has a Time Nexus of their own. For Jael, little or no time has passed. He will be surprised to see you all grown up.'

Suddenly, Jace couldn't overcome the urge to pinch himself on the arm. "Ouch!" he heard himself cry.

"What was that for?"

"I was just trying to see if I'm dreaming."

Shadow began to growl, and then Evin laughed, "Oh no, this is very real. Yeah, it seems strange, but I know I'm not dreaming. Don't you remember what Johan said?"

"How do you know about Johan?"

"Shadow told me."

Jace shook his head in disbelief as Evin grabbed his hand and turned him sharply to the right, pointing to the gray, rocky horizon. The dog began to howl like a wolf as they saw streaks of light move across the sky, curving downward toward the planet's surface.

"Falling stars will show the way—" Jace heard himself saying.

"That's what Johan said, isn't it?"

"That's one of the things I've remembered. Another is 'Don't jump to conclusions.' Am I doing that right now?"

'That was for Materna,' rumbled Shadow, 'And your rashness there almost ruined everything.'

Jace hung his head, staring at the strange ground beneath his feet. It seemed to pulsate like a beating heart.

'The other saying is for here. Yours are the first human eyes to see these falling pieces of meteors—yours and Evin's.'

"Shadow, what are you—really? Is this dog's body just a disguise?"

'Now Jace, you need to trust more. Can't you sense that I'm not like the Red Dragon?'

"So, *are* you an angel instead of a demon? I've already been fooled by one demon—the one in Branden."

'It's the black color, isn't it? Humans associate black with evil.' Shadow stepped up to Jace and pushed his head under the young man's hand. 'Tell me what you feel. Do you sense any evil in me?'

All he could feel was warm dog-flesh, and a firm bony skull. Then suddenly the black dog was gone and in his place was a shimmering golden shape. "You look like liquid light!" Those were the only words Jace could find to describe what he saw. "I saw something like this before Johan appeared in the stone circle."

"You see now?" asked Evin.

"Why didn't *you* just tell me?"

"Would you have believed me?"

"Well, probably not. I guess I needed to see for myself. But I still don't know what you are, Shadow."

'Guardian—or angel—those are both appropriate words,' Shadow growled.

"Please don't be angry with me. I'm only human."

'I know, and humans are full of doubts and questions. But it appears to be how you learn, and without that capability of learning, you wouldn't have come as far as you have.'

"Okay, Shadow. I saw the stars fall. Is that the way we're supposed to go?"

'Yes, but it's not on this planet. This is merely a way-station. The System has hidden their Nexus very craftily. Now we *do* need your friends.'

No sooner had the dog sent these thoughts to him, than the other three men appeared, their faces full of shock and wonder.

"Evin?" cried Danny. "What are *you* doing here?"

"Shadow brought us, Dad," the boy answered in a matter-of-fact voice.

"Shadow?" Danny lost his balance and fell to the ground, his face a picture of total disbelief.

"What's going on, Jace?" came Jon's voice. "How did you get here ahead of us?"

"I think he's been in a Time Nexus," Stephan said. "I sense it."

"You're right," said Evin.

"Evin? How do you know anything about this?" Danny asked, trying to sit up again. "You're not even in school yet."

"It's Shadow, Dad. He's no ordinary dog."

"I guess not. Stephan, *what* is going on here?"

"I think Johan has sent us an assistant in the form of your dog."

"We thought he was just a stray when he showed up on our porch one night, so we adopted him. Come to think of it, that's when Evin started asking a lot of questions."

Evin smiled at his father but didn't speak.

Finally, Jace spoke up. "Shadow showed me what he really looks like, Jon—like Johan did, when Celestia and I first saw him in the stone circle."

"The what?"

"Sorry Jon. I haven't had time to tell you about that. Celestia told me now Johan visited her on Materna, along with Jace and Raina."

"Raina?"

"Evidently, she needed to be in on some information about the plan," shrugged Stephan.

"Maybe it had something to do with Branden," mumbled Jace. "He's the traitor."

"He is?" cried Jon. "But he's been such a loyal Rebel soldier."

"Johan said he had a black hole in his heart," Jace added. "We prayed for him, but maybe it was too late—like Johan said."

Jon was shaking his head slowly. "It must have something to do with his wife Morgan's death."

The word 'death' made Jace shudder, and the vision of his lazer striking Laken in the back filled his mind. "Are you sure Laken is okay, Stephan?"

The man patted his back. "Yes, I'm sure, Jace. And soon I may need to send for him. Right now, though, we have other things to think about."

At that moment, Shadow began to howl again, and Evin pointed toward the horizon where more meteorites were flashing through the planet's atmosphere.

"Falling stars will show the way," Jace repeated. "That's what Johan told me."

By now, the dog was running in circles around all of them. Danny jumped up and tried to stop him, but his son cried, "No, Dad. He's telling us to get ready—he wants to take us across a GAP."

"Our dog is a GAP-crosser?"

"One of the best, Dad."

Danny looked like he was about to faint, but Shadow came up right beside him and let him lean against his side. Everyone watched in amazement as the big black dog seemed to triple in size before their eyes. Soon, he was towering over all of them, sheltering them beneath his body. Each of them leaned against one of the animal's legs—Stephen and Jon at his forelegs, and Jace at the left hind leg. Evin was holding tightly to his father's hand and bracing him against the right hind leg.

Then the ground dropped away in a sensation they all were accustomed to. When the feelings of icy vertigo ceased, all were standing in a densely forested area with a black wolf-like creature standing just ahead of them. Off in the distance loomed a massive stone fortress.

"What's that?" Danny whispered.

"I'd say it looks like a System prison," said Jon.

"More than that," added Stephan. "This is the System's secret Time Nexus, isn't it, Evin?"

"Yes, sir. That's what Shadow tells me."

"How does he talk to you, Evin? I can't hear anything."

"Dad, don't you remember Feier?"

"Jael's feier-cat, of course. He was telepathic. So that's how Shadow communicates with you."

"Yeah, Dad. And Jace can hear him, too."

Danny turned in surprise to see Jace nodding.

"So, is Jael in there?" Jon asked.

"Can anyone sense anything?"

"I can't," Jon replied. "Can you, Danny?"

Danny was shaking his head.

"Shadow says it's because of the Time Nexus," said Evin.

"How does Shadow know Jael is in there?"

"He says Splash told him. The horse saw where they took his master. He'd almost found them in the forest, when the Patrol attacked—"

"When I was under the fir tree," Jace sighed.

"Great," Jon cried. "So now Jael's horse is telepathic, too?"

"No, sir," said Evin. "He only talks to Shadow."

Jon threw up his hands and began to stalk away, but Stephan reached out and stopped him. "I sense truth here," he said softly. "It may seem too strange for belief, but if you think back over your life, many other strange things have happened—right?"

Jon nodded silently. Now Danny stepped to his side. "Yeah, you did some pretty amazing things with Ginna and me. Remember? Just because your life has been simple and Earth-bound recently doesn't mean these wondrous things beyond the world have ceased to exist."

"Yeah, I guess I forgot." He patted Danny on the shoulder. "And I have no reason to doubt Jace—or any of you for that matter. So, what do we do next?"

"Shadow says we need to help Jace get inside the fortress somehow," whispered Evin.

"Why Jace?"

"He gives two reasons: one is, Jace has half of Jael's DNA—"

"And the other is that Johan gave him instructions," Stephan finished for him.

Evin nodded. "In the circle of standing stones. And Shadow says we really need Laken—so he and Stephan can connect across the Nexus."

Jace hung his head. "So, I guess I've really messed things up, haven't I?"

Stephan patted him on the shoulder. "I'll just have to go back for him, that's all."

"You make it sound so simple," said Jon. "You must know a lot more about GAP-crossing than I do."

"It's more advanced in my universe, Jon. So, don't worry—I'll be back in a flash."

And just like that, he disappeared in a shower of sparks.

CHAPTER TWENTY-THREE
CELESTIA AND RAINA

As I slowly woke, I couldn't remember where I was. The first thing I noticed was the sleeping mat below me, and wondered if I was still on Earth. The second thing was Laken's warm body sleeping beside me—but this startled me. We'd promised each other to wait until we were married—and there'd been no chance to find Johan yet.

Then everything came flooding back into my mind: The System attack on Luna—our flight with Stephan to Materna, his home in this alternate universe. The traitor Branden's death, and my collapse into Laken's arms. But then everything was a blank.

"Am I alive, Laken?" I heard my voice ask. "Are you? Where are we? And why are you here with me?"

He stirred beside me, turned over and looked into my eyes. "To start with, we're in your parents' quarters. And for the why—don't worry, I'm here to protect you, not molest you," he chuckled. "And you're very much alive, my brave warrior."

I sat bolt-upright at this, remembering how Branden had crumpled to the ground before me. "How can I face Raina? I've made her a widow."

He began rubbing my back in sweeping circles. "You didn't kill him—the demon did. All you did was drive the demon out."

"Branden whispered something to me before his last breath."

"What did he say?"

"That he could be with Morgan."

Now Laken was sitting up too, and put one arm gently around me. "See, you did the right thing for his soul."

I leaned heavily into his embrace. "I'm glad you were here when I woke, Laken. I would've gone into a panic otherwise."

"I knew you'd need someone," he smiled, still massaging my back. "And don't worry—I didn't take advantage of you."

This made me turn and look into his dark brown eyes.

"Now do you trust me?"

I nodded and reached my hand up to stroke his cheek, where I could barely see the stubble of his day-old beard.

"You need to shave," I smiled.

"Well, I've been kind of busy."

Before I could tease him about this, two women walked into the sleeping room. Looking up, I immediately recognized my mother. But I felt a shock when I saw the person with her—she looked like my grandmother, but she couldn't be. Irina, along with her husband Dominic, and his son Donmal, had died on Luna—helping us escape the attack—brought on by the traitor.

Fortunately, Laken spoke up then, for I was speechless. "Celestia, this is Karina of Materna. Stephan sent her to help us while he's away."

Mom smiled at the woman beside her, then at me. "She looks like a younger version of my mother, doesn't she? Except she prefers to keep her hair in braids. Mother quit braiding her hair when my father died—long ago in the Galactic Wars."

Karina smiled at Mom and then turned and nodded to me.

"Pleased to meet you," I murmured, as best I could. "I've been calling Stephan my granddad. What should I call you?"

"I guess it doesn't matter. But Karina will be easier, I think." Her warm smile seemed to give me just enough strength to stand. As I reached out my hand to take hers, I felt warmth begin to flow into my body.

Thankfully, Laken stood with me, because I was surprised how weak and tired I felt. All my energy was drained away.

Mom must have seen me wobbling, because she quickly seated us all on some floor cushions. "I'll get some tea going," she said.

After taking several sips of the steaming, soothing liquid, I was finally able to ask, "How can I explain all this to Raina?"

"Perhaps Jace can help," said Mom.

"I don't think so," I sighed. "He leaped into Dad's GAP-circle with Stephan and Danny. Who knows where they are now?"

"Oh my, that does complicate things," Mom cried. "Raina often says Jace is all she has left. When Jael disappeared, she was devastated. I'm afraid this time, with both Jace and Branden gone, she may break down altogether."

"But this time Celestia is here," said Laken softly.

"What difference can *I* make?"

At this, Karina reached over and took my hand, again sending me a strange warmth. "Don't try to use your own power, Celestia. Let the True King work through you—as you've done before."

I eyed her curiously. "Has my mother been telling you about me?"

But then I saw Mom shaking her head.

"Stephan has told me," smiled Karina. "Have faith."

Then Laken reached over and took my other hand. "We're with you. You're not alone."

I turned and leaned into his chest. "Thanks. Say, why *did* you stay and sleep with me?"

He smiled slightly, glancing at Mom. "I stayed because I'm sworn to protect you. There was a possibility of the demon coming back."

"Oh!" I cried.

"Don't worry—you're safe."

"Thanks to you, my noble knight."

"What's a knight?"

"Oh, some ancient warrior I read about in an antique book. Their creed was to protect the weak and stand up for the right."

He smiled then and kissed me lightly on top of the head.

***

As I feared, Raina collapsed to the floor sobbing as soon as we told her about Branden. Fortunately, little Morgan was at Daiah's with Lexi and the other children at the time.

"Jace!" Raina cried. "Get Jace—he's all I have left now."

Mom knelt beside her and took one of her hands. "We can't," she murmured. "He's crossed the GAP with Jon, Danny, and Stephan."

"But why?"

"I'm not sure," Mom began. I knew she was hesitant to mention Jael to Raina—much less how Branden had deceived them.

I quickly joined her, kneeling on the other side of Raina. "Do you remember the stone circle where we saw Johan?"

She nodded mutely, but her tears still flowed freely.

"Johan gave Jace something important to do, something only he could do."

"What?"

"Only Jace and Johan know. Same for me. Johan's words weren't revealed to me until I needed them—to free Branden from the demon."

"But Johan told me to *love* Branden. How can I do that now?" She began sobbing on my shoulder.

I stroked her hair, noticing a few strands of gray appearing among the red. 'She seems young to be going gray,' I thought. 'It must be the stress.'

"Raina," I said, taking a deep breath, "If you truly love Branden, you can be happy that he's been freed to join Morgan in Heaven."

I felt her head nod against me, but she didn't speak.

"Somehow, I know the King has a plan in this," murmured Mom. "I've seen twists and turns like this many times before."

"Oh, I'm so tired of everything," Raina cried loudly. "Ever since the Disaster on Terres, it's been one heartbreak after another. Wasn't it enough that I lost my whole family? If the King is trying to teach me something in all this, I wish he'd get it over with. How much more death, grief, and trauma—even rape—do I have to endure? Why can't he just leave me alone?"

Tears began filling Mom's eyes at these angry words.

"I know, Raina. I've had my share of death and trauma, too."

"But you still have Celestia and Jon." The bitterness in Raina's voice increased. "I don't have anyone."

I sighed and tried to keep my voice calm. "Yes, Raina, I'm here—for now. But we don't know for sure where my dad is. Hopefully both he and Jace are safe with Stephan."

"I'm sure they are," said Karina softly.

Suddenly a picture came into my mind, and words came from my mouth before I even thought:

"I think people who experience the most pain also have the most capacity for joy."

"That seems totally contradictory," she sighed.

"It's as though the pain digs a deep well into our soul," I continued. "And later, when God does send joy, it can fill that well to overflowing. But those of us who don't have this well, only feel the joy washing over—like water in a shower—and very quickly it's passed on by."

No one spoke when my voice stopped, but I looked toward Laken and saw his eyes smiling at me. 'Where did those words come from?' I wondered. 'Perhaps they were part of the message Johan told me in that strange language.'

Raina lay back on the floor and stared at the ceiling for a long time. Finally, she spoke, "I wish I had your faith, Celestia. Sometimes I think I can't go on. And I wish the King would just take me away."

"We've all felt that way sometimes," I whispered. "Please don't think I'm some spiritual giant with a strong faith, because I'm not."

"It scares me when I feel like all I want to do is die," she murmured. "What do I have to live for, anyway?"

Just then, as if on cue, we heard the door of her room open. Looking up, we saw Lexi in the doorway, carrying Morgan on her shoulder.

"Mom said I should bring her," she said softly.

"Daiah always has good timing," said Mom.

Without realizing what I was doing, I stepped up to Lexi and took Morgan from her. The little girl curled comfortably on my shoulder and looked back toward her cousin who'd been holding her. And then I found more words coming from my mouth, seemingly of their own volition:

"There are times when I'm just hurting so much God seems nowhere near. But now I see those are the times he's holding me—like I'm holding Morgan now."

"Yes, I see," Lexi said in excitement. "Morgan can't *see* you, when you hold her this way. All she can see is what's behind you."

I nodded and then turned so Morgan could see her mother. "I know there have been times when God carried me like this, though I couldn't see him at the time. It was only later when I looked back—"

"Mommy," Morgan suddenly interrupted me, wriggled out of my embrace, and ran to the figure lying on the floor. "Mommy, what's wrong?"

Raina wiped hastily at her tear-stained cheeks and tried to sit up. She seemed weak and about to fall back down, so I knelt down and braced her with an arm around her waist.

Looking up at Morgan's confused face, I tried to say as calmly as I could, "Your daddy has died, sweetheart. I'm so sorry."

Morgan knelt down and crawled into her mother's lap. "Why are you crying?"

"I'm sad because I loved your daddy, and I'll miss him. But now he gets to be in Heaven with his first love—the one we named you for."

"But why did Daddy die? Was there another battle?"

I looked at Mom, where she sat on the other side of Raina, but she just shrugged. Laken had been standing in a corner most of this time, letting the women try to do the comforting. But now he came over and laid his hand gently on my head. The same warmth I felt from Karina's touch now seemed to flow into me from Laken. My mouth began to form words:

"Some very bad men made Branden do something terrible, Morgan," I sighed. "He caused the attack on Luna, when we had to leave there so fast."

"Daddy's not bad," she protested.

"No, your daddy was a good man, but the bad men forced him. And when he tried to stop them, they killed him."

I saw Laken smile and nod slightly.

"So, Daddy is with Morgan in Heaven—you're sure?" the small girl whispered.

Raina nodded to her, and I heard Laken's voice say, "Yes, we're sure."

I slowly stood, trying to keep myself from bursting into tears. Mom moved onto a floor cushion, so Raina could begin to rock Morgan gently.

"I love you, my Morgan," she whispered. "When you're with me, I'll always have a part of your daddy here, too."

"I love you, too, Mommy."

By this time, Laken was leading me out the door. Once again, I was leaning heavily on him, feeling as though something had drained me.

"You did great," he murmured. "Just the right amount of explanation for a child."

"I hope so. I wonder how long it'll be before someone tells her that her father was the traitor."

"I think you gave her enough ammunition to defend herself—and him," he smiled.

"I feel like I need to take another nap," I sighed.

"May I join you? I'm exhausted, too."

"Well, if you think you can resist temptation again."

No sooner were these words out of my mouth than sparks filled the air and the shimmering image of Stephan's face appeared, followed by the rest of him.

"Granddad, what are you doing here?"

"We need Laken," his voice said gruffly. "I'm sorry, but there's no time to explain."

"I was supposed to be with them, but Jace's firing on me broke the circle," said Laken.

"It's all worked out now." Stephan's voice was calmer now. "Shadow says we need Jace, too."

"Shadow? Who's that?" Laken asked.

"You'll see soon enough."

I was gripping Laken's hand fiercely. "Do you have to go?" Tears crept into my voice, but I held them back.

Stephan reached over and patted my shoulder. "I'll take care of him. Please don't fear."

As I turned to look into my alternate-universe grandfather's green eyes, I felt Laken's hand slip out of my grasp. There was a light touch on my cheek—was it his lips or his hand? Then suddenly sparks reappeared all around me. And I was alone.

***

When I finally awoke from sleep, it was another morning. I was lying alone on the sleeping mat, but Mom was snoring beside me on hers. Slowly I sat up, feeling a little less weary, and wondering how long I'd slept.

As I began to look for something to eat, Mom sat up and rubbed her eyes. "Finally up, I see," she said. "You've been sleeping for a day and a half."

"That long? Why didn't you wake me?"

"It seemed better to just let you sleep."

"Oh. Is Laken still gone?"

"Your father, too," she nodded. "There's some fruit and grain in the lower cupboard, if you want." She stifled a yawn.

"Yeah, I'm famished. Is there any cheese?"

"I think Jon left some in the cool drawer."

Sure enough, I found a small chunk of red cheese, and devoured this along with a blue-colored fruit and some flatbread. The food here, like the vegetation, was different in color and texture from Earth, but the flavors were tasty even if not like what we were used to.

"I think I'll go see Daiah," I said when I finished, knowing I must do something besides think about Laken. "It seems like ages since I've seen her, and so much has happened. Do you know if she's talked to Raina?"

Mom shook her head. "Sorry, Hon, I've been occupied with other duties. Karina needed me to introduce her to the heads of each family. We only saw Daiah briefly when I was doing that."

"How did she look?"

"Like usual—you know Daiah."

"Yeah, she's the compassionate one who often thinks of others before herself."

"Well, I wish you luck. I don't know how things will be with Branden's children—Siene and Toren."

"I know. Thanks, Mom." These words were spoken as I was already on my way out our door.

Daiah and I hadn't seen much of each other since the evacuation to Luna. But when I tapped on the door of her room, and she saw me standing there, she immediately gave me a warm embrace.

"Celestia, it's so good to see you. Are you all right? You've been through so much lately, with losing your grandmother, and then your father taking off on the GAP-mission."

"I'm okay." But even as I spoke these words, I knew she could tell I was only trying to put up a brave front. "Laken's gone, too. Stephan came back for him."

"Come in and join us for some tea," she smiled, knowing it was best to change the subject.

As I stepped inside her room, I saw Raina there and Daiah's daughter Lexi. Every time I saw Lexi she seemed to have matured even more. She wasn't a child at all anymore. Each of them nodded to me as I found a floor cushion to settle on. I tried not to look too closely at Raina's face, but I could tell by her red cheeks and nose that she'd been crying. Her eyes were dry now, though.

"We've been discussing how much we should tell the children about the situation with Branden," said Daiah, as I began to sip the delicious tea. "You did a wonderful job of explaining things to Morgan—in a way she could grasp and accept."

"It was the King, not me," I put in hastily.

"Well, so far that's the story she's told Siene and Toren—that some very bad men forced their father to betray us. And when he tried to stop them, they killed him."

I tried to smile. "I guess it's close enough to the truth."

Raina was nodding. "Well, he was deceived by the System and the demon—who are definitely very bad, even if not technically human."

"I just hope someone else doesn't start talking too much about demons and frightening the children," I sighed.

"Well, at this point, we three—and Laken—are the only ones who know about the demon."

"And my mother," I added.

"And Karina, but I think we can trust her."

"What about Jace?" Raina asked in a sudden whisper.

"I'm not sure how much he knows," I replied. "He jumped into Stephan's GAP-circle before I faced-off with the demon."

Daiah looked deeply into my eyes then with her usual sense of perception. "Are you sure you're all right now, Celestia? That must have been very frightening."

"The King gave me strength," I sighed. "But I sure have been tired. I think I've been asleep for most of the past two days. And I miss Laken so much."

Silently, Daiah took my hand, and comfort flowed into me. I smiled into her eyes but didn't speak.

Then she turned to her daughter. "Lexi, you spend more time with the children than the rest of us. What do you think? Should we tell them more?"

Lexi sat for a few minutes, deep in thought. "I think for now it's better to let them just get used to the fact Branden has died. That's enough for a child, especially one as young as Morgan. Siene and Toren have been through the grief of losing their mother, too."

"But do you think the loss of both parents now will be even more traumatic?" her mother asked.

Lexi shrugged. "All I know is what I went through when you told Andre and me that our father was dead."

Even though this had been several years ago, I still heard the break in her voice as she said these words.

After another silence, Daiah said softly, "Grief never completely goes away. It just changes forms over time—right Raina?"

Raina nodded, but I saw new tears dripping down her cheeks, and knew she couldn't trust her voice to speak.

Lexi stood then. "Why don't I get the children, and we'll have a prayer circle?"

"That's a good idea," I nodded. "It's been a long time since we even had a Gathering."

"Everyone has been focused on just surviving," said Daiah. "I'll talk to Karina about organizing one."

Soon Lexi returned with her brother Andre, and Branden's three children. I was pleased to see Morgan immediately climb into her mother's lap. Siene and Toren sat on each side of her. Maybe the time they'd spent together in the wilds of Earth before coming to Indonia had formed a bond which was now being renewed. I found a spot next to Siene, while Andre and Lexi sat on each side of their mother. Then we all joined hands.

As I closed my eyes I thought, 'This could be a GAP-circle, except we have no coordinates. And we aren't even in our own universe. I wonder if we can even cross GAPs here. But God is still King of all.' This thought gave me comfort, and I was the first to speak:

"We thank you, Lord, that you are always with us—no matter where we are: 'Where can I go from your Spirit? Where can I flee from your presence? If I go up to the heavens, you are there'—"

" 'If I make my bed in the depths, you are there'," Daiah joined in. " 'If I rise on the wings of the dawn, if I settle on the far side of the sea'—"

Then I heard Lexi's maturing voice: " '…even there your hand will guide me, your right hand will hold me fast.' Lord, please hold our loved ones who aren't with us—keep them safe forever with you."

"Our dad and our mom," whispered Siene beside me.

"My father and all who are with him," I added, finding I couldn't even say Laken's name.

"Jace—" That was all Raina could say. But then suddenly, her voice became stronger as she continued the

Psalm I'd started: "Lord, please keep me from hiding in darkness again. 'If I say, "Surely the darkness will hide me and the light become night around me," even the darkness will not be dark to you; the night will shine like the day, for darkness is as light to you'."

And then I felt chills as I heard Morgan singing a song her mother must have taught her:

"The Lord is my light and my salvation;
Whom shall I fear?
The Lord is the stronghold of my life:
Of whom shall I be afraid?"

By the end of the song, all of us had joined in. "Thank you, Lord," I murmured.

"And thank you, Morgan, for reminding me of our favorite song," whispered Raina.

CHAPTER TWENTY-FOUR
INTO THE FORTRESS

Jace and his companions stood among a thick growth of trees and brush growing just over the crest of a rocky summit. It was fortunate this side gave the most shelter, for it also gave the best view of the System fortress they were up against.

"What should we do first?" asked Danny. His young son, Evin, was standing close beside him, holding onto his hand while their dog, Shadow, stood guard next to the boy. At the moment he looked like an ordinary black dog—perhaps a cross of a Black Lab and a German Shepherd, but everyone present knew there was much more to him than met the eye.

Jon thought for several minutes before he answered his long-time friend. "You know, Danny, I've never faced anything like this before. I'm not even sure if we're in our own universe—or Stephan's. And I know next to nothing about Time Nexes. Your dog knows more than I do."

Stephan gave a slight chuckle at this. "Well, it takes

a brave man to admit something like that. It shows what honesty and courage you're made of, Jon."

"Don't overestimate me. I've just gotten lucky a lot."

"Shadow says I have to go because I have my father's DNA," said Jace then.

"And he's right. But you need someone with you who has more experience in Nexes."

"Like you or Laken?"

Stephan rubbed his chin thoughtfully for a few moments and nodded. "I could go, and for now I need Laken with me, too. But that would mean Shadow would have to stay here—and where Shadow is, Evin must be, to translate his communications. And despite Shadow's knowledge, I'd feel more comfortable with an experienced and courageous adult with them—like you, Jon."

"If you say so. But I think I'm the one who has the strongest link with Jael."

"Perhaps Danny can fill that role for us if we do split up."

"I can try," replied Danny. "I had about as close a contact as two people can. I was inside Jael's mind for several years of his time."

Jon nodded and smiled, "That surely counts for something, even if it was just an experiment of mine. But Stephan, do you think we should split up at all?"

"I've been mulling it over a lot. There's more strength in numbers, but we can be stealthy in smaller groups. And if one group runs into trouble the other can be a backup..."

He fell silent in mid-sentence, but no one else spoke. Jace was wondering if he'd make it through this mission alive. Even Evin looked scared, but Shadow rubbed up against him, and the young boy gave Jace a fleeting smile.

"Laken, I need your help to analyze this Time Nexus. So that means you, Danny, Jace, and I must try to find a waste outflow," Stephan said at last. "Even in these days, there has to be a place for the sewage to go."

"Wouldn't they be recycling everything?" asked Laken.

"Well, it's energy-expensive. I'm guessing they need all the energy they have to maintain the Time Nexus."

"Let's hope so. What do you want me to do?" Jon asked

"This is the best vantage point we've found so far. I think you should be our reference point, so we know which way to head when we get out."

"If we get out," muttered Danny.

At this, Jace took Danny's hand. "God will help us. And we'll all help each other."

Danny squeezed the young hand back. "You're right. I'm sorry. You sound like your father, you know—that's the kind of thing he would say."

"It's okay to be afraid," Stephan said quietly. "It keeps us alert."

"I've never been a soldier, that's all," Danny sighed.

"I think Jon and Stephan are the only ones who have," said Laken.

"Okay," Stephan resumed, his voice commanding now. "Evin, tell Shadow to stand as close to the edge of the forest as he can. With his black color he'll be the least visible. You need to stay on his back—don't get off for any reason."

Evin nodded silently and climbed onto the large dog's back. As he did Shadow grew in size, and Evin seemed to shrink slightly.

"Jon, I need you in this tree hanging over the edge of the ridge, with this signal flare." He handed him a small cube-shaped object. "Don't fire it off until you see mine— watch for purple, a color the System never uses. The only weapon I can leave with you is this long-knife. Shadow will have to be Evin's defense. If worse comes to worse, take care of your own escape and leave Shadow to do his job. Don't try to intervene in anything he and Evin are experiencing, no matter how bad it is."

Jace saw his uncle nodding, but knew this would be a difficult order for him to follow. He knew Jon's first reaction in battle was to protect others before himself.

"Okay, the rest of you follow me." Without another word Stephan began to head down into the ravine below them.

Jace wondered why he hadn't explained any of their half of the plan, but then he thought, 'Perhaps that's so the others can't give away any information about us, even if they're tortured.' This made him shudder. Apparently,

Stephan was a very experienced soldier, and by the way he was walking carefully and silently ahead of them, he knew how to travel without being detected.

'He's used to being obeyed without question, too,' Jace added to himself. He knew better than to make any unnecessary sound.

Just then, Stephan stopped and signaled with his hand for them to follow him down a steeply dropping path. At the bottom they found a large circular opening, and by the smell, they knew they'd found the sewage outlet.

Before they moved a step further, however, Stephan placed the lazer-pistol in Jace's hand. He looked up at him in surprise and mouthed silently, "Are you sure?"

"You know how to use it," Stephan whispered in his ear. "Stay close to Laken—he's unarmed and Danny has only a knife. I have hidden weapons of my own, such as the Sword of the Spirit…"

This made Jace feel strange—that Stephan trusted him with a weapon. But he was nervous, remembering how he'd used it to shoot Laken in the back. Regret began to roil in the pit of his stomach, as he realized he was now ordered to protect the very man he'd attacked. 'At least now I have a chance to redeem myself,' he thought.

Just as he expected, there were small rodents gazing at them with gleaming eyes as they stepped carefully through the stinking effluent. This seemed to be a given, no matter what universe you were in—there had to be scavengers. Here, though, he began to wonder if some of those red-looking eyes were natural or part of some artificial security system. He tried to slow his pounding heart.

Soon they came to a bend in the tunnel, and voices were echoing towards them. Stephan stopped him with a firm hand on his chest and nodded toward the pistol. Jace made sure it wasn't set on stun this time.

Then, with a movement so quick he barely saw it, Stephan rounded the bend and gave a hard shove. A body fell toward him, and without hesitation, Jace fired the lazer. The body glowed bright green, and then lay still. This was definitely a more powerful shot than he'd sent into Laken, and this made him breathe a slight sigh of relief.

There was no time for more, though, for another body came hurtling toward him, and this one was on its feet, trying to grab him. Again, he fired the lazer, and the form fell right across the toes of his boots. By the size and shape, he thought this one might be female.

Before he had a chance to think, something was pulling Laken away from him. Remembering the order to keep his companion close, Jace grabbed for his passing arm, but missed. This was when he saw the flash of steel from the knife in Danny's hand. A sudden loud cry and a spurt of blood showed he'd found a mark in his assailant's arm. Using the brief pause, Jace aimed and fired at what he knew would be the heart level. With a thud, this attacker fell, as well.

Out of the corner of his eye, he saw Laken give him a quick grin and a thumbs-up sign.

By now Jace was panting for breath. Fortunately, these three seemed to be the only guards at this junction, and Stephan motioned for them to follow him down a tunnel turning to the right. He'd only gone a dozen steps before he stopped and looked Danny in the eye:

"Do you sense anything yet?"

Danny closed his eyes tightly, apparently trying to clear his mind of the recent battle. At last he whispered, "There are life-forms ahead of us, but none behind."

"Well, that's a start," shrugged Stephan. Then he turned to Jace. "Have you ever been able to sense your father's presence?"

"Just as I was reaching puberty, I thought I could once."

"Anything now?" Laken asked.

Jace tried closing his eyes the way Danny had, but felt nothing unusual. Then he opened them, and to his surprise, he saw his father's face hovering above Danny. "That way," he cried. "I just saw him—behind Danny."

"You're sure? I don't sense anything," Danny said.

"It was just for a second. Maybe it was only wishful thinking—I don't know." Jace's voice showed frustration, and he still surged with adrenalin from their battle.

"Never mind," whispered Stephan calmly. "You're both pointing the same general direction. Come on."

***

It seemed they'd been walking in stinking slop forever when they finally came to some stone steps and climbed out of the sewage. Jace resisted the temptation to wipe his boots, knowing they'd probably have to come back through this stuff anyway. Laken glanced over at him and made a face.

Soon they came to another bend in the tunnel, but now Stephan apparently had a different strategy. He stood with his back flat against the wall and barely peered around the corner. Then he slipped back and pulled a small sphere from one of the inner pockets of his jacket. Without even glancing at his companions, he tossed it around the bend and then pulled them down to the floor with him.

A small explosion shuddered the ground beneath them, and an acrid-smelling smoke billowed over their heads. Stephan kept their faces and his pressed into the stone floor until the smoke cleared. Then he let them rise to their feet and follow him around the bend. Five bodies were splayed in various awkward positions on the floor.

"Are they dead?" asked Laken.

"Yeah—that's the effect poison gas usually has," he half-smiled. "Five was too many for us to take on hand-to-hand. Besides, we need these—" He picked up a set of small plastic tags with black ciphers on them. "One of these should open Jael's cell."

"But which way now?" Danny asked.

"You still aren't getting anything?" said Laken.

Jace looked from one to the other of his companions, and when he looked back towards Danny, it happened again—he saw a flash of his dad's face.

"I can see him whenever I look away and back at you, Danny."

"What?"

"I don't know what it means. Maybe he's like—trying to contact you."

Just then the floor began to vibrate beneath their feet, and then they heard the sound of marching boots.

"Quickly," cried Stephen, "Get behind me."

As they did, he spread his arms so his jacket sleeves became a kind of cape that fell in front of them. Jace could sense Stephan bowing his head and pulling a hood low over his face. While all of them stood pressed against the wall, as still as statues, a squad of about twelve soldiers marched right past them.

Once they were far enough away that their boot-steps faded completely, Stephan finally heaved a long sigh. "Sure glad I brought that rock-camo."

Jace glanced at Danny and saw that his eyes were round and bright with fear, and wondered if his looked the same.

Then Stephan took Danny's hand and closed his eyes. This only brought a frown to his face, so he took Jace's hand with his other, but still he seemed dissatisfied.

"Laken, maybe you should try," he said.

Laken nodded and placed Jace's hand and his on top of Danny's head.

"There," he whispered. "I feel something. Move this way," he gestured toward the junction in the hall.

As silently as they could, they crept toward the area where the soldiers had appeared. Jace's head pounded even harder, knowing they were most likely moving toward danger. When they turned the corner, however, they saw nothing but a long empty hallway paved with large rectangular stones. Along both sides of the hall were small doors with tiny square windows, each with a cover to keep all light out. All the doors were closed.

Stephan began trying the keytags he'd taken from the dead guards. Some of the doors began to swing open, but no one came out. At one door, Jace stopped long enough to glance in, but all he saw was a still form lying there. Stepping inside, he saw it was a female.

"Anyone in there alive?" he heard Stephan ask.

Reaching down with a shaky hand, he felt for a pulse but found none. "No," he called back.

"Shh, not so loud." Laken stepped into the cell and took his hand. As he did this, a kind of static electric shock ran through his fingers and up his arm.

"What's that?"

"Did you feel something, Jace?"

He nodded.

"Concentrate. Which way should we look next?"

Jace closed his eyes again, and this time he seemed to see a ray of light stretching across the floor and through the wall into the next cell. Silently, he pointed in this direction. Laken kept hold of him, and they ran out into the hallway, and grabbed Danny.

"This way," he hissed to the others.

"Yes, I feel it now, too," Danny whispered.

None of the keytags worked in the next cell-door—or the one after that—and Jace was beginning to think he'd imagined everything. But at the third door, a keytag finally worked. The hinges of the door creaked loudly.

"This hasn't been opened in a really long time," said Laken.

"But we're in a Time Nexus—no time passes here," protested Jace.

"Stop talking, you two," hissed Stephan.

The cell was blacker than night. They couldn't see their hands right in front of their faces. Finally, Stephan lit a small laser light and beamed it slowly around the cubicle. In the far corner a figure was huddled, silent and still.

Jace was the first to creep over and try to find a pulse. "He's alive!"

Stephan helped him prop the form into a semi-sitting position, and then all of them looked from Danny to the prisoner and back. The resemblance was uncanny. Except for Danny's darker hair and eyes, they might have been twins.

"Dad?" whispered Jace. "Can you hear me?"

The eyes stared blankly, appearing to see nothing. 'Perhaps his eyes have been deprived of light so long they've gone blind,' thought Jace.

"Who are you?" a weak cracked voice asked.

"I'm Jace, your son."

"I have a son? I don't remember that."

"Do you remember me?" Danny murmured.

Again, the prisoner shook his head. Then the raspy voice said only one name. "Jon. He's the one I need."

For an instant, the rescuers looked at each other in confusion.

"But Shadow said my DNA was needed," whispered Jace tensely.

"Well, you were the one who found him," said Laken.

"I think I know what's going on," Stephan said then. "He's been in this Time Nexus for so long that his mind has reverted to his childhood—before he even met Danny. The only rescuer he remembers is Jon. I should've anticipated this."

"But Stephan, we can't go all that way back," cried Danny.

"No—and we don't need to. This is where your dog helps us."

***

Jon was clinging tightly to his perch in the tree. It seemed like a long time since the others had left, and this position was getting more and more uncomfortable. Glancing down into the darkness below him, he could barely make out the odd-shaped outline of Shadow with Evin straddling his back.

Then suddenly, the dog loped over and stood directly beneath his tree. "Shadow says to come down quickly," came Evin's young voice. "We need to talk."

Halfway thankful for a change of position, but fearful of what this could mean, Jon slithered down the tree's trunk as quickly as he could. "What's wrong?"

"Stephan says Jael has reverted in his mind to his childhood on Terres. He doesn't recognize any of them and insists that the one he needs is you."

"How can that be?"

"Stephan thinks the Time Nexus has stripped Jael of all but his oldest memories."

"Ah, the ones of his childhood, when his family was gradually torn apart by the System."

"Yes, Shadow agrees."

"So, he thinks he's back on Terres, and needs me to help him escape and find Martina—like I helped him after the Terres Disaster."

This time Evin merely nodded, and the dog's dark eyes were staring deep into Jon's.

"But Stephan looks like Jael's own father—he's his parallel. Why doesn't he recognize him?"

Evin paused for a moment, apparently communicating

this to Stephan through Shadow. "Stephan says Jael was too young when his father left to have strong memories of him. His deepest bond after his siblings left was with you, who became like a brother to him."

"That's right—I remember now," whispered Jon. "I called him 'Little Brother'. But how do I get to them? I shouldn't leave you."

"Shadow could take you."

"No, I'm not leaving you alone out here, Evin."

"Wait! Stephan is saying he can do an exchange of you and my dad. So, Shadow can stay and take care of me."

"But—how does that work?"

"Don't worry. Shadow can do things with the GAP we've never even heard of, especially with Stephan's help."

"Why didn't they just cross the GAP to Jael in the first place?"

"They didn't know his exact location, and a blind crossing could have attracted the wrong attention."

"How do you know all this?"

"Shadow," was the boy's only answer. Then he grabbed Jon's hand and placed it on the dog's large head. "Shadow says to hurry. We may not have much time before the guards discover them. Don't try to think about anything or cross the GAP yourself—just let Stephan and Shadow take control."

Jon was apprehensive and confused at this sudden change of plans. Luckily, he thought at the last moment, to give the signal flare to Evin. Then it was as though his body ceased to exist for an instant. This was like no feeling he'd ever experienced in a GAP-crossing before. The next thing he knew, he was in a dark, stone-floored cell.

The instant he felt his feet touch the stones, a small laser-light shone in his face.

"Jon," a weak, but familiar voice murmured. "You came for me. Please—you have to help me find Martina. Has the Double-Star come yet?"

Jon knelt by the form of Jael. "It came long ago, Little Brother. But be brave—we'll find your sister. I know where she is."

At this, Jael showed the most movement since they'd found him—he sat up gingerly, on his own power, and gave Jon a weak hug. Jon wrapped his arms around the frail body and lifted him up.

"His muscles have atrophied through so little use in this small cell," said Stephan.

"What do we do next?" Jon asked.

"First, Laken must go back to the Crimson Dome on Materna."

"Why there?"

"It has a special link to several Time Nexes—and hopefully this is one of them. There's no more time to explain—the rest of you follow me."

In an instant, Laken's form disappeared in a shower of sparks.

Just then the sound of running feet reached their ears, followed by shouts:

"Prisoners escaping!"

"Doors left open!"

"Guards are dead!"

In a flash, Stephan grabbed Jace with one hand and Jon with the other. "Concentrate on Shadow!" he cried, as the din in the hallway increased.

Jace barely had enough time to get hold of his father's hand—where he lay limply in Jon's arms. Then they were in the GAP.

Just as soon as their feet felt the ground again, Shadow was leaping over them, with Evin clinging to his back. Then they saw why. A flaming ring like a hole in the sky appeared behind them, and through this fiery circle came slithering the frightful Red Dragon.

"Look out!" Jace cried, for Jon and Jael still had their backs to the Dragon. Jon froze in confusion, so he ran toward them and shoved them both to the ground.

"What the—?" began Jon, but then he saw the dragon, too.

Meanwhile, Shadow was trying to bite holes in the creature's massive, leathery wings, but it kept evading him.

"Shadow, come guard!" called Stephan's commanding voice.

Immediately, the black dog settled to the ground between the Dragon and all the rest of them. Jace reached up his hand to feel the comforting strength and warmth of his fur. Jon moved closer to him, too, still holding Jael.

Then a terrible sound reached their ears, and fear made their blood run cold:

"S-s-so!" the Red Dragon hissed. "You thought you'd steal my greatest prize! How many ages have I tried to capture this one—Dani-El—this Ja-El—the anchor of El Shaddai—"

"El—what?" Jace whispered to Jon, who was closest to him. "What's he mean?"

" 'El' is one of the most ancient names for the True King—so names like Jael and Daniel have God in them, and carry special power," said Jon. "I knew there was something unique about Jael from the first time I met him."

"And Daniel—Danny—is a forerunner of my father, isn't he?"

"Right Jace—and so was the Daniel in The Book."

"Does the Red Dragon want Danny, too?"

"Maybe so. This dragon is really a form of the great Serpent, Satan. Perhaps that's why Shadow was sent—to protect them."

"They belong to the King!" bellowed a powerful voice just then. "You have no right to either of them."

Jace was surprised when he saw Stephan. He was now twice the size he'd been before, and wearing a coat of blazing, silver armor. In his hand was a flaming sword, and words echoed from it:

"How you have fallen from heaven, O Lucifer, son of the dawn! You have been cast down to the earth, you who once laid low the nations! You said in your heart, 'I will ascend to heaven, I will raise my throne above the stars of God: I will sit enthroned on the mount of assembly, on the utmost heights of the sacred mountain… I will make myself like God, the Most High.' But you are brought down to the grave, to the depths of the pit."

On hearing these words, the Serpent roared in fierce anger. "Ah, so now you're revealed—the Once-and-Again Stephan, who thinks he's a jewel in God's Crown," he mocked. "You were the first of the Earth-Believers to be martyred, and yet you keep coming back for more—again and again—when will you learn to give up?"

"I'll never give up, as long as you continue the war, you Deceiver of Worlds. The Sword of God's Word shall slay you."

Just as Stephan was saying this, a bolt of orange flame zigzagged toward him. At the last moment, he was able to dodge it, but the Serpent had several more prepared to throw, in one of his huge clawed hands.

Without turning his head, Stephan called out, "Jon, get out the cube I gave you. It has the coordinates for Materna."

"You said it was a signal flare. I gave it to Evin when we had to exchange places."

Jace thought he saw Stephan's shoulders slump slightly as he called out, "Evin, where are you?"

"On Shadow."

"Then give the cube to Shadow—*he* will have to take you all across the GAP. And Danny, you must get behind Evin and concentrate every ounce of strength you have on Laken—that's why I sent him ahead of us—to be a focus point."

Danny scrambled onto the black dog's back while Jace climbed up one of the dog's legs. Then he reached down to help Jon, who was still carrying Jael. Both of them fit onto one of the massive paws. "We're ready," he shouted up to Danny and Evin.

In the split second, before they entered the GAP, Jace saw Stephan glance their way to be sure they were all safe. And in that instant, the Serpent hurled a lightning bolt that caught a tiny crack in the silver armor. Orange flames and red blood spurted everywhere.

Then came the bitter cold of the GAP, the sudden darkness—and that was the last he saw of Stephan.

CHAPTER TWENTY-FIVE
CELESTIA AND HER MOTHER

Mom and I were sitting in the garden, as we had for each of the seemingly endless days that Dad, Laken, and the others were gone. It probably hadn't been as long as we felt, but the days here on Materna were longer than on Earth. And when you've nothing to do but sit and wait, the time slows to a crawl.

"Einstein sure was right," Mom sighed.

"Huh? Sorry, I must have been dozing off in the sunlight."

"Time is relative. It doesn't always pass at the same rate."

"Oh, yeah. I remember hearing that at school."

"It was a totally revolutionary idea in the early Twentieth Century, you know."

"Like crossing the GAP was in Laken's time. I wonder where he is, and what he's been up to." I tried to say this casually, but my voice cracked.

"I know you're worried about him. I'm worried about Jon and the others, too."

I squeezed Mom's hand tightly.

"When Laken returns, you'll be the first one he'll seek out."

"The hardest part is not knowing anything," I sighed. "Do you think something's gone wrong?"

"All we can do is pray."

This just made me sigh again. "It seems like I'm praying all the time, Mom."

"Well, it does say somewhere in The Book, 'Pray without ceasing,' you know."

I couldn't think of a snappy comeback for her, so I just stared up at the strange purplish-blue of Materna's sky. The colors in this alternative world were so different from what I was used to. Sometimes I could stare at them for hours. But now I'd spent too many hours with nothing to do except wait.

Mom sighed and shook her head as if to clear it. "I need to get a grip on myself. Where they are, only a short time may have passed—even though it seems like hours and days to us."

"I know—Einstein again," I sighed. "Let's talk about something completely different, instead. I've been doing some research on the meanings of names. Laken showed me a program on this minipad." I pulled the small device from my tunic pocket.

"Where did you get that?"

"Laken said Karina gave it to him—since his tablet couldn't function in this universe. When I started searching, I learned a lot about names. Apparently, they can have similar meanings in alternative time-lines. Back in ancient times, people put a lot of stock in what names meant. Naming a child was a big deal, and it's really interesting what some of them mean."

"Okay," Mom tried to smile. "What's your name mean?"

"Oh, that's an easy one: Celestia means 'Heavenly'."

"I know what it means. After all, I gave it to you. And I also know your father's name 'Jon' means 'Gift of God', which he truly is—sent by God to help a lot of people, including my little brother and me."

"What about your parents' names, Mom?"

She fell silent, and I realized this probably hadn't been a good question, since both her parents were now dead. But she smiled slightly and said, "You tell me."

"Well, 'Stephan' means 'Crown'," I read from the new data I'd pulled up on the minipad. "And 'Irina' comes from an ancient Greek word that means 'Peace'."

"'Thanks. I didn't actually know what my mother's name meant. Ironic, isn't it, that a person who had so many sad things happen to her had a name meaning 'Peace'?"

"Well, sometimes people learn to find peace through their tears," I whispered.

"What about their twins?" she asked, partly to change the subject.

"Well, 'Dominic' means 'Of the Lord'. That's interesting."

"How do you mean?"

"Well, if you put the twins' names together you get 'Crown of the Lord' for Stephan and Dominic."

Mom's mind was on her mother, for she said, "My mother's counterpart here seems fairly peaceful. But her name is 'Karina'. What does that mean?"

I tapped on the tablet screen and suddenly chuckled. "Would you believe that 'Karina' is derived from an ancient Greek word that means 'one of two'? What a great name for a twin—especially one in an alternative universe."

Mom didn't seem to hear my answer, though. She was probably thinking about the past. "I really don't remember my mother's sister. She and my Uncle Dominic ran away to the Wilds of Terres when I was very young. Say, what does my name mean?"

"You mean you've never asked?" I said quickly, as I flipped to another screen. "It says here it's the feminine form of Martin, which is derived from the name of the ancient Roman god of war, Mars."

"War, huh?" sighed Mom. "Well, trouble does seem to follow me. At least I have a planet that shares the name."

"Oh, yeah—Mars, the planet that's in the next orbit out from Earth—back home."

"Are you getting homesick?" She looked into my eyes as she said this. "I know I am. All this waiting and not knowing is getting hard."

"Well, let me just share two more names," I said,

avoiding her question. "These are the ones I really want you to see." I turned the screen of the tablet toward her, and in block letters were two short words:

"JA" and "EL"

"Jael?" Mom murmured.

I nodded. "It's a very special name. First, 'EL' is from ancient Hebrew—the oldest part of The Book was written in this language originally. It means 'Lord'. And 'JA'—also sometimes spelled 'YA'— is derived from the name God gave himself."

"Gave himself? How do you mean?"

"Well, one of The Book's characters, Moses, met the Lord in a burning bush, and asked him what his name was. God replied 'I AM'."

"I am what?"

"That's all—just 'I AM'—God just *is*, and always has been—he has no beginning and no end—he's eternal."

"So, my younger brother's name means 'I AM' and 'Lord'?"

I nodded. "That seems really powerful—like the Lord has some special mission for him—if they find him."

"I think they will. There's a reason for this name. I'm sure of it. My parents probably had no idea of this meaning when they named their youngest son—" She paused for a moment, gazing far across the hills beyond us. "Oh, look," she said then. "Here comes Karina. Maybe she's heard something from Stephan."

Just as she said this, Karina was reaching up her hand to wave at us. But her face suddenly turned pale and she clutched at her chest, screaming as if her heart were being wrenched out. Then she fell to the ground.

Both of us ran to her, expecting to find her having a heart attack. Instead we found her sobbing uncontrollably.

"What's wrong?" She didn't seem to hear me.

Mom managed to get her to her feet and pulled her to the nearest garden bench. By the time we got there, she was trying to speak:

"He's dead!" She stopped and gasped for air.

"Who's dead?" Mom cried.

But Karina didn't seem to hear her. Instead she went on, as though she was speaking in a trance, "That evil Serpent, Satan, has pierced him with one of his fiery darts. I felt it in my own heart."

"Who—" Mom began to ask again, but this time I stopped her.

"She can't hear you," I whispered in her ear. "I'm not sure where she is, but it's not here with us."

"Oh, my sweet Crown of the Lord—" Now Karina was murmuring as if to herself. "I'm so sorry that I didn't marry you, like you asked. Oh, please forgive—but it's too late now."

"I think she means Stephan," I said softly to Mom. "Didn't his name mean Crown?"

Mom was nodding, and at the same time rubbing Karina's shoulders. Gradually, she seemed to relax a bit.

Then she shook her head suddenly and looked around in confusion. "Where am I?"

"In the garden," I said to her.

"Near the red dome?"

"Yes," I nodded.

"Please take me inside the dome," she sighed. "I need to be covered by the blood of the Lord. Oh, my dear Stephan—I'm so sorry."

I wasn't sure what she meant by her words, but as soon as she said them, there came a sharp cracking sound. I closed my eyes in fright, but in the next instant a familiar voice washed over me like warm water:

"Celestia!"

"Laken?"

His hands grabbed me and pulled me into a firm hug.

"Oh Laken, I was afraid you were gone forever."

He didn't reply, but just held me tighter. Mom and Karina were standing behind me, seemingly holding each other up.

"What's happened?" Mom demanded. "Karina says she just felt Stephan die."

"It must have been after I left," sighed Laken. "He told me to get back here to the Crimson Dome as fast as I could. An instant ago I was there, and now I'm here."

"Yes," Karina cut in. "The dome is the only refuge from the Evil One—only there are we protected by the blood of the King. We must get inside now."

Laken glanced quickly around the grounds, but no one else was in sight. Then he pulled me forcefully toward the nearest entrance to the domed building. He didn't have to tell Mom and Karina to follow—they were right on our heels.

Just as we reached one of the entry doors, there came a crackly snapping sound, and a huge black dog appeared before us, flashing with sparks. Again, I ducked in fear—what new evil creature was this? Two small figures were on its back, and a couple more were clinging to one of the stout black legs.

Suddenly, however, there came a voice I recognized shouting my name.

"Dad, is that you? Where are you?" I responded.

"Here—under Shadow—uh—the dog."

"Shadow? The dog we met at Danny's?" This couldn't be the same animal who'd met us in their yard, barking and wagging his tail.

But no one replied, except Laken who cried, "Quickly! All of you come inside the dome."

No sooner had he said this than a crash like thunder nearly deafened us. Looking up, I saw a huge red dragon, the Serpent we'd seen at Mendeleev Portal.

"There he is," cried Karina. "The fallen angel himself."

At this, we all crowded through the opening. We'd barely made it through when the dragon's body crashed against the red dome above us. Long streams of dark red liquid began to drip down the outside of the dome. Angry bellows shook the roof above us, but it held fast, and none of the blood reached us.

"We're safe here—under Kristos' care," murmured Karina.

"There is no other name given in Heaven or Earth by which we can be saved," Laken added softly.

I was still clinging to Laken's neck and shoulders. My muscles refused to move.

"Are you all right?" he asked.

Slowly, I managed to nod my head. "What was all that? What does it mean?"

Laken glanced at Karina before he answered. "This place was built for the first Believers of Materna, wasn't it?"

She nodded. "It's the safe haven, the shelter of the King. It's the only place we can truly be protected from the evil Serpent. That's why Stephan brought all of you here from Luna."

"Is everyone here?" I asked in surprise.

"Yes," said Karina. "I was warned in a dream last night to gather you all. You and Martina were the last ones I was coming for."

"And just in time," Laken sighed.

"But what happens now?" asked Mom.

"The Serpent has lost this battle, I'd say."

Karina nodded. "But he won't give up that easily. The real war is just beginning."

Suddenly her face turned pale, and her knees buckled. Laken and I caught her and laid her on one of the soft couches nearby.

Now, at last, I was able to see the others around me clearly. The dog seemed to have shrunk to the size of an ordinary black Labrador—the one we'd met in Colorado. Danny was helping someone climb off Shadow's back, and soon I recognized his younger son, Evin, the redhead.

Jace moved away from one of the dog's legs and pulled me into a hug that nearly choked me. "It's okay Jace," I gasped, "You're safe now."

We both turned as my dad gently laid a frail-looking figure on another one of the couches.

Mom was on her knees at his side almost instantly. "It's him, isn't it? Jael? Can you hear me?"

"He's really weak," Dad said, taking Mom's hand. "They had him in a Time Nexus, and his mind has atrophied. We're lucky he's still alive."

"He didn't even know who I was," Jace said sadly.

"The System had him?"

"It seemed that way," added Danny. "But the Serpent made it clear that Jael was *his* prize prisoner, and fought us fiercely to re-take him."

"Definitely," said Dad. "He came right for us."

"We're fortunate Evin and Shadow were sent to help us," said Danny. "Especially when the Red Dragon—"

"The Serpent—the Dragon—the Devil—he killed

Stephan, didn't he?" Karina's mournful voice reached us from a nearby couch.

"He died to save us." Dad moved to her side. "I'm so sorry."

"He and I will meet again someday," she sighed.

"We all will," I nodded.

Mom meanwhile was rubbing Jael's arms and legs gently and crooning to him like a little child. Then at last, his eyelids began to flutter open to reveal those green eyes I remembered so well.

"Mother?"

Mom looked up in confusion. Then Jael's eyes rested on me, and he said:

"Martina, is that you?"

"No, I'm her daughter—"

"Shh," said Jon. "He's back in his childhood right now. To him, you look like his sister, and Martina looks old enough to be his mother."

"Oh."

"What will he think of *my* mother then?" whispered Jace. "Raina to him should be a young girl."

"I don't know what—" But just as Dad started to say this, Raina burst around the nearest corner, crying:

"Is it true—what I heard? Is Jael really alive?" She rushed to the figure on the couch before any of us could say anything, gathering him close in her arms. "Oh, my darling—my love—I've missed you so much."

Jael was trying to struggle from her grasp for a few seconds, but then something changed and his body relaxed. He rested his head on her shoulder and sighed. "Red hair—there was something about red hair. I thought I remembered—but now I—I've forgotten."

Mom gently took Raina's hand and whispered in her ear, "His mind is back in his childhood, Raina. He may not remember you."

"Maybe not now," she sighed. "But someday he will. The King brought him this far, and he'll help me bring the rest of him back, too—in his time."

CHAPTER TWENTY-SIX
CODA

Many Materna days had passed, perhaps even weeks—if they had those here. Laken and I were walking the rolling hills beyond the garden as we often did.

"I wonder how much longer we'll have to stay here."

"My, Celestia, you *must* be homesick—to want to leave a beautiful place like this and go back to the wars and tribulations of Earth."

"Well, it *is* nice and peaceful here, I'll admit. But all the colors are so different—it's just not home."

He smiled and took my hands in each of his. "I guess I've never had that problem. I've been so many places and times—whatever one I'm in is home."

I eyed him suspiciously. "Are you sure you don't remember your other lives? Sometimes you sound like you do."

He glanced down before he answered me. "Okay, I'll admit there are bits and pieces of memories, but nothing complete—not like what I'm experiencing now.

And I swear to you—when we first met on Earth, back in 2123 Tacoma, I had no memories of having lived any other lives."

Before I replied, I gave him a quick kiss. "All right, I believe you, Laken Meta."

We started walking back toward the garden then, hand-in-hand. As we got closer, I saw Raina guiding Jael carefully along one of the flowered paths. "Jael seems to be gradually getting better," I said.

"Yeah, he does. If anyone can help him heal, it's Raina. She's so devoted to him."

"Well, she's known him almost all her life, you know. Mom says they met when they were only seven or eight Standard Years—before they'd even started school on Terres. And besides that, she has Daiah's help—who learned a lot about healing when she was in Indonia."

"And this quiet, peaceful place is exactly what Jael needs, isn't it?" He turned and looked right into my eyes as he said this.

"Okay," I nodded. "You've made your point." Suddenly, I had an irresistible urge to hug him tightly. "Oh Laken, I love you. I was so afraid when Stephan took you. I hope I never lose you like Raina lost Jael."

"Well, she's getting him back now," he whispered into my hair.

"But at what cost?" I found tears beginning to seep into the corners of my eyes. "Laken?"

"Hmm?"

"How long will it be until we see Johan again?"

"With Johan, it's hard to say. Why do you ask?"

"I was thinking of what you said about his performing a marriage."

He pulled me tighter to him—in fact, he took my breath away. "So your answer is 'yes'?"

"Yes!" I gasped. "But you'd better let me breathe—"

He released me and stepped back. Then he smiled and kissed me on top of the head—like he had on a moonlit hilltop in Indonia, so far away, but not so long ago.

"You do have stars in your eyes, my Celestia."

Then he began to lead me by the hand. Before I could say anything, we crossed another path and were met by Danny and Evin, with Shadow, their dog.

"We've been looking for you two," began Danny, "to say good-bye. It's about time we were heading home. Jael has finally recognized me. I'm glad his memories are beginning to come back."

I was glad they'd found us. It would've been sad if they left without saying good-bye.

"That's great news about Jael," Laken smiled. "I have a feeling the True King still has need of his special talents, especially now that the Serpent is abroad again."

Then he turned to the small red-haired boy. "Evin, you're a very special young man, too." He solemnly shook the redhead's hand. "Be sure to listen for the Lord's guidance as you go. Believe me, I've learned—sometimes the hard way—what happens when you don't."

I was silently wondering if he was thinking of some of his escapades in the Twenty-second Century, so I decided to change the subject:

"Laken, you've gotten me interested in the meanings of names. Have you noticed how the sound of 'Evin' resembles 'Stephan', especially when it's spelled with an 'f'—'Stefan'?"

"Wow!" Evin was wide-eyed. "Stephan was an awesome Guardian and warrior."

"Actually, though," I smiled, "The name 'Evin'—also spelled 'Evan'—is a form of 'Jon' in an ancient language called Welsh."

"Really?" Danny said in surprise. "Sandy and I had no idea. We just liked the sound of it."

Laken nodded. "People pay more attention to the sound of names than their meanings. The true power of names is something almost forgotten now."

"Say," I said softly, "I wonder—since Danny is a forerunner of Jael, and Evin means 'Jon'—perhaps they're another special combination like Jon and Jael."

"Could be."

"What does my name mean?" asked Danny.

" 'Daniel' means 'God is my judge'."

"Wow, that has a powerful sound, doesn't it? How about my other son's name, Dain?"

"That's another form of your name. But your wife, Sandra, has an interesting history to her name."

"What is it?"

"Well, Sandra is derived from 'Cassandra', who was a princess in very ancient times. She had a gift of prophecy, but no one ever believed anything she predicted."

"Oh, that's sad. I'm not sure I'll tell Sandy that one."

"Perhaps not," Laken smiled. "So, are you two looking for Jon, so he can take you back to your own place and time?"

Evin spoke up. "Actually, Shadow says there's no need to trouble Jon."

"Your dog?"

Now it was Danny's turn to smile. "I guess no one's told you. Evin and our dog can communicate telepathically—like Jael and his feier-cat did."

"Really." I was more intrigued than surprised.

"He crosses GAPs, too," said Evin. "That's how we escaped when Stephan was killed."

"Oh, I just assumed my dad did that," I said.

"He was busy carrying Jael," said Danny. "And Evin—uh—had the coordinates. It's a long story."

"Shadow says he can take us back to the same night we left," Evin cut in. "Mom won't even know we've been gone."

"But you and Shadow left a few days after I did, remember?"

"That's true, but only a few. Hopefully, Mom hasn't had too much time to worry about you."

"Not like Raina and Jael," I murmured, half to myself.

Laken was shaking Danny's hand by now. "We couldn't have gotten Jael here without you three. Thank you."

"It was mostly Shadow," Danny shrugged. "Stephan said Johan sent him as another Guardian to help with Jael's rescue and to protect us all."

While he was speaking, Shadow doubled in size right before our eyes.

"This is no ordinary dog," Laken nodded. "Especially if Johan sent him to you."

"Oh, we know that," Danny laughed. "So, is he ready to do his thing, son?"

"Yeah, Dad."

"Okay, up you go." Danny boosted Evin onto Shadow's back, and then climbed up behind him. "I've already said good-bye to Jon, Martina, Jael, and Raina—but I have a feeling it's not a forever farewell."

"In the True Lord's Kingdom, they never are, Danny," I smiled.

He nodded and gave a quick salute to us. Then he put his arms around his young son's waist and closed his eyes. For an instant, there were sparks in the air where they had been—and then everything was gone, except for an echoing cry of a bird flying overhead. Looking up, I caught a glimpse of red and gold before it disappeared.

"It seems like GAP-crossings are different here, aren't they?"

"Well, it is an alternate universe. Or maybe Johan is up to something new. That reminds me. I have a lot of things I need to tell your dad about my last meeting with Johan."

"You mean when we went through the Portal in Mendeleev Crater with Stephan?"

He just nodded and appeared deep in thought.

"Uh—Laken?"

"Yes?"

"When I told Danny we'd see them again—that partings are never forever in the Lord's Kingdom—I was thinking of Heaven. But do you think we may see them again in this life?"

He looked thoughtful for a few moments and then grinned. "Oh, I'd say there's a strong possibility."

"WHERE ALL WORLDS END"

CHAPTER ONE
THE SECRET IN THE LOFT

Evin Parker bit his lower lip in an attempt to stop the tears gathering in his eyes. 'Not now,' he thought angrily. 'I need to concentrate.'

But despite his best efforts the tears soon filled his eyes and began to trickle down his cheeks. Glancing to his left, he saw his older brother Dain fighting back tears of his own. And it didn't help that he could hear his mother sobbing softly.

'What good are funerals anyway?' he said to himself. 'Why can't we just pick up and go on?' But even as he thought this, Evin knew it wouldn't be easy to get over his father's death. His mind began to run through the past five years—since they'd come back from the alternative universe with Shadow, their big black dog.

'I wonder if Dad was exposed to something there that caused his brain cancer,' he thought. 'But maybe not. Aunt Ginna, Dad's sister, once reminded us that their mother—the grandmother we never knew—also died of cancer.

Part of Evin's mind was desperate to find the answer to his dad's illness, but it wasn't easy to travel in the GAP. You couldn't just *go* somewhere in the space-time fabric—no matter how badly you wanted to. Shadow made this clear to him in one of their telepathic conversations. Evin was the only one Shadow communicated with in this way, so he could pass things along to his older brother or his parents if he chose to.

'There are things I don't tell them,' Evin mused. 'Have I kept too much back?'

'No, you haven't,' came the familiar low growl in his mind.

'Where have you been, Shadow? I've been searching for you for hours.'

'No need to be angry,' the thoughts came to him. 'I know what I'm doing, and I will tell you whatever you need to know.'

He turned and stared angrily at the black furry face behind him. 'Why do you always get to be in control? Maybe I need to decide for myself what's important now—after all I'm already thirteen years old.'

Suddenly he realized he'd said those last few words aloud. People were staring at him from where they were arranged around Danny's grave. Evin looked down at his shoes, embarrassed. Mom reached over and took his hand.

"Yes, Evin," she said. "You're a teenager, too—like your brother. I'm just sorry your dad will miss it—" Her voice dissolved into tears.

Other voices around them began to sing, and Evin recognized one of his father's favorite songs:

> *Work, for the night is coming, work through the*
> *   morning hours;*
> *Work while the dew is sparkling; work 'mid*
> *   springing flowers.*
> *Work when the day grows brighter, work in the*
> *   glowing sun.*
> *Work for the night is coming when man's work is*
> *   done.*
>
> *Work, for the night is coming under the sunset skies:*
> *While their bright tints are glowing, work, for*
> *   daylight flies.*
> *Work 'til the last beam fades, fades to shine no*
> *   more;*
> *Work while the night is dark'ning when man's work*
> *   is o'er.*

He tried to join in the singing, but his voice refused to cooperate. Then as silence fell around him, he felt the arm of his older brother coming across his shoulders. "Come on, Ev," said Dain. "We can go home now."

They walked back across the hills and fields to the house. It wasn't far—only about a mile—since their mother decided Dad should be buried on their own land instead of in a church cemetery. Evin wasn't sure he could go into a church right now, anyway. Each time he thought about God, the huge question 'Why?' seemed to totally fill his mind with an endless ache.

Once they reached the house, Dain pulled him aside toward the barn. Inside, the smell of hay and horse manure filled his nostrils.

"Guess we'd better muck out Splash's stall today," said his brother.

"Yeah, and it's my turn," Evin sighed. He reached up and ran his hand along the black and white pinto's neck. The horse let out a nicker, and he reached into his pocket for a sugar cube—he always kept some there for his friend.

"We can do it together this time," whispered Dain, and Evin felt a slight warmth in his chest. "Let's climb up into the loft and take a break first, though."

So, the two boys climbed up the ladder to the hay loft above the stalls. They had just the one horse, who'd appeared seemingly out of nowhere, much like Shadow. Evin suspected Shadow had brought Splash to them—hadn't people in the other universe thought he might be Jael's horse? But Jael didn't live in this time—the early Twenty-first Century. Danny, his father, had known Jael very well, though. That was why the young woman and the older man had come to get Danny, just over five years ago. They said they needed his help to locate Jael. And they *had* found his father's friend—in a System prison, hidden in a Time Nexus.

"It all seems like a strange dream now."

"What does?" his brother asked.

"Oh, all the GAP-crossing and time travel Shadow took me on."

"Maybe it *was* just a dream, Ev."

"But I still hear Shadow's voice in my mind."

"Are you sure it's not your imagination?"

"Of course, I'm sure!" He couldn't keep the anger out of his voice. People asked him this way too often.

"Hey, it's okay."

He found himself calming down as Dain patted his back.

"I believe you," Dain said softly. "Dad did, too."

"Well, he'd traveled in time before—inside Jael—and knew things about GAPs no one else from our world could."

"I believe you—and Shadow."

Evin sighed and looked up into his brother's green eyes. With a start he realized he'd seen that color before—in

Stephan's eyes. But now Stephan was dead, killed by the Red Dragon.

"What should we do now? I keep thinking of that song, 'Work for the Night is Coming'. If we need to work, how can we find out what to do?"

"I say we wait and see what Shadow tells us."

"But just sitting around and waiting is so hard."

"Here, Ev, I need to show you something."

"What?"

Dain brushed aside some of the hay, revealing the bare wood of the loft's floor. There were strange markings rubbed into the boards, and small stones arranged in a circle around them.

"What is it?" Evin said again. Below them, Shadow began to growl suddenly.

"Quiet, boy," he called to the dog. "He wishes he could climb up here, too," he shrugged to Dain.

"I'll find a way to show him this someday," Dain whispered. "He probably can shed some light on the parts I'm not sure about."

Evin crossed his legs into a more comfortable sitting position, but he didn't speak again, since he'd already asked the same question twice. Dain would tell him what he knew—in his own timing.

Dain was running his hands thoughtfully across the stones, his eyes closed. "Dad showed me this," he finally said. "A couple of years ago—I think he already knew then the cancer would take him."

He blinked hard to stop the tears again, and saw Dain was doing the same, as he said, "It's sort of like a miniature stone circle, isn't it?"

"Yeah," Evin said into his brother's silence.

"Didn't you say Jael's son told you instructions he got from some strange old man he met in a stone circle?" asked Dain at last.

Now Evin found his heart beginning to race, but he had no words to say.

"I don't know if this will help us reach that other place or not," continued Dain. "All I know is what Dad told me, when he arranged these stones and drew these letters."

"Can you read them?"

"Dad explained it this way—here, let me show you."

Again, he passed his hand gently over the stones. "They're like a stockade, see?"

"You mean like one of those old-time forts?"

His brother nodded. "A place to go for safety in time of attack— see, we're protected from all sides."

"By what?"

"Dad said it was a presence—like God—who encircles us."

"I wish I felt that presence."

"Dad said we couldn't always feel it, but it was still there. And he said not to give up hope, but to keep standing our ground."

"Standing our ground? Against what?"

"I bet Shadow can tell you the answer to that," Dain said, looking his younger brother squarely in the eye. "Ask him—"

'Shadow?'

'I'm here, Evin,' the dog rumbled. 'Yes, the True King will never leave you or forsake you—he's promised that.'

"But what are we standing against?" Evin heard his voice asking this question out loud.

'You've seen him—remember the Serpent?'

He closed his eyes and shuddered. "How could I forget the Red Dragon?"

"There's more," Dain said just then. He pointed his finger at a small figure drawn with charcoal in the middle of the circle. "See this?"

"It looks like a stick person." Evin tried not to chuckle.

"Well, it's not so easy to draw on these rough planks, I guess. But see his arms?"

Evin looked more closely and found himself nodding. "One arm is held up like he's making a fist."

Dain nodded and pointed to letters on the figure's left. "Can you read that?"

"*Semper Paratus*? What does that mean?"

"It's Latin," said his brother. "It means 'Always Prepared'. It's the motto of the U.S. Coast Guard."

"But we're in Colorado—nowhere near a coast."

"Still we need to be prepared for whatever the True King calls us to do."

Evin looked up quickly in surprise. He'd never heard Dain talk about these things before.

"You believe, don't you?"

"Of course, I do. Just because Shadow talked to you, and took you with him doesn't mean I'm not important in all this."

"I'm sorry. I didn't mean to make you feel that way, Dain."

"After all, I am the firstborn—"

"Then you have the potential to be a GAP-crosser—don't you?"

Dain just nodded silently and pointed to the stick figure's other hand. "See this?"

He looked closely and saw a tiny sword in the figure's right hand.

"What's the sword mean?" he asked.

"Didn't Stephan have one—at the battle with the Red Dragon?"

"He did have a shining sword—and he said it was the Sword of the Spirit."

The words were barely out of his mouth before Shadow began howling below them.

"Sounds like Shadow remembers, too," Dain whispered tensely.

"Stephan's sword spoke words from The Book—he also called it 'The Sword Which is the Word of God'." Again, Evin heard himself saying aloud the thoughts Shadow sent him.

"We have three things here to remember," Dain sighed. "Dad told me to show this to you, after—"

"After he died?"

Dain nodded mutely. Both boys were fighting tears again.

"So, the first is to stand our ground, right?"

"Yeah. And the second is to always be prepared."

"And, what's the third one?"

Dain put his hand across Evin's as he spoke again. "Dad said we need to be ready to go the distance—whatever it takes."

"Like Stephan did." Again, Evin spoke aloud the words the black dog put into his mind.

"From what you've told me, Stephan was ready to give himself for the rest of you."

"And he did. He died to save us from the Red Dragon. But what do all these things have to do with us now—here in Twenty-first Century Colorado?"

"I don't know for sure—yet," Dain said softly. "But I have a feeling the battle isn't over.

"Yeah, that Serpent is still alive, Shadow's just reminded me."

"I won't be surprised if sometime, someday, one of those GAP-crossers is going to come back here—and we need to be ready."

"And since Dad is gone, it's all up to us now, isn't it?"

THANK YOU

Thank you for joining me. If you liked the story and have a minute to spare, I would appreciate an honest review or comment on the page or site where you purchased the book.

Reviews from readers like you make a huge difference to helping new readers find stories similar to The Peaks series: *Beyond the World.*

- Amazon
- Barnes & Noble
- Goodreads
- iBooks

Thank you!

M. F. Erler

ABOUT THE AUTHOR

M.F. (Mary Frances) Erler is a music teacher, outdoor educator, and author of fantasy fiction and non-fiction. Her teaching career has spanned over 25 years, and she has been writing most of her life. Her first Christian-based science-fiction book, "The Peaks at the Edge of the World" has been re-written and revised in 2017.

Erler has been writing most of her life. In fact, some of the characters in *The Peaks Saga* were initially conceived in her youth. Her lifelong goal has been to bring spiritual ideas into fantasy-fiction, in the spirit of writers like J.R.R. Tolkien and C.S. Lewis. She enjoys public speaking and sharing her faith journey. She is an approved speaker for Women's Connections, a Stonecroft Ministry.

Now that she has published the ***The Peaks Saga***, she is embarking on a new venture in historical fiction, where her modern-day characters time-travel back into the lives of their ancestors. So, in the future, watch for more tales in *Journeys Beyond the Peaks.*

Her books are designed to appeal to young adults and all who are young at heart. Among her many hobbies, Erler especially enjoys travel. She has been to several countries, including China, New Zealand, the British Isles, and Western Europe, as well as Canada, Mexico, Jamaica, and 43 of the 50 States. Her favorite mode of travel is cruising, but her current favorite place is her home in Montana.

Along with fantasy, true science, and science fiction, she is also a student of history, comparative religion, ecology, and music. Previous publications include non-fiction articles in *Today's Christian Parent,* and *Social Studies and the Young Learner,* as well as poems and short sketches in Standard Publishing Program Books. In addition, she has produced *Music in God's World,* a music curriculum for preschools, and *Wonders of Creation, an Environmental Education Curricula* for use in schools and camp settings. She has worked as a newspaper reporter and columnist, and was writer for various U.S. Forest Service publications, including being in charge of producing the book, *Targhee Lodgepole-Tragedy or Opportunity?*

She has a Bachelor of Science in Environmental Education and Biology from Colorado State University, and a Masters of Music Education from Concordia

University-Chicago. In her senior year of high school, she was awarded a prize for her writing by the National Council of Teachers of English, the Quill and Scroll Award for Journalism, and a National Merit Scholarship.

Her love of singing has led to participation in many choirs and Acapella groups, which enabled her to perform at two International Sweet Adelines conventions in Nashville and Houston. She sang with these women's barbershop groups for 18 years. Hobbies include reading, singing, playing several musical instruments, and teaching piano and guitar lessons. She and her husband have two adult children. All make their home in the northwest.

You are invited to connect with Frances at:
mferler@peaksandbeyond.com
Or follow her blog at PeaksAndBeyond.com
(MFErler.blogspot.com)

THE PEAKS SAGA

PEAKS AT THE EDGE OF THE WORLD
Finding the Light

SEARCHING FOR MAIA

MOUNTAINTOPS AND VALLEYS

WHEN THE WORLD GROWS COLD

THE FOUNTAIN AND THE DESERT

BEYOND THE WORLD

WHERE ALL WORLDS END